I0604936

ENDGAME

THE SHORTEN CHRONICLES BOOK 6

ROSALIND TATE

TOB PUBLISHING*

® The Shorten Chronicles is a registered trademark
Copyright © Rosalind Tate 2025

The Shorten Chronicles

*In the first and second books of the Shorten Chronicles, **Stranded** and **Escape**, Sophie and her beloved dog, Charlotte, fall into a parallel universe, a century back in time. Sophie struggles to adapt to living in Shorten Manor but the heir to the estate, Freddy Lacey, is besotted. At the end of **Escape**, Sophie, Charlotte, and Hugo manage to return to the 21st century. Sophie and Hugo confess their love for each other, act on their feelings and sleep together, but then Freddy turns up. He's followed them through time.*

*In the third book of the series, **Exile**, Freddy finds out that Sophie is with Hugo. In despair, he dashes recklessly across universes, and they all find themselves in a terrifying medieval kingdom. Charlotte's DNA is enhanced, giving her a human lifespan and an advanced understanding of language. Sophie acquires a temporary, deadly power and trapped in a bear pit, she and Freddy give into temptation to fend off the bitter cold. When they finally return to modern London, Sophie discovers she's pregnant.*

*In **Intermezzo**, a fun, rom-com novella (exclusive to Rosalind's Fantasy Bookshop: https://bookshop.rosalindtate.com), Sophie marries Hugo but gives birth to Freddy's child, Bella. Freddy and Sophie become platonic friends. Charlotte the labradoodle accepts this unusual state of affairs with aplomb, adores the new baby and, with her enhanced DNA, listens to audiobooks featuring canine sidekicks.*

*In the fourth book of the series, **Defiance**, Freddy insists on taking Bella to his family in Shorten. As a civil war rages, Freddy falls in love with Clarissa. Janus, the Roman god whose ship enables them to travel between universes, tricks Sophie and Freddy into returning to modern London without their daughter. If they are* *ever to see Bella or Clarissa again, they need Hugo and Charlotte's help to track down the only artefact that can kill Janus: his walking staff.*

*In the fifth book of the series, **Hunted**, Sophie and Freddy go to ancient Rome to find the walking staff that can end Janus and reunite them with their daughter. With Hugo and Charlotte's help, they find it but before they can complete their plan, a time traveller destroys the staff, throwing it into the River Tiber. Distraught, back in modern London, they discover that in this version of modern London, Sophie's parents weren't killed in a road traffic accident, and she's reunited with them.*

***Endgame** is the final book in the first **Shorten Chronicles** series, set in 1889. The last chance to find the walking staff and end Janus.*

Even the very wise cannot see all ends.
J. R. R. Tolkien

CHAPTER 1

For five weeks the sterile air inside Juno, the unchanging temperature of seventy Fahrenheit, and the hum from whatever powered the ship, haunted Sophie's waking hours as well as her dreams. The length of the journey depended on activity in the black hole they were passing through. Some took less than a day, others lasted months. Juno would eventually land in a parallel universe where time passed slower than at home, where it was 1889, but if she took too long, her passengers wouldn't disembark. They'd be dead.

Sophie paced to and fro, not seeing the vast cargo bay. Instead, she pictured her toddler. Bella's rosy cheeks, her solemn blue eyes, her unsteady, r first steps. It had only been ten months since she'd seen her daughter, though it felt like forever. Far away in Shorten, Bella would soon celebrate her second birthday. So much time lost.

To be reunited, her mother had to track down the device that guaranteed safe passage. But first, she had to survive this crossing between universes. A gamble with unknown odds.

Hugo stood up from the metal bench and stretched. 'We're not dead yet.'

Her husband's capacity to guess her emotions was practically telepathic, and Sophie gave him her chin-up smile. Hope was treacherous. Too little and it withered into nothing. Too much, and it deepened the despair when hope ran out. Her eyes flicked to four bottles of water, upright on a shelf. All that was left.

On a nearby bench, Freddy fidgeted and folded his arms. Resigned? Philosophical? 'Sophie, sit down. Conserve your energy.'

Freddy was Bella's father, and Sophie's closest friend. Which was just as well, as Sophie was married to Hugo. Unusual relationships, but they worked.

Both men were sporting a short beard and moustache, to blend in with 19th century fashion. Sometimes, when Sophie was distracted, it surprised her. The beards were cool, though Hugo's made him look mysterious, not quite himself.

She sat beside him. Enough water for a day, maybe two. Whether conserving their energy would make any difference once it was gone, she had no idea. She traced the outline of her daughter's key-rattle on the necklace under her T-shirt. She'd pocketed the rattle in Shorten Manor and ever since had treasured it. Basic old keys on a ring, the edges and angles cold and hard, but it helped her focus, cope with the fear.

On the floor, Sophie's large brown labradoodle was lying on her stomach, reading a paperback, using her front paw to press the button on a new page-turning machine. The previous one had been taken by unknown travellers in Juno, back while its owner had been in ancient Rome. When Charlotte pressed, turning a page, the paper rustled, and the machine clicked. Portable and light, it had been a boon on this endless crossing. Having no opposable thumbs, Charlotte needed it to read her cosy mystery books. Obviously.

Clink, and the rustle of another page. Charlotte was channelling canine stoicism. Yes, her enhanced DNA made her remarkable, but she'd always been calm and resolute. Sophie briefly closed her eyes. Be more like Charlotte.

They'd left Charlotte's beloved companion, Jack the retriever, convalescing in modern London. Unaware chocolate was poisonous to dogs, he'd eaten a family-sized chocolate cake, with cherries and frosting. Though Charlotte hated being separated from him, at least he was safe.

Sophie stared into the cargo bay that stretched off into the distance. Racks attached to the barrel-shaped walls held countless boxes of discarded travellers' junk: old clothes, rusty coins, and papyrus with scribbled unknown languages.

For the nth time, Sophie scrutinised the section of the hull in front of her, willing the exit to appear.

Hugo squeezed her hand. 'I love you.'

Sophie kissed him. 'And I love you.'

Freddy rolled his eyes. 'One of the many reasons my Clarissa's so wonderful is that she's not embarrassingly soppy.'

'If we survive this,' said Hugo, 'I resolve to be even more soppy.'

This was a long-running joke. Banter could quieten intrusive thoughts — for a while. 'I want to be the soppiest version of me,' said Sophie, 'in all the universes.'

'That's ambitious,' said Freddy, 'given the number of versions and universes.'

Parallel universes often contained the same individuals. Similar or very different, depending on the choices they made throughout their lives. The three of them knew from Juno that other versions of them hadn't survived a crossing in this ship. That knowledge alone would have persuaded most people not to travel. Yet the prize was beyond priceless: a safe way back to Bella, and to Freddy's fiancée.

Freddy was on this mad quest for his fiancée and daughter. Hugo, though, was only here because he so loved his stubborn wife. Sophie balled her fists, pricked by familiar guilt.

A soft click. 'Juno has landed at your destination.' The automatic ship's message was flat and unemotional, but Sophie squealed in relief.

Charlotte jumped to her feet and Freddy exhaled. 'Thank God.'

'I wonder if Juno makes the same announcement if her passengers have stopped breathing?' Hugo's deadpan expression and gallows humour didn't hide his relief. He enveloped Sophie in an exuberant bear hug, and she relaxed against him. Now they'd landed, her legs were shaky.

The ship's hum had stopped, replaced by an eerie silence. A narrow panel of the hull changed into red bricks and rippled into an archway. Through the arch, hazy in dawn fog, were silver birch trees and a neat lawn. Further away was a low fence. Latticed railing, the sort used in formal parks.

Charlotte moved cautiously towards the exit, wrinkling her nose at a bitter scent.

Burning coal? 'You'll be back with Jack before you know it,' said Sophie.

Charlotte's expression remained the same. She understood the odds. The likelihood they'd all be together as a family was vanishingly small.

Before this crossing, Sophie had been staying with her parents, appreciating every moment. Dead in one universe, they were very much alive in the universe she now called home. She would survive this 'last roll of the dice,' as Hugo called it. See her parents again, and her daughter. They'd survived the crossing!

Adrenaline surged in an energising wave. 'Juno, is H. G. Wells in your database in this universe?' During his time travels, the famous science-fiction writer had acquired the device that could safely convey them to Shorten — and to Bella.

Click. 'H. G. Wells is not in Juno's database.'

'Please search for Bertie Wells, author, and George Wells, author,' said Sophie. He might be using a different pseudonym.

'Done.'

'Can you tell us the result?' Sophie couldn't hide her frustration. Juno's software answered specific questions, never volunteered info.

'Neither name is in Juno's database.'

'Sophie, you're being irrational.' Freddy sighed. 'Asking the same questions won't change the answers.'

Einstein's definition of insanity. Repeating an action and expecting a different result. Sophie shot him a defensive glare. 'Now we've landed, Juno's systems might have picked up more facts.'

'Apart from travellers' tales, the database hasn't added new facts in two thousand years,' said Hugo. 'Arriving in this universe won't have changed that.'

They were right. Her fear was making her irrational, hoping facts she knew to be true would magically change.

In Sophie's universe, Wells' cousin had drawn the device as she saw it: a beautiful walking stick. That was an illusion. The real object was a metal cylinder. Wells' cousin had added her initials to the drawing and the date, *June 1889*, so the cylinder would still be there a few days later, in July. But Wells and his souvenir might not be in this universe. There were many universes where time passed at the same rate, where it was July 1889. This one had been randomly selected by Juno.

Outside the ship, it was getting light, yet the mist hadn't lifted. A silent spooky park. 'Juno, please confirm we're in London,' said Hugo.

'Destination confirmed.'

In accordance with Sophie's instruction, Juno answered Hugo's questions, despite him lacking the rare gene which allowed his companions to call this ship and travel. The gene had been passed down by the race who'd built the ship. Little was known about them, including their name. Calling them the builders seemed apt.

Sophie stepped away from the exit. 'Fingers crossed, Wells and the cylinder will be here.' Having the gene, she'd see the walking staff as it really was. No fancy carving or polished wood. Just a long grey tube and on the top, a transparent ball.

'If it's not here, we'll have to try a different universe.' Freddy sounded resigned but resolute. 'Most versions of 1889 should have Wells in them.'

Charlotte vigorously shook her head and Sophie stroked her. They'd barely survived this crossing. The thought of trying another one…

Juno's sister ship could protect passengers from the passage of time but using that vessel wasn't an option. The entity that controlled it, Janus, was trawling time and space to kill them. If they were ever to travel freely in his ship and live, Janus had to die.

Charlotte trotted closer to the arch and sniffed.

'Hold on,' said Sophie. 'We've got to dress the part.'

Charlotte turned and nodded.

Sophie went into Juno's loo. The facility resembled a design common in ancient Rome when Juno had been in service with her builders. There was a scrubbed bench with a hole and set on a shelf, layers of fabric served as toilet paper. A copper mirror gleamed above a basin and twisting a tap produced a sanitising green light. Shame it didn't dispense water.

After swiping the lime-green privacy curtain closed, she hauled off her T-shirt, stepped out of her shorts, and removed her bra. She kept on her modern knickers and pulled on black tights. Not everything had to be historically accurate. The boots, though, had to look right. Fortunately, finding ones with buttons and a kitten heel hadn't been difficult.

The boots had to be fastened *before* the corset. Once the stays were snug, bending from the waist was near impossible. She put on a thin shift that reached her knees and drew the corset down over her head. The stays pinched in her waist, supported her breasts and cushioned the weight of the petticoat and skirt she had yet to put on. Next came a flimsy sleeveless top that softened the corset's shape.

She moved Bella's rattle free, and her daughter's trusting face filled her mind. A deep, steadying breath. You can do this. Be brave.

CHAPTER 2

In the ship's main bay, Sophie turned her back to Hugo so he could lace up her corset. 'Not too tight,' she said, expecting him to make a quip about how sexy she looked in Victorian underwear.

But he didn't reply and when he'd finished tying the laces, he just kissed her bare shoulder, his face shuttered.

'This is the worst bit.' She hugged him. 'Before the start, worrying how much could go wrong—'

Click. 'You have designated supplies,' said Juno.

Freddy's brow creased. 'What do you mean?'

'Supplies designated as yours on landing.'

A light flashed some way down the cargo bay and though half-dressed, Sophie hurried towards it with the others. Hugo and Freddy were wearing trainers and their rubber soles squeaked on the metal floor. Sophie's boots sounded clumpy, and Charlotte's paws made an unsettling skittering noise.

Directly under the light was an open cardboard box containing a stack of cream vests. On top of the vests was a yellowing note with a ragged edge.

'This is my handwriting,' said Freddy, 'though it can't be.'

Hugo peered at it. 'Written by another version of you?'

Freddy read the note out loud. *Bullet and stab proof.* He picked it up. 'Juno, when was this left here?'

'Seven weeks and four days ago.'

'Juno, how come you didn't give these to other travellers?' said Hugo. The ship's supplies were a common resource.

'These items are designated private,' said Juno. 'Assigned to named travellers.'

'We can make any of our belongings … *designated*?' asked Sophie.

'Yes.'

Hugo grabbed the box. 'Nice to know.' On a previous crossing, unknown travellers had made off with their supplies.

'Juno, why didn't you tell us about the vests earlier?' said Freddy.

'Designated items are released after arrival. When travellers require them.'

Sophie swallowed. Right. If they survived the crossing. 'Juno, will the body armour work for Hugo?' Lacking the builders' gene, it might not.

'The clothing protects all individuals who wear it.'

Hugo's eyes registered his relief.

Click. 'You have a second designated item.' A light appeared further along the bay.

Under that light was a chunky bronze box and Sophie lifted the lid. Nestled on a blue velvet cushion was a gold bracelet. She gave a low whistle, and Charlotte stood on her hind legs to see. 'The bracelets that the time police wore in Rome... it's the same design.'

The mysterious couple had pulled Sophie out of the river Tiber and resuscitated her, but they'd also thrown her precious cylinder in the river, claimed they were protecting the timeline.

She examined the bracelet. No green gems, only rubies, and some sockets were empty, the holding clasps broken. And there was a note with it. Though it had been a while since she'd written anything by hand, Sophie did a double take. 'That's my writing. *Bracelet functions broken but locates the cylinder when it's...* I can't make out the last word. Scribbled in a tearing hurry.' She exhaled. 'I didn't write this, or I don't remember writing it. Must have been done by another ... me.'

Freddy frowned.

'I know.' Sophie shuddered. 'Creepy.'

Hugo gingerly took the bracelet from Sophie and Charlotte sniffed it. 'Juno, how does the wearer operate this to find the cylinder? Or does the bracelet find it automatically and inform the wearer?'

'Unknown.'

Hugo ran his finger over the gems. 'Juno, will this work for me?'

'No.'

He returned it to Sophie, and she kissed him on the cheek. 'One day, we'll come across awesome sci-fi toys *you* can use.' She folded the scrappy note, then slipped on the bracelet. The rubies were different shapes and shone and sparkled in the artificial light of the bay. It fitted perfectly on her wrist. Crafted for the other version of her?

'We shouldn't need to track the walking staff. If it's here, it'll be in Wells' flat.' Like Wells' cousin, Hugo saw the walking staff illusion, not the cylinder.

Not all the builders' technology appeared differently to individuals without the gene. Long ago, to impress the ancient Romans, the builders had used the cylinder to summon Janus from their ship. That Janus had just been a puppet, controlled by the builders, but for everyone who saw him, he'd been a mesmerising, terrifying sight. Eight feet tall, a divine warrior defending Rome, his armour had gleamed, and the sun had danced on the razor-sharp steel of his sword.

'The bracelet must help us locate the cylinder,' said Freddy, 'or the other you wouldn't have left it.'

Sophie nodded but her mind was still on the Janus puppet, centuries before a software upgrade made him sentient. 'It's surprising Wells had the presence of mind to steal the cylinder in Rome.' The builders had kept their field equipment close.

Hugo bit his lip. 'If not many versions of Wells stole it, that would reduce the odds of us finding it.'

'Even if only a tiny percentage managed it,' said Freddy, 'there are so many versions of Wells, that wouldn't materially affect the odds.'

As they retraced their steps towards the exit, Sophie pictured the cylinder: the transparent ball on the top, the see-through cover with a discreet lip to click it open, and inside, the three buttons in a line. The middle button summoned Janus out of his ship and viewed with the lip nearest to the operator, the button on the right returned him. It was the first button that reset the ship's systems. Handy for sorting glitches. But if used now, that button would send him right back to factory settings. The sentient malevolent god would once again be a mindless algorithm and his ship an obedient vessel. And that vessel would safely reunite them with Bella, and Freddy's fiancée.

Sophie's longing for that day was a physical ache. She knew it was the same for Freddy.

He sensed her gaze. 'The versions of us who left the bracelet and vests, I wish we could meet them.'

'I'm not sure I'd want to,' said Sophie. The idea of other

versions of them, of her, making different choices, living different lives, was … disturbing.

Hugo set the box of vests on the floor and removed one. 'This smaller size must be for you.'

Sophie took it. The material was silky smooth and stretchy. It smelled of nothing, felt clean, but looked worn. There was a slight, ragged tear in the neckline, as if it had caught on something.

'If this body armour works, the technology's impressive,' said Hugo. 'The 21st century equivalent weighs ten pounds or more.'

'How do you know?' Sophie was joking. Countless obscure facts were squirrelled away in his brain.

Hugo played along. 'Just general knowledge.'

Sophie slipped the vest over her corset. The garment protected her thighs and core and fitted snugly. Tailor-made for the other Sophie?

'This armour might give us an edge over Wells,' said Freddy.

Janus himself couldn't directly hurt them. Trapped in his ship, he'd previously sent different versions of Wells from other universes to kill them. The original author at home had been a gentle academic and author. Janus had selected flawed versions, men prepared to murder and maim.

Sophie pulled the vest further down over her thighs. If they were up against the Wells who belonged in this universe, it didn't mean this would be easier. They'd hoped to select a universe where Wells was out of his mind on opium, or an invalid, or both. Unfortunately, with Juno's outdated database, selecting this universe had been as much of a gamble as the crossing.

Charlotte's vest covered all of her, except her head and lower legs. Sophie fastened Charlotte's summer dog coat over the vest. Dark grey, the coat might attract less attention.

'The vests and bracelet are like the shield and sword a knight collects before a quest,' said Freddy.

Sophie straightened. 'You're an incurable romantic.'

'Thinking of this as a quest makes me braver.' Freddy tugged the vest to cover his hips.

'And all quests end, one way or another,' said Hugo. 'Which in an odd way is comforting.'

'In a quest story I read before university, the hero had to stay brave, all the while knowing that when he completed it, he'd die.' Sophie tied the 'lobster tail' underskirt, with flexible steel hoops at the back, around her waist. 'I don't remember why, but at the end he survived.'

'I don't believe Janus can see all ends,' said Freddy, applying Gandalf-wisdom to the Roman god.

The lobster tail was crazy big. Large bustles were the fashion. Sophie pulled on the petticoat which hid the ridges. 'Remind me why you think he can't see all ends.' Janus was master of time, had omnipotent knowledge of the past, the present, and the future.

'There are too many universes for him to control. Gives us wriggle room.' Freddy looked sheepish. 'That's supposition.' With a starred first in mathematics from Cambridge University, he relished working through problems. This, though, was beyond even him.

From the storage shelf, Sophie picked up a matching navy skirt and jacket that when worn, appeared to be a single dress. She'd found them on eBay, left over from a period drama. The skirt had pockets. Anachronistic but useful. Sophie pocketed the bracelet note.

The fashionable line of genuine late 19th century skirts would have been spoiled by pockets. This skirt was fuller at the front to accommodate them and at the back, it followed the shape of the bustle. Unlike in Shorten, the jacket fastened at the front. The wearer's shoulders appeared narrower, thanks to the long sleeves with a puff shape at the top.

'We should have bought you the second jacket too,' said Hugo. Styled for the evening, it had been too expensive.

'Whether we succeed or fail, this should only take a day.' Freddy fussed with his bow tie.

Hugo tucked his pale blue shirt into his trousers. 'No plan survives contact with the enemy.'

'Who said that?' said Sophie. 'I mean, apart from you.'

'A 19th century general. Or more bluntly, to quote Mike Tyson, everyone has a plan until they get punched in the mouth.'

'The American boxer.' Freddy made a face. 'I suppose he'd know.'

Sophie moved a silver brooch from her T-shirt to her jacket. Brought from Rome, the curving gold lines joined at the centre on the display side and stretched out four ways. On the back was carved *AETERNUM*. Eternally. The lines symbolised her and Charlotte, and Hugo and Freddy, bound by love and friendship. And if objects harnessed protective energy, the brooch and Bella's rattle were a powerful combo.

Hugo helped arrange her hair up in a neat bun, and she fixed a dainty boxy hat with a short pin, so the front peeped over her brow. Freddy and Hugo were dapper in dark three-piece suits and grey ties. The jackets were longer than modern ones, reaching their knees.

Hugo plonked on a top hat. He'd never been a fan of hats.

'We look like unremarkable Victorians.' Freddy transferred the vest note from the pocket of his shorts to his jacket.

Sophie tugged on navy gloves. When she'd first found herself in Shorten, wearing gloves while out and about had been compulsory. Now, that infuriating convention reminded her of a safer time and place.

She grabbed the carrying handle of a large Mary Poppins carpet bag. Inside were basic supplies including spare underwear, a packet of codeine, a first aid carry case taken from Juno, shaving stuff for Hugo and Freddy, poo bags for Charlotte, and a dog-travel device that poured water into a shallow bowl. Sophie folded her T-shirt and shorts into the bag, to sleep in, and added Charlotte's page-turning machine.

Hugo took a notebook from his trouser pocket and tore out two pages. He gave one to Sophie and one to Freddy.

'Keep this safe,' said Hugo. 'It'll ensure you can get home by yourself.'

They might not all survive. Sophie swiped away the thought and scanned the note. *21st century universe 666, designation ending 3940279473939.* The core number 666 had been assigned to their universe many centuries ago, evolving into myth and theology. She pushed it into her skirt pocket with the bracelet note. Juno had confirmed their home universe when they'd boarded.

Freddy slipped his paper into a jacket pocket. Hugo had copied the Shorten designation when they'd crossed to Rome. Freddy put on his hat and turned towards the exit. Charlotte was already there, gazing out. The park was still deserted and foggy.

'Juno, where are we in London?' Sophie asked.

Click. 'Within the Marble Arch monument in Hyde Park.'

'What's the date?' said Freddy.

'Thursday, 4th July 1889.'

'American Independence Day,' said Sophie. A happy anniversary for America and, hopefully, happy for them.

'Local time?' said Hugo.

'05.37 am.'

Everyone except Charlotte adjusted their analogue watches.

CHAPTER 3

Out in the park, the huge Marble Arch monument, built to celebrate British victories over Napoleon, was half hidden in mist. Juno was nestled within it, her shape mirroring the larger triumphal gateway. Flanking the central arch were smaller arches.

Sophie coughed. Tiny particles of coal in the warm air tasted bitter on her tongue.

Freddy scanned the park. 'What beastly fog.' Above them, invisible birds were chattering in ghostly trees.

Charlotte barked and inside a minor arch of the monument, a shadow moved. A raised arm? A pistol?

The sound of someone clapping, and something hit Sophie square on the chest, the force of it flinging her backwards, the bullet absorbed by her vest.

Clap.

'Back into Juno!' Hugo's order was a panicked gasp.

They scrambled towards the ship. The entrance was still open and only yards away but getting there took forever. Clap, clap.

Everybody threw themselves in, landing on the bay floor.

Freddy landed on top of Charlotte who'd got there first. Sophie squirmed around, holding the bag up as a makeshift shield.

'Juno, shut the door,' Hugo yelled.

Silence.

'Juno, shut the door,' Sophie said in a rush. If the shooter came in, they'd be finished.

The brick exit changed into solid hull with a click, sealing off the park, and Sophie took a quivering, relieved breath. 'Juno, obey Hugo as you would me.'

They'd been out of the ship for just minutes. Losing Hugo's status with Juno had wasted precious seconds, could have cost them dearly. She put aside the bag, staggered to her feet, and touched a tiny hole in her jacket. Her breastbone hurt but there was no blood. 'Saved by the magic vest.' Charlotte was unhurt, and Sophie wheeled around to check on Hugo and Freddy. 'Are you okay?'

'No.' Hugo was clutching his arm, his face ashen.

Sophie hastily peeled off her gloves and removed his jacket. His shirt was stained red below his elbow. Sophie rolled up the sleeve, revealing a shallow gash on the outside of his arm. 'Superficial. Luckily. We need a bandage though.'

Freddy hurried over to a rack holding medical supplies. Sophie had a carrycase of Juno's first aid stuff in her bag, but they might need that in 1889.

She cleaned Hugo's injury with wipes, cut off a good-sized bandage with scissors, and secured the dressing. The bandage was slimy with antibiotic paste and stuck on without tying. She used the last of the water to rinse his shirt sleeve and helped him get his jacket back on.

Freddy returned the medical stuff to its rack. 'That could have been the Wells that comes with this universe, or the version Janus has sent.'

Every assassin changed the timeline, and to adjust for a

myriad of consequences far into the future, Janus could only send one assassin to a universe at a time. He was sending assassins to other universes to kill other versions of them, so consequences were complicated, even for a god.

Sophie sat on a metal bench beside Hugo. She wanted to slump. Impossible with her corset. Charlotte was lying down, silent and alert, facing what had been the exit.

'This Wells was quick off the mark,' said Freddy.

Armed with Janus' itinerary as well as a pistol, he knew where they'd go and what they'd do — before they did.

Hugo winced. 'Wells didn't know about our body armour, which means Janus doesn't know. How can he not know?'

'Proof he's not infallible.' Freddy sat down heavily on a bench.

'Why didn't Wells finish us off in here?' said Sophie. Charlotte turned her head to stare at her mistress and the question hung in the air.

'At home, guns with silencers make that clap noise,' said Hugo.

Sophie took that in, beyond grateful for their body armour.

'I didn't spot the pistol,' said Hugo. 'Did you?'

Freddy shook his head. So did Charlotte.

'I saw it,' said Sophie. 'For a split second.'

'How big was it?' Hugo asked her.

Strange question. 'Regular size.'

'A silencer attached to the barrel makes a weapon much larger.' Hugo spread his hands. 'A foot long.'

'It wasn't that big,' said Sophie. 'I'd have noticed.'

'A built-in silencer for a handgun has yet to be invented. Wells must have acquired it from beyond the 21st century.' Hugo flexed his injured arm. 'Lucky it hasn't got nastier extras. Radiation, poison…'

'Shame Juno doesn't stock the normal sort.' Sophie rubbed her bruised chest.

Hugo looked up from his arm. 'We should ask her.'

'Juno, do you have weapons?' said Freddy, as if he were ordering afternoon tea.

Click. 'One, left by a traveller.'

Sophie bit her lip. A poor soul who hadn't survived a crossing. 'Please show us where it is.' Getting info out of Juno was like pulling teeth.

A light flashed some way down the bay, and they all trooped towards it, including Charlotte, evidently satisfied Juno's exit was secure.

On a rack beside a worn string sack of bullets was a small handgun with a battered metal handle and a round barrel.

'Like something from the Wild West,' said Hugo.

Charlotte sniffed at the sack.

Freddy picked up the gun and spun the barrel, showing empty cavities. 'I can use this.' He'd hunted on the Shorten estate since he was five.

They returned to the bay near the exit and familiarised themselves with the pistol. It was compact and light enough to fit into a pocket.

Sophie put the ammunition in the carpet bag. She didn't want to kill this version of Wells, or anyone. Her parents' principles still resonated, including the quote from her mother's faith book. *When you see the light in each and every person, you should never extinguish it, for a greater good or self-defence...*

But to take the cylinder and reach Bella, they had to defend themselves, and half-measures could get them killed. Sophie raised her chin. 'If Wells confronts us, we won't have time to load the pistol.'

'It doesn't have a safety mechanism,' said Hugo.

Freddy slotted bullets into the weapon. 'If we leave a single chamber empty, in front of the hammer, that should stop accidents.' He slipped it into his trouser pocket.

CHAPTER 4

Four hours later, just before ten am, Sophie and Freddy flattened themselves on one side of where the ship's exit would appear. Hugo and Charlotte did the same on the other side.

Sophie took a deep breath. 'Juno, open the door.'

The arch appeared. The fog outside had lifted, was a high, soft veil against a clear sky. Children were playing noisy chasing games, and couples were strolling, arm in arm. The men's suits and hats matched Hugo and Freddy's, and the women's clothes were like Sophie's. They'd fit right in — if they could get past the shooter.

Freddy held the pistol in both hands and stepped out first. Hugo and Sophie emerged behind him with Charlotte. The monument's small arches were empty, and they hastily checked the park.

'No sign of him.' Freddy returned the weapon to his pocket.

Sophie could still taste coal dust in her mouth. The smog that reeked of it, shrouding the sun, might linger all day. Yet no one else seemed bothered. People stared at Charlotte's grey dog coat, covering her pale vest, and Charlotte pretended not to notice.

A line of trees edged the park, obscuring the road beyond and dampening the sound of clattering hooves from the traffic. The air was ripe with horse dung. Smelled no worse than diesel fumes.

A young woman walked by, pushing a sturdy metal pram. Its four wheels were larger than modern buggies, with delicate inner spokes. Just visible at the front of the pram, under a leather fold-up awning, was a baby, its cheeks rosy and plump. Sophie briefly closed her eyes. Don't think about Bella. Focus on finding the cylinder. She turned back her sleeve and tapped the stones on the bracelet, hoping one would somehow point the way to Wells' home. 'No idea how this works.'

Hugo clumsily unfolded a map of 21st century London, using his good arm. He'd crossed out anything built after 1889. 'It's just a few miles' walk to Wells' flat.' He sighed. 'Going there is suicidal so, hopefully, unpredictable.' They could only defeat Wells — and Janus — by not behaving logically, changing the timeline and subverting Janus' itinerary. 'We know the cylinder's there. Catch-22.'

'Catch what?' said Freddy.

'It's the title of a novel,' said Hugo. 'The hero is a World War II pilot who wants to get out of flying dangerous missions against the Nazis.'

Freddy adjusted his hat. 'Not very heroic.'

'By requesting an assessment to prove he's insane, the request itself demonstrates he's sane,' said Hugo. 'So, he can never be relieved of duty.'

'Why number 22?' asked Sophie.

'I can't remember,' said Hugo, 'but we're in the same boat.'

Sophie sighed. 'All we can do is keep an eye out for Wells or the criminals he'll hire.'

'And we have the pistol.' Freddy patted his pocket.

Hugo turned slowly around. 'The monument at home in 1889 was at the edge of the park, not inside it, and this park is much bigger. I wonder what else is different?'

'Which way?' said Freddy, keen to keep him on track.

Hugo traced the route on the map with his forefinger. 'Down through Marylebone, then alongside Regents Park.'

Sophie attached a lead to Charlotte's collar for appearances' sake, and Charlotte accepted it with a shrug. Leaving the grass and trees behind, they went left, on alert for Wells.

On the road, a cacophony of clip-clops mixed with the sharp rattle of wheels. Black hansom cabs with a single horse and only two passengers, weaved easily around larger hackney cabs.

'In Shorten, the London taxis were painted cool colours,' said Sophie, remembering a red cab they'd taken to Clarissa's house.

'Perhaps black's the cheapest paint?' said Freddy.

A constable was standing on a concrete box in the centre of the road, blowing a whistle as a speeding carriage whipped past him. His trousers and jacket were navy, and his jacket was fastened with shiny, silver-coloured buttons. His high collar was stiff, with a symbol stitched in white. A letter or number? The leather belt around his waist had a buckle, used to secure his truncheon, and his custodian helmet was also dark blue. Tall and rounded with a slight brim, it had a metal badge, displaying the man's district designation and the royal crown. The outfit was ludicrously smart for directing traffic.

A carriage glided through the mayhem. It had darkened windows, the Victorian equivalent of tinted privacy glass. Next came a cart filled with ironmongery, pulled by a tired horse. It clattered beside a red bus with an open top deck.

'Do you see the colours the same as home?' Sophie asked

Hugo. Without the gene, he sometimes saw them differently, depending on the universe.

'Slightly faded, but that could be the fog.'

As Sophie walked, a summer breeze caressed her face, and her skirts made a pleasing swishing sound. 'This is stressful though also amazing.'

Hugo rubbed his injured arm. 'It is.'

Freddy looked thoughtful. 'This isn't so different from how the city will be in 1910.'

'Did you visit London then?' Hugo asked him.

Freddy nodded. 'I was six, only remember bits.'

Other pedestrians were dressed as befitted their social station. Women in brown, shapeless dresses, squished hats and worn boots, rubbed shoulders with ladies in bustle skirts and matching jackets fashioned from rich silk, satin, and velvet. The better-off carried plain umbrellas or parasols trimmed with lace. Men were hurrying to work, their cheap suits paired with bowler hats. Manual workers wore ill-matched tatty jackets and trousers. A few men sported top hats.

Lining the street were flower shops, stores selling bric-à-brac, butchers, fishmongers, and milliners. On the floors above the shops were signs advertising rooms to let.

Sophie paused by an apothecary window with glass jars of dried herbs, roots, and plants under a black and white sign: BREW IN TEA. The jars were labelled in neat copper-plate: lavender to sooth, peppermint for headaches, willow bark to ease pain.

Further on, shops were interspersed with large town-houses. Maids and housewives hurried along with provisions, dodging small children in rags, and earnest young men strode towards unknown appointments. A few couples and families were simply enjoying a day out, heading for Regents Park.

This was the heart of an empire where the sun never set and, for those with money, a time of security and prosperity. But Sophie couldn't relax and take it all in. Her brain was too busy picturing Wells.

With Janus' itinerary listing everything they'd do, he'd be ready for them.

CHAPTER 5

Fitzroy Road was a residential street. Modest compared to the homes in Marylebone, the identical Georgian houses still had three floors and a basement. Freddy led the way up the short flight of stairs to number 46, took the pistol from his pocket and cocked it.

'Are you sure this is the right house?' asked Sophie. There was no panel with flat numbers and names.

'I'm sure.' Hugo knew everything there was to know about the science-fiction author, including where he lived.

Freddy rang a bellpull and held the gun behind his back. The door was opened by a grumpy woman with grey-flecked hair.

'Can I help you?' The woman's brown skirt and jacket were neat and unfussy, the bustle on her skirt smaller than Sophie's.

'We're friends of Mr Wells,' said Freddy.

The woman eyed Charlotte. 'Keep it on a lead. First floor. No guests after six.' She gestured for them to go in, closed the front door, and disappeared into a sitting room.

Hugo and Freddy took off their top hats and headed up the stairs. Sophie and Charlotte followed.

Freddy knocked and a sing-song voice shouted in response. 'Coming.'

After half a minute, H. G. Wells opened the door. His face was plumper than the versions in Rome, but his outsized, droopy moustache was instantly recognisable from 19th century photos at home. And he was younger. Early twenties, the same age as them. Over his trousers and pale, long-sleeved shirt, he wore a lilac apron, splattered with flour. He dragged flour-flecked fingers through his brown hair, spreading the powder across his parting. If he was armed with his futuristic weapon, he was making no effort to find and fire it.

Freddy blinked, wrong-footed by the apron and the flour, and moved the pistol into his pocket. 'Apologies for disturbing you.'

'Please don't worry.' Wells hadn't noticed the pistol, his attention on Charlotte. 'What a charming jacket your dog is wearing.'

Wells' voice had a higher timbre than the other versions. Charlotte put her head on one side, assessing him. Sophie assessed him too. Unless he was an incredibly accomplished actor, he had no idea who they were, and didn't perceive them as a threat.

'You're from another lost-and-found agency?' Wells' tone was hopeful.

This Wells was so different from what they'd expected, everyone was struck dumb. Finally, Sophie nodded. Whatever was going on, they needed to stay alert. Grab the cylinder and get out.

'Do come in,' said Wells.

In the hall was a closed wooden packing box and resting on it was a pretty lilac hat. Presumably, the hat belonged to

Wells' cousin. Wells strolled past it and gestured them through to a shabby sitting room.

Sophie perched beside Hugo on a dark green sofa near a cold fireplace. White crochet antimacassars protected the back and arms, like covers on train seats. In front of the sofa was a splendid low table. The round top had exquisite marquetry inlay, with circles of many hues of wood edged with gilt. A battered carriage clock sat on the mantlepiece. The clock wasn't ticking, and the hands were stuck on midday.

The room smelled of lavender and wax, as if recently polished. Freddy perched on a different sofa, Charlotte at his feet, and placed his hat next to him. His sandy hair had a faint line around his head, a dent where the hat had been.

Wells looked them up and down. 'Your agency must pay well.'

'I beg your pardon?' said Freddy, flummoxed.

Wells gestured at Freddy's and Hugo's hats. Top hats were expensive. Unlikely to be worn by men employed by … what type of agency had Wells mentioned? Lost-and-found… Recovering stolen goods? Sophie cleared her throat. Go with it. 'We only recover items for the most discerning clients.'

Wells' eyes narrowed. 'I won't pay if you haven't found it.'

'Found what?' asked Freddy.

'Why, the walking stick of course.' Wells' oversized moustache twitched.

Hugo's expression was carefully blank, Freddy's face fell, and Charlotte went still. Wells and the cylinder were in this universe, but Wells didn't have it. Stolen? Sophie stared at her lap, the jolt of disappointment making her eyelids prickle. She'd been so fixated with taking on Wells, it hadn't occurred to her the cylinder wouldn't be here. Wells' cousin had dated her sketch June 1889. Instead of 4th July, they should have chosen 1ˢᵗ June and if necessary, waited for Wells to bring home the cylinder.

She briskly wiped her eyes. The cylinder was missing, and other elements were too. The last version of Wells she'd come across in Rome had been desperate and dangerous. All she got from this man was mild curiosity, though his eyes were like the other versions, an unusual cobalt blue.

He gave them a probing look. 'I have six shillings put by, though you don't have it, do you?' He studied his flour-specked slippers. 'Commonplace to others, unique to me.'

Right. Wells saw the cylinder as it really was but didn't know what it could do.

'Which agency are you from?'

'It's new,' said Hugo, thinking fast.

'I won't pay more,' said Wells. 'The agency lady who called after breakfast apparently wanted ten shillings.'

'Apparently?' Freddy tapped his fingers on the arm of the sofa.

'My cousin answered the door. The lady wanted payment in advance.' Wells sat down in an armchair and shook his head. 'My cousin gave her short shrift.'

They needed more info on the cylinder. Maintain the fiction they were from an agency. 'We only take payment if we find the item,' said Sophie. They might yet track it down. 'Where did you lose it?'

'I included that in the notice.' Wells wiped his brow with his hand, smearing more flour. 'I left it on a bus.'

'More details would be helpful,' said Hugo, smoothly.

'I was coming back from work. The Mortimer Terrace route. Last Tuesday in the late afternoon. A passenger fainted and in the fuss of helping him… I was tired, the end of term and all that.'

Wells at home had been a teacher at a boys' school. So far, so similar.

Wells sighed. 'It hasn't been handed in to the bus company. Let's hope it proves a useful walking aid to whoever took it.'

He didn't seem particularly bothered. Why wasn't he distraught?

'Isn't it too heavy to use as a walking stick?' said Hugo. 'I mean, for someone other than you?' Hugo had speculated in Rome that for people without the gene, the cylinder would be too hefty to move, never mind steal.

'My cousin carried it easily.' Wells narrowed his eyes again, suspicious.

Every parallel universe had different physics, biology, and chemistry, ranging from tiny differences to big ones. That affected how individuals missing the gene interacted with the builders' equipment.

Distract him. 'We understand you're an author,' said Sophie.

'Why does everyone keep saying that?'

Freddy caught Sophie's eye and she gave a slight nod. Time to take the gloves off. Metaphorically. As a female guest in Wells' home, convention dictated her actual gloves had to stay on.

'By "everyone," you mean Janus,' said Freddy.

Wells gulped. 'You've travelled with him?'

'We have,' said Sophie.

Wells paused, taking that in. 'You're not from an agency.'

'We're not,' admitted Hugo.

Wells jumped to his feet, his face as pale as the flecks of flour. 'I feel the need for tea.' His voice was shaky. 'Would you care for a cup?'

'Thank you,' said Sophie, automatically, still evaluating him. 'That would be kind.'

'I'll fetch water for the dog.'

'She'd prefer tea,' said Freddy, 'in a bowl.'

'A bowl,' Wells echoed vaguely. He went over to a chest of drawers and fetched a worn cloth which he carefully laid out over the posh table.

'It's a lovely piece of furniture,' said Hugo.

Wells beamed. 'I bought it a week ago.' He hurried out, presumably to the kitchen.

Hugo lifted the side of the cloth to examine the decorated table edge. 'This must have cost a pretty penny.'

'He doesn't seem worried we've travelled with Janus,' said Freddy.

'Just surprised,' said Hugo.

Charlotte looked to her mistress for guidance. Instinct told Sophie this Wells was harmless, but caution could save their lives. 'This might all be an act, so he can take *us* by surprise.'

CHAPTER 6

Ten minutes had passed since Wells had left the sitting room. Freddy waited beside the doorway, his pistol ready. Sophie, Hugo, and Charlotte lined up behind him. Wells came in and with great care, put down a laden tea tray on the expensive table. He straightened and cast around for his guests.

Sophie sagged in relief. A confused host, not an assassin. She rushed forward with Charlotte to distract him, giving Freddy time to pocket the pistol. Hugo strolled over to the window, holding his sore arm.

'Let me help you with that.' Sophie set out the crockery, her cheeks warm with embarrassment. Okay, you could be too paranoid.

Wells gave her an appreciative nod and smiled at Charlotte who was sitting demurely beside the table. 'The bowl wouldn't fit on the tray.' He left and returned, placing the bowl on the boarded floor.

'Would you mind being mother?' asked Wells, addressing Sophie.

She only hesitated for a moment, distracted by the old-fashioned saying. 'Of course.' She poured milk into small cups, and then tea from a pot. She poured the rest of the tea into Charlotte's bowl. Charlotte preferred Earl Grey, but she drank the regular sort.

'I never expected to meet anyone who'd encountered Janus,' said Wells. 'I should have realised there'd be others.' He took a delicate sip of tea, practised at keeping food and drink away from his moustache. 'Introductions are in order, are they not?'

Freddy introduced them, including Charlotte. 'When did you begin your adventures?'

'Adventures? I'm not sure I'd call them that.' Wells cleared his throat. 'It started in February last year. I didn't get home for weeks.'

Sophie ground her teeth. The cylinder had been safely in this flat for well over a year.

'You previously rented a smaller flat,' said Hugo, 'on the same road.'

Wells stared at him. 'How on earth do you know that?'

'Where we come from, you're famous,' said Hugo.

'I have no wish to be famous.' Wells put down his teacup. 'A fortune teller told an acquaintance of mine he'd be famous. He later committed suicide, was famous for a day. His picture was in *The Times*.' He swallowed. 'What happens to make me famous?'

'Nothing bad,' said Hugo.

'With fame comes scrutiny. Perhaps it's for the best the object is lost.' Wells paused. 'Where are you from?'

'The future,' said Freddy, keeping things simple. Wells was stressed enough. Not the moment to explain parallel universes.

'The future,' Wells echoed, accepting this. Unsurprising, given what he'd been through.

'How did your time-travelling begin?' said Freddy.

'In Derbyshire, in a pub. I got rather inebriated and after closing time, I sneaked into the basement for more wine. The cellar was dimly lit, and I stubbed my toe on a storage box.' He steeled himself. 'At the rear of the cellar was a scruffy door, arched and painted green. I hoped it would lead to a room with better wine.'

'The entrance changes its appearance to fit in with its surroundings,' said Sophie.

'Your experience will inspire a classic horror story. *The Door in the Wall*.' Hugo's tone reflected his respect for the author's work, but Wells looked bemused.

Sophie's mind shifted to Shorten, to when she'd fallen off a horse and been convalescing. At her bedside, Hugo had read to her *The Door in the Wall*. The short tale had ended badly for the hero. Stepping across what he'd thought was a supernatural threshold, he'd fallen down a shaft to his death.

'There was a second cellar,' said Wells. 'The wine wasn't real. My hand passed right through the racks.'

'The ship probes travellers' brains,' said Freddy, 'creates an interior that matches their expectation.'

'I travelled in a *ship*?' Wells' mouth dropped open. Sharing this was traumatic. 'The door swung shut behind me, so I opened it and went out. Found myself in ancient Rome.'

'You believed you were in the pretend cellar for a few moments,' said Freddy. 'You may have been there for days or weeks.'

Wells finished his tea, taking his time. 'I walked a few steps, the green door vanished, and I assumed I was dreaming. Eventually, I accepted I was awake and I was consumed by crippling panic. I had no idea what to do.'

'Perfectly understandable,' said Sophie, wanting to comfort him. She didn't pat his hand. After all, they hardly knew him.

'In the cellar, when you noticed the green door, what were you thinking?' Hugo asked him.

'The wretched crate I'd stubbed my toe on. It had the classical horn of plenty on the front, contained bottles of olive oil.'

'Janus twisted your thoughts,' said Freddy. 'Used the image from antiquity to take you to Rome.'

'I've tried to make sense of it, but I didn't connect that image with the destination,' said Wells. 'What did Janus stand to gain?'

'He gets his kicks from travellers' fear,' said Hugo. 'Enjoys toying with them.'

Charlotte nodded. Fortunately, Wells didn't notice. Charlotte was usually careful not to nod in front of strangers. She'd evidently concluded Wells wasn't a threat.

'Did you go to Rome?' asked Wells.

'We did,' said Freddy. 'Truly memorable.'

'We'd love to hear about your visit.' Hugo sounded mildly curious, as if enquiring about a regular holiday. Didn't want Wells to clam up. 'Did you stay long?'

'Only a week or so. I used my rudimentary Latin. Sold my pocket watch, lived in a room above a bar, and had enough to eat. My moustache brought unwelcome attention, so I had it shaved off at the baths. After a few days, I almost enjoyed being in 99 AD.'

Sophie set down her cup. Wells had been in a version of Rome four years after they'd time-travelled there.

Wells' full lips wobbled, his splendid moustache trembling in sympathy. 'The glory that was Rome!'

'Did you go to Janus' festival?' prompted Sophie.

'I watched him stride out,' said Wells. 'The crowd was enjoying the spectacle, so I relaxed. Then something frightened a donkey by a cart, the animal bolted, and the revellers panicked. Most people ran towards the road, careless of who they trampled. I fled in the opposite direction and stumbled across a metal object. I picked it up on impulse.'

'Wasn't the object guarded?' Freddy asked him.

'Guarded? Everyone was desperate to escape the crush.'

Sophie thought back to the riverbank in Rome when she'd been in the protective sphere. She and the time police couple had been unaffected by anything or anyone outside. Faced with being crushed by the crowd, the builders' team may have hurriedly created a similar sphere, leaving the cylinder.

Wells took a handkerchief from his apron pocket and wiped his brow. 'Inside Juno's arch, the green door was there, looking like part of a rundown shed.' He drew a calming breath. 'I went into the pretend cellar and heard a booming voice.'

'Did you say Janus' name out loud?' said Freddy.

Janus only conversed with travellers who did. A builders' safeguard, to stop him terrifying accidental travellers.

'I put the metal object on the floor...' Wells bit his lip, trying to remember. 'I said something like, what a strange Janus souvenir.'

'What did the voice say?' Freddy was aiming for casual and failing.

'That I should leave the keepsake with him, and I promised I would. But then I concluded that keeping the object would prove this nightmare had been real. Prove I was sane.' Wells sighed. 'I stepped out with the object, though not into the pub. I was in a ravaged landscape, strewn with dead men and dead horses. Then the door vanished, just as it had before. I came across soldiers who nearly shot me. Fortunately, I cried out and they realised I was English, like them.' Wells stared into space. 'They assumed I was a war reporter and complained about the French weather.'

'Did it rain while you were there?' said Sophie. The cylinder broke in contact with water, might be useless.

Wells shook his head. 'I asked how long they'd been fighting in France. That's how I discovered I'd travelled to the future, to 1917.'

For Wells, 1917 was the future, not the past.

'Were you thinking about the real pub before you found yourself in France?' said Hugo. 'Was the wine in the cellar French? Janus needs something in a traveller's mind, however tenuous, to select a destination for his own amusement.'

'All the wine was French,' said Wells. 'I pictured the bottles, and a vineyard. I suppose there could once have been vines in that hell. So many terrible explosions, I was terrified I'd be blown to pieces, but by some miracle the door appeared. I went through and told Janus I wished to return to the real pub cellar. Seconds later, I put the object under my arm, threw myself out, and banged my hand on the wine racks. I couldn't stop shaking.' He gripped the arms of his chair. 'If you're from the future, you must know about the French war.'

'The war wasn't just in France,' said Hugo. 'It's called World War 1 or the Great War.'

'Janus sent you there too?'

'Luckily not.' Remembering medieval Georgia, Sophie added, 'We have experienced other times and places. Some were … unpleasant.'

Wells hugged himself. 'It's strangely comforting that I'm not the only person this has happened to.'

Charlotte blinked her understanding.

'It's made me appreciate my humdrum life,' said Wells. 'Some good came from it.' He sighed. 'Everyone else saw the metal object as a walking stick. I soon stopped questioning that. I had no desire to be locked in an asylum.' He considered them in turn. 'You know when I last had it, the bus route and the date. Can you find it?'

I was coming home from work... Sophie leaned forward. 'Why did you take it to work?'

Wells shifted in his chair. 'Some days my mind seeks out dark thoughts. Holding that object reinforced my conviction that the strange events hadn't been a crazed delusion.' He scrutinised them. 'But you coming here, that's proof.' Wells sat up straighter. 'I'm determined to prevent the terrible war. Years in advance, I shall write to the papers and cajole politicians in public and in private.'

They'd been baffled why the Great War had never happened in Shorten. There was probably a complex chain of reasons, yet here was proof that the Wells in this universe would try to prevent it. Maybe succeed. 'Did Janus say he'd help you stop the war?' said Sophie.

'I decided once I was home.'

'Did he offer you your heart's desire?' asked Hugo. They'd speculated Janus had made spurious promises to persuade other versions of Wells to kill for him.

Wells appeared confused. 'He just said I was a wonderful author.'

Sophie wanted to protect this Wells. 'Janus will offer you fame and fortune. Don't believe him. It's a ruse to make you work for him.'

Wells looked wildly around. 'How can he do that? Is he here?'

'He can't leave his ship,' said Freddy. 'He'll beguile you with promises when you go back to him.'

'Go back!' Wells' words came out as a squeak. 'Why would I do that?'

'To visit the future,' said Hugo. 'Find inspiration for your novels.'

Wells' cobalt eyes darkened. 'I will *never* go back. Besides, I have no interest in writing fiction.'

'Really?' said Sophie.

'If you don't wish to be famous, you could write under a pen name?' said Hugo.

'Writing a book of recipes has some appeal.'

'Some authors get rich writing cookbooks,' said Sophie, thinking of celebrity chefs at home.

'I don't need money,' said Wells. 'I've invested in the stock market with my knowledge of the future.'

'About the war?' said Freddy.

'Indirectly. Every chance they got, the soldiers smoked, mostly Greys cigarettes. I bought shares in the company and a week afterwards the company was bought up and the value of my shares rose ... significantly. That, and with further investments, life is more comfortable.' He gestured at the table. 'You seem relaxed about your own travels. Can you go to the past, stop me losing the object? I'd be grateful for its return.'

Sophie suppressed a sigh. They couldn't find the cylinder for themselves, let alone return it to Wells. They could risk crossing in Juno to a date between May 1888 and May 1889, but in another universe, a different Wells might have returned from his travels outside of those dates or without the cylinder. Or never been born.

She got to her feet and turned the bracelet on her wrist. There must be a way to figure this out.

CHAPTER 7

Outside 46 Fitzroy Road, Freddy put on his hat. 'I'm glad I didn't shoot him.'

'I'm glad too,' said Sophie. There was no way this Wells had ambushed them by the arch. She scrutinised the quiet street, checking for the different version, hand-picked by Janus.

'Wells stole the cylinder in Rome, and countless other versions must have too,' said Freddy. 'Why would Janus send them there, knowing they'll acquire the only thing that can end him?'

'Arrogance? Boredom?' Hugo put on his hat, using his good arm. 'He's been immortal for a long time.'

Freddy stomped down the road, his lips compressed in a grumpy line. 'This Wells is a good chap, if careless.'

Charlotte trotted by his side and Sophie caught up with them. 'Preventing the Great War will make a civil war more likely.' The conflict in 1920s Shorten had blighted countless lives. 'I half hope he succeeds.'

'His determination may inspire others,' said Freddy.

'Nice Wells was obviously baking bread or a cake,' said

Hugo. 'But I think we also caught him doing something … private.'

'With his cousin Isabel?' Sophie slightly turned back to the house. 'Do you think she was there, out of sight?' In due course, he'd marry her.

'No,' said Hugo.

'Someone else?' said Freddy. 'Wells in Shorten had many mistresses.'

Did he sound envious? Sophie rolled her eyes. 'He's not exactly a looker and didn't strike me as a womaniser.'

'When Wells opened the door, his hair was smoothed flat,' said Hugo, 'as if he'd been wearing a hat.'

Sophie hadn't noticed. 'So?'

'The lilac hat on the packing case matched his pinny,' said Hugo. 'Just before we called, I reckon he was wearing it.'

'It was a lady's hat,' said Freddy.

'There were rumours about our Wells at home,' said Hugo. 'Gossip he was actually female because he had a reedy voice.'

Freddy shook his head. 'Every Wells we've come up against has been male.'

'Perhaps at home, and here, he was seen in women's clothes and people drew the wrong conclusion?' said Hugo.

'I can't see the attraction of lady's clothes,' said Freddy. 'They look … uncomfortable.'

'That may be the point,' said Hugo, eliciting a puzzled frown from Freddy.

'We need to stay *on* point.' Sophie stopped and peeled off a glove. 'This is why the other me left us this.' She tapped the rubies on her bracelet. Nothing happened. 'Maybe it works at a specific time of day?' She was clutching at straws.

'The walking staff operates within a fixed radius around Janus' ship,' said Hugo. 'If the bracelet uses the same technology, perhaps to track the walking staff, it has to be close to it?'

Sophie squinted at him. 'Surely that defeats the point of a tracking function?'

'We should check London, street by street,' said Freddy.

'That would take months or years.' Hugo sounded weary. 'Dad's sovereigns won't stretch that far.' They only had two, the last of his father's collection.

'This is a job for Sherlock Holmes,' said Sophie, sounding upbeat. Shame he was fictional.

'We must return to Juno, try an earlier date.' Freddy set his mouth.

But in his eyes, Sophie saw a reflection of her own fear.

Half an hour after leaving Wells' flat, Sophie shortened Charlotte's lead and waited with Freddy outside a bank. Hugo was changing a sovereign for notes and coins to buy supplies for the crossing. The smog was down at street level and further along the road, objects and people were fuzzy. Sophie folded back her sleeve, exposing the bracelet. 'Why would another version of me give us a useless trinket?'

'She wouldn't.'

'We need to brainstorm this before risking another crossing.'

Freddy sighed. 'With every passing day, I miss Bella more. And Clarissa.'

Sophie knew exactly what he meant. The longing was building, becoming more unbearable. She removed a glove and tried to twist a gem. It wouldn't budge. One by one, she tried the others. Nothing. Maybe she needed to give an instruction at the same time?

'Find Janus' walking staff.' She touched the gems,

repeating the words, then held the whole bracelet, ensuring her skin was in contact with all the stones.

'Try saying something different,' said Freddy.

'Show me the location of the device that summons Janus.' The twinkling rubies mocked her with their silence. 'Why didn't the other me write more detailed instructions?'

'If she could, I'm sure she would have.' Freddy randomly pressed gems. 'So many versions of us in almost identical universes must be doing what we're doing, or trying to.'

'Don't think about it. It'll send you insane.'

'I wonder how the other you acquired the bracelet,' said Freddy.

'The body armour is from a long way in the future. The bracelet could be too?' Sophie slid on the glove, frustrated.

Charlotte tugged on her lead, wagging her tail. Since her DNA upgrade, she'd rarely wagged her tail, had to consciously decide to behave like a regular dog. Right now, she wanted to greet a girl in a ragged shawl selling matches from a tray. But the girl backed away and Charlotte took the hint.

Hugo came out of the bank and gave five shillings to the girl. She was so surprised she nearly upended her tray. The currency here was the same as in Shorten and five shillings was a lot.

'You said your sovereigns won't stretch far,' Freddy whispered to Hugo.

'We can spare a few shillings. You don't know about the match girls?'

Freddy shot him a blank look.

'They work in horrible conditions,' said Hugo. 'Many develop a fatal jaw disease from white phosphorus in the matches. At home, they went on strike in 1888. Though the company made some changes, it'll be decades before the phosphorus is outlawed.'

The girl closed her hand over the coins. 'What should I do?' she asked Hugo.

'Domestic service is hard, but you won't die of phossy jaw.'

She snapped her tray of matches shut and marched away.

Had Hugo saved her life? 'Maybe one person can make a difference,' said Sophie. 'Like Wells trying to stop the Great War.'

'Who knows?' Hugo divided the cash into three.

He and Freddy stored their portion in their trouser pockets. Sophie dropped hers into a small purse in her bag.

Freddy strode over to a grocer's. Inside, tins of food were stacked on wooden shelves but there were no trolleys. Stocking up would take a while. He chewed his lower lip. 'We'll need wheelbarrows.'

Out on the pavement, Hugo examined his map. 'Now we know Juno will reserve our supplies, we can load up in stages. We should sort our water first. There's a public fountain near Marble Arch.'

'Transport it in beer barrels.' Sophie pointed across the road. *The Barley Mow* was painted a striking red and a lit gas lantern over the entrance gave the air a cosy glow.

Freddy nodded. 'There'll be a pub closer to the fountain.'

They walked towards Hyde Park, Charlotte trotting to heel on the lead.

'If Bad Wells' ambush is anything to go by, he'll wait until there's fewer people around.' Sophie mentally crossed her fingers.

They reached the park with no drama, and Sophie let herself relax a little, though the mist was thicker. 'I wonder if the smog ever clears?'

'Breathing it in probably does as much damage as smoking.' Hugo headed to a white structure, the size of a garden Wendy house. It had an angled roof and at the front, in a stone basin, water bubbled from a pipe. Above the basin was carved, *The Fear of the Lord is a Fountain of Life.* 'The government thought clean drinking water would lure the poor away from pubs.'

'Did it?' Sophie asked him.

'A bigger benefit was preventing the spread of disease—'

Something pinged, and they all jumped.

'The bracelet!' Sophie pulled back her sleeve. The oval-shaped ruby was flashing, the light clear through her glove. In her mind, streets, numbers, and names appeared. The images were superimposed on her vision, like a display on the dashboard of a plane. She put her hand to her brow. 'I can see a map, and a red dot on a road.'

Hugo cast around, searching for the map.

'It's inside my head,' said Sophie. 'Whooh, the strangest feeling…'

Hugo guided her over to a park bench. She sat down, shut her eyes, and the map came into sharper focus.

'Is it the cylinder?' said Freddy.

'I'm not sure. And the names of roads and places are incomprehensible hieroglyphics.' She'd barely finished the sentence when the writing changed. Had the characters transformed, or could she just read them now? 'Barlby Gardens. No idea where that is.' The map zoomed out. 'It's still in London, north of here. And the dot's moving slowly, as if whoever has it is walking. The person who took it from the bus?'

Charlotte nodded. She was sitting near to the bench, facing away from her mistress, on guard.

'We should wait until the dot stops moving,' said Hugo, sitting beside Sophie.

'The map's frozen, like when the internet's rubbish.' Pain was building behind Sophie's eyes. 'Okay, it's back online, and the dot's moving faster. Must be on a bus, or a cab or carriage. Coming this way.'

Sitting bolt upright on the bench, Sophie continued with a running commentary of street names. 'East of here, on Park Street, heading south. Brook Street, just beyond the junction with Davies Street.' She rubbed her temples. 'The dot's stopped … no, moving again, slower.' She swore under her breath. 'It's disappeared inside Claridge's.'

'The hotel?' said Freddy.

'Yes, it's named on the map.'

'I had afternoon tea there a few years ago,' said Hugo. 'I mean … in the future.'

'The map's gone.' As if a door had slammed shut. Sophie gingerly stood up, nursing a thumping headache.

'Come on.' Freddy hurried towards the road. 'Let's hail a cab to Claridge's.'

'Hang on,' said Hugo. 'With Janus' itinerary, whenever we get there, Bad Wells will be waiting.'

'No point delaying. Better to take a cab.' Freddy flagged one down.

Hugo scowled but got in. Sophie climbed in with Charlotte. On the ceiling at the rear of the cab, a flap opened and the driver asked for their destination.

'What's the fare to Claridge's?' said Hugo.

'Half a mile, so eightpence.'

'Rather expensive,' said Freddy.

'First time in London?'

'No,' said Sophie. They'd get charged more if the guy thought them out-of-towners.

'All cabs charge the same rates. For journeys up to a mile, it's eightpence. After that, fourpence a mile.'

'Very well,' said Freddy.

The cab clattered at a stately pace, and Sophie's anxiety level rose. What if the bracelet was taking them straight to

Bad Wells and into a trap? No. How mad was that? Not being able to trust another version of yourself…

A lurch and the cab stopped. Hugo passed coins through the hatch, and the driver unlocked the doors from his seat with a clunk. A Claridge's porter opened the cab door and helped Sophie out. His jacket was jade wool with brass buttons, and he wore a matching cap. Neither he nor the other porter gave Charlotte a second glance, even with her dog coat.

Their cab was one of many. The horses pulling them snickered and snorted as passengers were dropped off and picked up. Across the road from the hotel, the fog obscured buildings and people, reducing them to shadowy shapes, and the skin between Sophie's shoulder blades itched. That primitive warning was rarely wrong.

Someone was watching.

Hattie Wells removed a vase of violets from her sixth-floor suite in Claridge's and took it to the outside corridor for the staff to remove. Despite her specifying no flowers, the chambermaids often left them. Their sweet smell was cloying, and they rarely thrived for long.

Back in her suite, she sat on a sofa in her comfortable housecoat. Sky blue, the garment had an extravagant line of white frills down the front and a short train. She put her stockinged feet on a coffee table and re-read the letter. The handwriting resembled her own, the letters formed with care, though the wording was clumsy and disjointed.

The letter was a private commission to eliminate four associated targets and retrieve an artefact. Two separate tasks. Retired Guild agents were often approached by dubious individuals, to settle old scores or prevent future calamities. Few accepted. The Guild executed those who unlawfully changed timelines. But she had to find a way to make a living. She could have churned out penny dreadful novels, with rehashed accounts of daring assignments, except they'd have attracted the attention of the Guild. Fortunately, knowledge gained from her previous security clearance had enabled her to tweak timelines to order. So far, undetected.

The envelope had been delivered by hand and the letter wasn't signed, which was normal — and wise. If the Guild caught her, she couldn't reveal the client's identity. The writer was flattering about Hattie's glory days in the Guild but that hadn't persuaded her. Hard cash had done that. The offered fee was truly enormous, with half paid in advance. Shortly after she'd posted the name of her charity's bank account, *Daisy Perfection*, to the provided post office address, the money had been paid, committing both parties. The funds would ensure the charity survived her.

Hattie turned to the second page of the letter. *Artefact can appear as a wooden pole with carved handle.* Historical artefacts were highly prized by collectors, even by those who couldn't see the real object, which was often mundane compared to the illusion. Hattie had learned about DNA in the Guild, only then understood that her rare gene allowed her to see original artefacts.

The targets' names and descriptions were brief:
Sophie Harrington. Female, fair hair.
Frederick Lacey. Male, light brown hair.
Charlotte. Female canine, brown fur.
Hugo Harrington. Male companion.
With no access to the Guild's database, private clients were obliged to rely on their own memories or incomplete documents. Hence the brevity. Sufficient, if the targets were together.

The final digits of this universe's designation had been supplied, which was usual, yet the inclusion of the itinerary was a puzzle. Private commissions didn't include itineraries. Where had the client obtained it? Not from the Guild. The last security breach had been centuries ago. And in addition, the itinerary was far too long. Guild assignments had come with two Events in the instructions, occasionally three, showing an artefact's location or a target's movements. More Events and the itinerary became progressively more inaccurate. Yet this itinerary listed sixteen, unevenly spread over eleven days.

Thursday, 4ᵗʰ July 1889. 05:39 at Marble Arch, 10.56 at 46 Fitzroy Road, 12.34 at Claridge's...

If targets evaded the Guild for long enough, their itineraries degraded, but the initial Event anchored the timeline and remained accurate. This itinerary, though, had been unreliable from the start, the targets leaving their ship two minutes early. Manageable, if worrying. Hattie always turned up well before Events. That had saved her life more than once.

Waiting inside the smaller arch, she'd had a clear line of sight and shot the first target squarely in the chest. Once the weapon locked on an individual's DNA, you couldn't miss. When the bullet bounced off, shock had caused Hattie to hesitate.

She'd never encountered a target wearing Guild armour. Presumably stolen from field agents. Dead ones. Safeguarding kit took priority over agents' lives. One of the reasons she'd left. She'd been right not to pursue the targets into their ship. Little was known about Juno, including her intruder systems. At worst, they could have proved lethal. At best, Hattie would have revealed her gender, squandering her best asset. Working for the Guild and later, on private jobs, targets had never identified their assassin until their last moments. Sometimes, not even then.

Hattie stared at the letter. The Event at 46 Fitzroy Road was for her a high-risk time-paradox. Something to avoid at all costs in a parallel universe. The client was ignorant of the risk or didn't care. Hattie had struggled to understand the Guild's lectures about paradoxes and antimatter, but the fate of agents who'd moved too physically close to their other versions had given her nightmares. Blinked out of existence, leaving no body to bury or mourn.

She'd arrived an hour early and keeping well clear of the other Wells' flat, she'd waited. At 10.53 am, her equivalent had left the house and sauntered down the street, swinging a shopping bag over his arm. The three minute difference from the itinerary meant the timeline was diverging too quickly.

Hattie knew not to look at him, but the urge to converse with him, join with him, swept over her in a shocking, roaring wave. She squeezed her eyes shut and resisted with all her strength. To no avail. Propelled by an invisible force, she glided towards him, a moth mesmerised by a flame. Inexorable. Inevitable. While he walked on, his back to her, she drew closer and closer, mentally fighting every step.

He strolled around a corner out of sight, and Hattie swayed, the suicidal urge to be annihilated gone in a blissful instant. Drained of energy, she rested her hands on her knees and caught her breath.

Long minutes passed before she felt able to approach his residence, indistinguishable from her own, far away in her home universe. The landlady directed her to the first floor and Hattie knocked. If Isabel wasn't in, Hattie wouldn't need to pick the lock. Her own flat key might fit.

Isabel was in, and disconcertingly identical to Hattie's cousin. If Hattie's facial features resembled the other Wells, Isabel didn't notice. This meeting was a lower-risk paradox, shouldn't harm her or Isabel, but the less time spent together the better. Hattie took her purse from her bag. She had more than enough cash to buy the artefact.

'You've come about the pretty walking stick?' said Isabel. 'Have you found it?'

Hattie's heart sank. The artefact wasn't here? How could

it not be here? The artefact was mentioned in an Event two days from now. She'd assumed that was an error.

As Isabel gestured to an armchair in the parlour, Hattie's training kicked in. *If the assignment goes wrong, if safe, stay in situ, gather information.* Hattie sat down and Isabel talked, assuming Hattie was from a lost-and-found agency. The other Wells had lost the artefact on a bus. Careless. He must have no idea how much it would fetch on the black market.

'It's a shame,' said Isabel. 'Beautiful workmanship. Would you like to see my sketch of it?'

'No, thank you.' Illusion technology held little appeal. Based on maths formulae, not art. Hattie inwardly sighed. Now, she'd have to retrieve the artefact during the other Event. More work for the same money. She stood up. Not knowing how lost-and-found agencies worked, she guessed. 'Ten shillings up front. Refunded, if I don't find it within a month.'

Given those terms, Isabel at home would have shooed her out. This one did too.

Hattie didn't remember the cab ride back to Claridge's, dwelling on nearly dying before the flawed Event. Luckily for her, the completion of private commissions wasn't reliant on an accurate itinerary. Observation and common sense worked fine.

Hours later, settled in her suite and wearing her housecoat, Hattie sat in the bay window that overlooked the hotel's entrance. Yes, there they were. The targets, fitting the description, were leaving their cab. She checked her pocket watch. 12.31. Four minutes late. Another minute's divergence.

Hattie got to her feet, took off the housecoat, and dressed. She selected the veiled hat that matched her purple skirt and jacket, pinning the hat at a jaunty angle.

The next Event was Grosvenor Square.

CHAPTER 9

$\mathcal{I}$n Claridge's spacious foyer, summer sunshine danced through tall, arched windows framed by jade velvet curtains, and a domed skylight provided yet more light. Interspersed between pale, classical columns were luxurious sofas, armchairs, and side tables. A familiar smell lingered in the air: beeswax, lemon, and pine. Sophie breathed it in. The hotel must use the same polish as in the Manor, thirty-five years from now. The atmosphere here was similar to the Manor. Calm, contented, and loaded.

Bad Wells would be easy to spot with the monstrous moustache, but he was nowhere to be seen. And no one was using the cylinder as a walking stick.

'This is as fancy as the hotel at home.' Hugo removed his hat, happy to be somewhere familiar. 'In the future, the floor is black and white squares, like a chessboard.'

'That might be a bit much,' said Freddy. 'I prefer the plain marble.'

Sophie perched on a couch, her back straight as her corset dictated. Hugo sat beside her, able to slouch and choosing not to. Charlotte dutifully settled at their feet though she'd have preferred a chair.

'Your hair's sticking up,' Sophie said to Hugo. His hat had sent his thick hair awry. He smoothed it.

Freddy leaned over and whispered to Sophie, 'Could you keep the pistol in your pocket? When I sit down, it makes my trousers too tight.'

'No problem.' She took the pistol, pocketed it, and he sat on the sofa opposite.

Across the foyer, a pug dog on a lady's lap gave Charlotte a snappy bark. Charlotte took no notice, watching a guest who was approaching reception. The woman's hat was boxy with a short veil obscuring half her face, and her purple skirt had a fashionable, oversized bustle. Charlotte sniffed and flicked her eyes towards her. Sophie said by Charlotte's ear, 'It is a gorgeous outfit.' Charlotte shook her head, frustrated she couldn't speak.

'We know the cylinder's nearby,' said Freddy. 'Can you decipher the last word on the bracelet note?'

Sophie fished it out of her pocket. '*Locates the cylinder when it's...* The final word begins with an o.'

'You wrote this. If you can't read it, nobody can.' Hugo squinted at it. 'Outside?'

Sophie looked closer. 'Could be, though except for visiting Nice Wells and in the cab, the bracelet's been outside since we left Juno. Doesn't explain why the map turned on and off.'

'You thought this had been written in a hurry,' said Hugo. '*The bracelet locates the cylinder when it's outside.* Strict grammar would mean the bracelet works when it's outside, or it could mean the bracelet shows the map when the walking stick is outside.'

'The bracelet can't track the cylinder if it's inside a cab or a building?' said Sophie. Unlikely, given its advanced technology.

'The note also says its other functions are broken,' said Freddy. 'Perhaps the tracking bit works but isn't reliable?'

'It kept working when the dot was moving faster. Could have been on the open top deck of a bus?' Sophie smoothed a crease on her skirt. She felt dowdy compared to Claridge's other female customers whose outfits were intricately quilted and flounced. 'A regular person who travels by bus couldn't afford a drink in this hotel, let alone a room.'

'They could work here,' said Hugo, 'though we can't exactly go poking around the kitchens and offices.'

Sophie racked her brains and came up empty.

'I'm starving,' said Freddy. 'We should have lunch.'

Hugo grabbed his hat. 'Let's find a cheap café.'

'The cylinder could be in the dining room?' said Freddy, and Hugo sighed, defeated.

They inquired at the reception desk and were directed across the foyer and down a corridor. 'They might not allow you in,' whispered Sophie to Charlotte, who shrugged.

But a waiter smiled at Charlotte, and she made an effort to behave like a normal dog, wagging her tail.

In the corner of the room, a young man was playing gentle waltzes on a grand piano. Diners were talking in low voices, the murmur punctuated by the clink of bone china. The smell of food and fresh coffee made Sophie's stomach rumble.

A couple in front of them were waiting to be seated. A waiter noted their names and carried the man's hat off to a cloakroom. Another waiter showed the couple towards a table.

Sophie checked the diners. Bad Wells wasn't here. Nor was the cylinder. 'We should buy bread and cheese from a shop.' Who knew how long they'd be in 1889? Couldn't risk running out of money.

'We're here now,' said Freddy. He gestured at Hugo's arm. 'In an ideal world, you'd have spent today resting.'

Hugo fixed him with a droll look. This was just an excuse for a posh lunch.

'And they're cool with dogs,' said Sophie. Some diners had pooches on their laps and under one table was an impressive wolfhound.

The waiter wafted away Sophie's bag as well as Hugo's and Freddy's hats, while another guided them to a table with sweet-scented violets arranged in a glass vase. The linen was crisp and white, the cutlery silver, and jade place mats, square with rounded corners, had a gold coat of arms in the centre, indicating the royal family were customers. Of course they were.

Sophie squeezed Hugo's hand, glad that Freddy had nagged them to eat here. A nook beside their table was perfect for a large labradoodle and Charlotte sat there as if holding court.

Following the convention that had prevailed in Shorten, Sophie peeled off her gloves. Freddy's mother had insisted gloves were always removed to eat and drink, unconvinced by Sophie's certainty that ladies in *Downton* kept them on.

Freddy picked up a menu and gave a contented sigh.

'This reminds you of home,' said Sophie.

'The Manor should be nearly finished.' Freddy's rambling house had been gutted by fire. Fortunately, Clarissa's wealthy father was funding the rebuild.

Sophie pictured her daughter in Shorten with a fresh wave of longing. Children grew up so fast, and time was passing quicker than ever. Don't think about it.

She scanned the menu. All in French. Unsurprising.

Menus in high-end restaurants in Shorten had been in French too.

Hugo was wincing as he perused the prices. Sophie's menu was price-free. As in Shorten, posh ladies never saw them.

'We don't need starters and puddings,' said Hugo.

Sophie would choose lamb with mash and peas. Charlotte could have the lamb—

The bracelet on Sophie's wrist pinged, and the oval ruby flashed.

Sophie stumbled out of Claridge's, holding Freddy's arm. The map in her mind was affecting her sense of space and her balance. She coughed, the ubiquitous smog irritating her throat.

She forced herself to focus on the dot on the map. 'The cylinder's moving fast.'

'Which way?' asked Hugo.

'Back towards Marble Arch.' Sophie paused. 'Okay, now it's stopped by Grosvenor Square.'

Charlotte set off, trotting faster than the dense, horse-drawn traffic.

'Let's go,' said Sophie, keeping hold of Freddy's arm.

It took ten minutes to walk to the western side of Grosvenor Square, a green with trees, surrounded by town-houses. Sophie pointed ahead. 'It's moving again, up there.'

Charlotte hurtled across the grass, and Sophie hissed in frustration. 'The map's gone. So has the dot.'

They sprinted after Charlotte.

'Can't be far,' panted Hugo.

A teenage girl was sitting on a bench. Families were

strolling, and children were playing hide and seek between the trees.

Charlotte skidded to a halt on a deserted residential street that ran beside the green.

Sophie caught up with her and turned around. Same families. Same children. Same girl on the bench. On the north side of the square a cab stopped, but no one got out or climbed in.

It began to drizzle, then strengthened into steady rain, and they sheltered under the trees with the families and children. The girl on the bench didn't move, apparently not caring that her cream outfit and hat were getting soaked.

A pigeon waddled past. Not that long ago, despite knowing that at the last second the pigeon would fly off, Charlotte would have chased it. Today, she simply watched it and grunted, her hungry noise.

'We passed a café on the way,' said Hugo.

When the rain eased off, they trudged back along the road. The café was on a corner, its windows overlooking both streets. The entrance opened onto the main road, the café an exaggerated V shape, narrowest at the front. Its wooden façade was a distinctive dark red and outside were wooden tables and benches, deserted in the rain. On a damp blackboard was scrawled, *2 thick slices of bread and butter for a penny! Kidneys, cold beef, and ham for 6d.*

'Sixpence is more our price bracket,' said Hugo.

'Why does it say 6d?' asked Sophie.

'It stands for denarius,' said Freddy, 'from the silver coin in ancient Rome.'

A fact Hugo didn't know. He looked impressed.

Inside the café, men in rough jackets and trousers sat at bare tables, tucking into eggs and bacon and pork chops. The smell of cooking oil and seared meat turned Sophie's stomach.

A plump woman with a sweaty face bustled up and glared at Charlotte. 'Can't bring that in here. I don't care if you put a dress on it,' she shouted, making herself heard over the customers' chatter. She jabbed a thumb towards a placard hanging from the counter. In addition to a list of nationalities and races of people who weren't welcome, it said, *No dogs.*

Sophie bristled. 'We'll eat outside.'

'I'll order,' said Hugo.

Sophie turned on her heel and left, taking Charlotte with her.

The outside chairs and tables were soaking. Sophie wiped water from the seats with the carpet bag and Charlotte watched with a resigned air. 'I think welcoming dogs into less posh restaurants is a modern thing. It's probably the same with babies.' Charlotte tilted her head. She missed Bella too.

Hugo and Freddy came out with trays of food and steaming cups of tea.

Sophie fed Charlotte bacon, two chops, and water from her travel bowl, then made herself a fried egg sandwich. The egg was runny and messy and delicious. She cleaned yolk off her chin with a thin paper napkin. 'The bracelet might be going off randomly.'

'That could be a good thing,' said Hugo. 'Skewing Janus' itinerary?'

Sophie moved her wrist and the gems sparkled. 'Or it's sending us down rabbit holes.'

'We have no other leads,' said Hugo.

Sophie transferred dirty crockery onto the tray. 'I guess I have to trust the other me.'

'We know the body armour works,' said Hugo. 'That makes it more likely the bracelet works too.'

'We should return to Claridge's.' Freddy added his empty plate to the tray. 'Watch for someone with the cylinder.'

'The illusion of the walking staff looks expensive,' said Hugo. 'The person who found it might have sold it by now. In which case, it could be anywhere.'

'When the dot was near Claridge's, it was moving slowly,' said Sophie. 'Consistent with using it as a walking aid.'

'If they're leaning on it, there's no point waiting in Claridge's for another waiter shift.' Hugo stood up. 'They'll have a sedentary job in an office out of sight.'

'I could ask for a job,' said Sophie. 'Nose around.'

Charlotte vigorously shook her head, frustrated, and Sophie stroked her. 'I wish you could talk.'

'You're too well dressed to need a job.' Hugo stretched his sore arm. 'They'll be suspicious.'

'Okay,' said Sophie. Think big. 'I'll tell them I'm considering buying the hotel.'

'You're not well dressed enough,' said Freddy.

'Yes, tone it down.' Hugo picked up the tray of crockery to return it. 'A relative would like to train as a bookkeeper.'

Sophie made her pitch at Claridge's reception desk and was directed to a service corridor and upstairs to an office. A young woman was firmly typing on a shiny, brown typewriter, the keys clunking and slapping against paper. A bell rang and the carriage slid back with a satisfying click. On a separate table, a man was checking a line of figures in a large ledger. He had a short, handlebar moustache and his bald patch was smooth and pale.

The room was stiflingly hot and something tickled Sophie's nose. Ink? Pencil shavings? She cleared her throat. 'Excuse me, who do I ask about a vacancy?'

The man glanced up. 'The manager's out.'

They might have seen the cylinder. 'I'm looking for a lost walking stick.' Sophie described the green heart-shaped handle and the gold letter T.

The woman didn't slow typing, but the man bit his lip. 'You're from one of those agencies?' His tone was defensive.

Sophie took a chance. 'We have reason to believe you found it.'

The man hesitated. 'It was on a bus.'

Finally. A stroke of luck. He'd been on the same bus as Nice Wells and taken the cylinder. 'I don't need your name,' said Sophie, smoothly. 'Please give me the item, so I can return it to the owner.'

'I can't. Housekeeping has it.'

Sophie's heart sank. Her luck hadn't lasted long. She hurried out of the office.

Downstairs, Hugo, Freddy, and Charlotte were across the foyer, and Sophie put up her hand in a 'wait' gesture. She approached a different receptionist. 'I've lost my walking stick somewhere in the hotel.' She described it.

The receptionist waved to a boy dressed like the door-men. 'Fetch housekeeping.'

A middle-aged woman came out a few minutes later, swerving around a group of fashionable guests. The women resembled an exotic flock of chirping birds, their gowns a kaleidoscope of purple, yellow, pink, and red.

The housekeeper addressed Sophie. 'I'm sorry, madam. The walking stick belongs to Mrs Alveston and has already been returned to her.'

Sophie's heart sank again.

'It's very strange. Someone else inquired about Mrs Alveston's walking stick not half an hour ago.'

'Was it a man the same height as me?' said Sophie. 'With a droopy moustache?'

'He was clean-shaven and tall.'

Not Wells, then. 'Mrs Alveston…'

'She's stayed with us for many years.'

The implied 'Who on earth are you to be asking?' was clear and Sophie gave the woman a curt nod. 'I'm sure it's an innocent mistake.'

The housekeeping woman walked off. She acknowledged the lady in the fetching purple gown who'd drifted away from her friends and was gliding towards the staircase.

Sophie joined Hugo on an emerald sofa. Freddy was sitting in a leather armchair, Charlotte at his feet. Sophie told them what she'd learned. 'A guest called Mrs Alveston claimed it.'

'Progress of a sort,' said Freddy. 'We should take rooms here.'

Hugo sighed. 'Absolutely not. It would clean us out.'

Freddy stood up and strolled over to reception. He soon returned, his face sulky. 'The minimum booking is two weeks.'

'Why would a wealthy woman claim a walking stick from housekeeping?' said Sophie. 'If this Mrs Alveston has need of a walking stick, she could just buy one.'

'Let's have a wander, find a helpful chambermaid,' said Hugo. 'If this is the same as posh hotels at home, the best rooms are on the top floor. Mrs Alveston's should be there.'

CHAPTER 11

Sophie and Hugo climbed Claridge's grand stairs to the highest floor. They'd left Hugo's hat and the carpet bag in the foyer with Freddy and Charlotte who were watching out for Bad Wells.

Everyone descending the wide sweeping staircase paid them no heed, assuming they were guests.

'I love the lack of security,' said Sophie. 'I wonder when they'll get a lift?'

'I wouldn't get into it.'

Sophie shuddered. Janus' ship disguised as an elevator had scarred them for life. 'Even if we end Janus, I'll be nervous about taking Bella across universes.'

Hugo shot her an understanding smile.

On the top floor, the doors were well spaced out, indicating generously sized rooms. A jade carpet in the deserted corridor muffled their footsteps as they turned right, reached the end, and looked around. By the stairs, a girl in a cream gown and hat was walking towards her room.

'She was in Grosvenor Square,' said Sophie.

'That can't be coincidence.'

As they hurried down the corridor, there was a piercing scream. A door opened, and the girl backed out, straight into Hugo.

'Help! Help!' The girl collapsed against him. She was hyperventilating, going to faint.

Hugo held her up, blinking in shock.

Sophie walked cautiously into the room the girl had just left. A young man and elderly woman were sprawled on the floor. The woman had no visible injury. Her eyes were closed, and one of her hands was splayed on her chest. The guy had a wound on his neck. Blood was seeping out from a small gash, turning the jade carpet beneath him a dull red. In his hand was a thin, blood-stained knife. A letter opener. On a writing desk by the window, a flower vase was on its side, violets floating in water that had soaked a mess of scattered papers. A silent image from a stylised horror flick. But this was real.

Sophie stumbled into the corridor, breathing fast.

Hugo was talking to the girl. 'What's your name?'

'Miss Alveston,' she stuttered. 'Gladys Alveston.'

'There are two dead people in there,' said Sophie.

'We must call the police.' Hugo put his arm about the girl's shoulders, steering her towards the stairs.

'I'll be right behind you.' The girl's surname was Alveston. She had to be related to Mrs Alveston. The cylinder might be in that room? There wouldn't be another chance to check. Steeling herself, Sophie went back in.

Apart from the bodies and the messy desk, the place was immaculate. By the door was a stand with hats and four regular walking sticks, polished and expensive. Mrs Alveston would only have seen the cylinder as a walking stick. Why hadn't she stashed it on the stand?

Sophie hastily searched the sitting room, then a connected bedroom, flicking clothes aside in the wardrobe.

Nothing. The cylinder was too long to fit in a drawer. Finally, she got on her knees to check under the bed. Still nothing.

She returned to the sitting room and tiptoed around the bodies, not stepping too close and staying well clear of the blood-soaked carpet.

The position of the elderly woman, facing the man, and the letter opener in the man's hand suggested an attempted robbery gone wrong. Too obvious?

A grey-haired bloke in a suit appeared in the doorway to the corridor, his brow shiny with sweat. 'Goodness!'

'I haven't touched them,' said Sophie. 'This is a crime scene.'

'I'm the manager.' He peered at her. 'Are you alright, madam?'

'A bit shaken up. The girl who found them is distraught.'

As he helped her down the stairs, Sophie was trembling. She was at best a witness, at worst a suspect. So was Hugo.

Down in the foyer, Sophie gently removed the manager's hand from her arm. He strode behind the reception counter and whispered to the woman on duty.

Sophie caught some of it. '...Brook Suite ... absolute discretion ... business as usual.'

The woman nodded, her eyes wide.

The manager hurried towards the hotel entrance, and Sophie made her way over to Freddy. Charlotte jumped up as she approached and pawed at her, trying to tell her something, then shook her head in frustration.

Gladys was sitting beside Hugo, staring at her lap.

Sophie hesitated. Make a quick exit or try to get more info?

Reading her face, Hugo said, 'The hotel has no phone. They'll have to send someone to the nearest police station.'

'Have you asked her about the cylinder?' said Sophie.

'She's in bits.'

'I'm really sorry to ask,' said Sophie, keeping her voice low. 'Have you seen a walking stick with a green heart on the handle? It might assist the police.' She was lying to this traumatised girl, but needs must.

Gladys didn't look up. 'Granny's not steady on her feet. I mean … she wasn't. She collected walking sticks. I thought she'd like it.' The girl spoke in a monotone. 'She thought it vulgar, so I gave it to my friend.'

'You met your friend in Grosvenor Square?' said Hugo.

'We can't marry.' The girl's voice was still flat. 'He has no money of his own. I gave him the walking stick to sell.'

'The dead man in your suite,' said Sophie. 'That wasn't your friend?'

'No, thank God.'

A waiter set a glass of brandy on the table and Hugo paid him.

'The police will find who did this,' said Sophie, with convincing confidence.

Hugo patted Gladys' shoulder. 'Drink the brandy. It'll help.'

Gladys took a hesitant sip and coughed.

Freddy stood up and put on his hat. 'We should leave before the police arrive.'

Leaving Gladys sipping her brandy, they made their way outside.

'Where now?' Sophie's teeth were chattering. Shock. She pushed her jaw shut with her hand.

'Let's return to the café,' said Hugo. 'Regroup.'

They turned left at the junction into Davies Street, and the skin between Sophie's shoulder blades prickled. She paused and checked back down the street. No one was following them.

The bracelet flashed and pinged, and the map came up,

but instantly vanished. Sophie sighed. 'Gladys' friend must have been outside for seconds.' Beyond frustrating.

They walked on. 'Tell us what you saw in that room,' said Freddy.

Sophie described it. 'I've had a chance to take it in. It seemed … staged.'

'You mean they weren't dead?' said Hugo.

'Definitely dead.' Sophie sucked in a sharp breath. 'The man was stabbed and the older lady may have had a heart attack.'

'There wasn't anyone else in the corridor,' said Hugo.

'If Bad Wells' itinerary includes Gladys,' said Sophie, 'he joined the dots and went to Mrs Alveston's suite, maybe trying to find the cylinder.'

Freddy chewed his lower lip. 'Could all be coincidence.'

Charlotte gave Freddy a sceptical glance.

'Motivation is the key to this,' said Hugo, 'and Bad Wells has that in spades.'

Sophie swallowed. Don't think about the bodies. 'If it isn't coincidence, Bad Wells means to kill us *and* grab the cylinder.'

They'd reached the café and it was closed. Hugo turned around, adopted his 'stay positive' face. 'Freddy, if Gladys' friend is selling the walking stick, where would he go?'

'A gentleman's outfitters. If the store exists here, we can start with mine.' Freddy looked at his watch. 'It's gone four. They'll be closed.'

'Why so early?' asked Hugo.

'I've never thought about it,' said Freddy. 'I suppose gentlemen are meeting their mothers or wives for afternoon tea?'

Another version of Freddy might be born here in fifteen years, into a society not so different from 1889. She'd half-forgotten that. 'You can still surprise me.'

Freddy drew himself up to his full height. 'It's not just Hugo who knows things.'

Hugo's lips twitched. 'We need somewhere to stay the night.'

'What about the Ritz?' said Freddy. They'd spent a memorable evening in the Ritz's cocktail bar in the 1920s.

Hugo rolled his eyes. 'Yeah, right.'

Their banter was meant to buck them up, but Sophie didn't respond. Her mind was back in Gladys' hotel room. Lives cut violently short by Bad Wells.

Charlotte gave her a hard stare and Sophie knew what she was thinking because she was thinking the same.

They were next.

CHAPTER 12

Further down the street from the café, Charlotte growled at a terraced house. Beside a sign saying, *To Let. Room on Ground Floor,* was another notice proclaiming the sort of humans that weren't welcome and it said, *No Dogs.*

Freddy's brow creased. 'Perhaps one unpleasant person owns all the buildings in this road?'

Hugo shrugged. 'Or they all have the same opinions.'

'Time to get creative,' said Sophie. 'I'll carry on along the street with Charlotte. Hugo, you can pay a week's rent in advance, and after dark we'll sneak Charlotte in through the window.'

A man pushing an invalid bath chair came towards them on the pavement and they moved aside to let him pass.

Hugo turned and stared glumly at the sign. 'No point in trying to find a different place. I suspect other rooms to rent will have the same restrictions.' He opened the gate that fronted the small garden.

'I have a better idea,' said Freddy. 'My great aunt Marion.'

'Sorry?' said Sophie.

'At home, she lives in this part of London … somewhere.' Freddy sucked his teeth. 'Although she might not be in this universe.'

'When did you last see her?' said Hugo.

'The Christmas before you arrived in Shorten. She was elderly then, but she'd be in her thirties now.'

'Why didn't you mention her before?' Sophie asked him, squinting at the darkening, misty sky. More rain wasn't far off.

'I foolishly assumed we'd be staying in a hotel. The bath chair reminded me of her. Hers is splendid.' Freddy hesitated. 'The thing is, she's rather eccentric.'

'Unless her eccentricity involves knocking off unexpected guests,' said Sophie, 'staying with her would beat paying a dodgy landlord.'

Charlotte, eyeing the *No dogs* notice, blinked her agreement.

'She told jolly stories from her travels abroad,' said Freddy. 'Then Mummy explained that though her adventures were real to my great aunt, they were just in her mind.'

Hugo took off his hat and put it on again. 'She'd put us up?'

'She saw relations at Christmas… but I can hardly tell her who I really am. A version of me that hasn't been born yet.' Freddy guffawed. 'Ha! I'll say I've come over from America.'

Charlotte wiggled a furry eyebrow, confused. She wasn't the only one.

'My great aunt's cousin was also called Freddy and looked a bit like me. In the 1870s, when he was a toddler, he and his family emigrated to America. He'd be about my age now.'

'And nobody has phones,' said Sophie. 'So, Marion can't check.'

'Her address was Garden Street,' said Freddy. 'We visited years ago.'

'When?' Hugo unfolded his map.

'I was fourteen.'

'There's no Garden Street near here,' said Hugo.

'Park Street?' said Freddy.

Hugo tapped the map. 'Park Street's over a mile long.'

'Her home was near Grosvenor Square,' said Freddy.

They followed another road into Park Street, then turned south, parallel to Grosvenor Square. Identical Georgian townhouses stretched into the distance and at equal intervals on the pavement were apple trees, their branches plump with fluttering pink blossom.

'Freddy, I don't suppose you remember anything particular about the house?' said Hugo.

'The name was something to do with thorns and there was a lady's head on the portico.'

'A lady's head?' said Sophie, alarmed.

'A gargoyle,' said Freddy. 'Mummy told me it represented Britannia.'

Every house had classical porticoes gentrifying their front doors, the columns smooth and gargoyle-free.

'If my great aunt is in this universe,' said Freddy, 'she might not live in the same house or even in London.'

Hugo sighed. 'Let's turn around. We may have more luck north of Grosvenor Square.'

They crossed a junction and further along, Georgian simplicity gave way to Victorian gothic. Wide bay windows curved out like ships' prows, each above the other on successive floors, and porticoes were bigger, with pillars adorned by cherubs, elaborate garlands — and gargoyles.

'There!' said Freddy.

Peering down from a portico was a grey stone face. Not a devilish or grotesque gargoyle but a simple woman's head, with shoulder-length straight hair, topped by a round helmet with a feather. The home it guarded was wide and tall, with five storeys and a basement.

Freddy pointed to a plaque on the half-height garden gate: *Thornbridge.* 'This is the right place.'

Beyond the gate, white lilies edged the lawn. Associated with mourning, they symbolised innocence restored to the soul after death. 'Who else lives here besides Marion?' said Sophie.

'There was just a butler and a maid when I visited,' said Freddy. 'Her parents died in a carriage accident when she was young. Her older brother inherited the family home in Derbyshire, and she was bequeathed the London residence. After the accident, she rarely left the house.'

'How old was she when her parents died?' Hugo asked Freddy.

'Nearly old enough to go to parties.'

Sophie thought back to Shorten. So, fifteen. Sophie had been two years younger when she'd lost her parents. Despite everything she'd been through since discovering parallel universes, she'd be forever grateful for finding her parents again, safe and well in a slightly different one.

Freddy's lips tightened. He'd only recently lost his father, shot in Shorten by a rogue member of the militia.

Sophie looked up at the house. 'Whenever you lose your parents, it's horrible.'

'My great aunt suffered a head injury in the accident,' said Freddy. 'It affected her mind. She never married.'

'You don't have to be crazy not to marry,' said Sophie, trying to lighten the mood by teasing with a well-worn joke.

Charlotte pawed at the gate, and Hugo swung it open. 'In the 17th century, the word spinster described a woman so good at weaving she was financially independent.'

'Ha,' said Sophie. 'I didn't know that.'

Freddy strode under the arch. He rang the bellpull and clanging, loud as a church bell, echoed far inside.

The door creaked as it opened. A guy in an immaculate butler's suit eyed them with suspicion. 'Can I help you?'

He was young to be a butler.

'My name is Frederick Lacey. We've come to see Miss Lacey.'

The butler's eyes narrowed.

'Apologies,' said Freddy. 'We're from America, been overtaken by events.'

'Miss Lacey doesn't receive visitors.' He shut the door in Freddy's face.

CHAPTER 13

Hugo put his hat beside him on the park bench and holding his injured arm, gazed across Grosvenor Square. 'It'll be dark in a few hours.' The smog was a grey haze above the trees, blurring into paler cloud.

Sophie ruffled Charlotte's head. 'Smuggling you into that guest house will be a cool adventure.'

Charlotte jumped onto the bench, narrowly missing Hugo's hat, indicating she'd rather sleep on the bench.

'It's not cold.' Sophie squinted up at the sky. 'If it doesn't rain, we could sleep here.'

'If Bad Wells comes calling, we'll be sitting ducks,' said Hugo.

Charlotte jumped off the bench.

'We'll feel yucky in the morning,' said Freddy, 'and have creased clothes.'

Hugo picked up his hat. 'More to the point, if we look down-at-heel tomorrow, Freddy's outfitters will think we're dodgy and won't share info about the walking stick.'

'Come on then,' said Sophie. 'Dog-hating house is better than no house.'

Charlotte stretched, appearing even larger than usual. A lapdog would have been easy to pass through a window. Charlotte … not so much.

'No,' said Freddy. 'I'll try again with that beastly butler. Be more forceful.'

More in hope than expectation, they followed Freddy back to Marion's house. Freddy marched down the path, passed under Britannia's gargoyle head, and rang the bellpull.

A minute went by, and he rang again. Finally, with a creak, the door opened a fraction.

'We have concerns about Miss Lacey's welfare.' Freddy's voice resonated with authority. 'If you don't let us in, we'll fetch a constable.'

Sophie's eyes flicked to Hugo, uneasy. Would Freddy really involve the police? Marion could end up in an asylum.

The door opened another smidgen, and Freddy inserted his foot in the gap. 'I appreciate we're unannounced. If you allow us to confirm her safety, we'll leave immediately. You have my word.'

The butler slowly opened the door, scanning their faces.

'Miss Lacey knows me,' said Freddy smoothly, easing his way past him.

Sophie awkwardly followed with Charlotte and Hugo.

The butler strode in front and turned to face them.

'You don't know me,' said Freddy, 'but I stayed in this house many years ago.' Freddy was bluffing. He wouldn't visit for twenty years, and then he'd be a teenager.

Sophie screwed up her eyes. Time travel made your brain hurt.

'Our dog is impeccably behaved,' said Freddy, deploying persistent charm.

Charlotte was staring straight ahead, keen to appear unremarkable. The butler frowned at her. Oozing suspicion, he reluctantly took Hugo's and Freddy's hats and hung them on a stand. Sophie put the bag down beside a narrow console table set against the wall. On the table was a beautiful bronze figurine of two hunting dogs.

The butler went into a room off the hall. Instead of announcing them to whoever was in there, he shut the door behind him.

Hugo raised his eyebrows.

'As I said, she's eccentric.' Freddy folded his arms. 'And her servants are too.'

'Is it the same butler?' asked Hugo. 'From when you stayed here?'

'I can't remember.'

Sophie sniffed. The ubiquitous floor polish.

Freddy gestured at a china doll with bulging eyes, propped up on a dresser. 'I remember my great aunt collected dolls.'

The doll was creepy, and Sophie turned away from it. Would Bella ever be into dolls? Their daughter had focused her affections on the key rattle, ignoring other toys.

The butler returned, his lips compressed in a knife-thin line. 'Miss Lacey will see you.'

He showed them into a drawing room and Sophie paused, taken aback. Every available surface was covered with dolls. Some on shelves, others on the floor around a planter pot with a tall fern. Still more were on chairs and sofas. The dolls were all clean and shiny. Regularly dusted.

A petite woman was sitting in a tartan armchair. She wore a black skirt and matching silk jacket and was holding a doll on her lap. Her hair was a striking natural red, tied up in a loose bun with an ebony ribbon. With her pale complexion, she looked like a doll herself.

'Frederick Lacey,' announced the butler. 'From America.'

Marion peered at him. 'Little Freddy?'

Freddy did a formal nod. 'Please accept my apologies for calling unannounced.'

Marion tilted her head like a delicate bird. 'Burgess, ask Harris to clear seats for our guests.'

The butler left and returned with a maid who gathered up dolls from two sofas, taking them to a storeroom on the next floor. That took a while.

Attached to the maid's narrow belt was a silver, latticed bookmark. Hanging off the bookmark on chains were tiny objects, also silver: a mesh purse with a clasp, a bottle with a stopper, a whistle, a pocket watch, and a notebook with an attached pencil. There were also iron keys. It all jangled as she tidied away the dolls.

Sophie thought back to an old movie with a formidable housekeeper in *Rebecca*. She'd worn a similar belt with keys. Miss Harris' array of tools resembled a Swiss army knife.

'I'm opening a shop.' Marion surveyed her remaining dolls. 'Do you think it will prosper?'

'Absolutely,' said Freddy. 'A splendid idea.'

Charlotte was staying close by Sophie's legs, unsure what to make of Freddy's great aunt.

'May I present Mr and Mrs Harrington,' said Freddy.

'How do you do?' said Marion.

Marion's mourning gown made her appear older than she was. If her parents had died when she was fifteen and Marion was in her thirties ... the accident had happened more than half her lifetime ago. How long did Victorians stay in mourning?

'What's the hound's name?' said Marion.

'Charlotte,' said Sophie.

Charlotte let Marion pet her.

'We were robbed on our voyage from New York,' said Freddy, conversationally, as if such an event were commonplace on luxury liners in the late 19th century. 'Could we impose on your hospitality, just for a few days?'

Marion gave a joyless laugh. 'My dear Freddy, you wouldn't be imposing. I'm not short of space. Harris will show you to your rooms and Mrs Dalton will cook dinner.'

Sophie smiled at her, grateful they could stay, but with Marion's issues, even staying a few days would be awkward.

CHAPTER 14

The maid's toolset rattled with her steps as she climbed the stairs of Thornbridge House. She showed her unexpected guests into two interconnected bedrooms.

The ironwork bed in each room was a small double. The chest of drawers and dressing tables were covered with protective pale doilies and the wardrobes were solid and dark. Beside each bed was a tartan rug, the red and green weave a bright contrast to the brown boarded floor. In the largest room was a buttoned, cream armchair. There was a faint scent of lemon and both rooms were spotlessly clean, as if waiting for them.

'You're the only maid?' Freddy asked Miss Harris.

'I am, sir. Miss Lacey likes everything shipshape.'

'When did you last have guests?' Freddy asked her.

'Before my time.'

'How long have you worked here?' said Hugo.

'Seven years.'

Sophie went over to the window. The back garden had a

wide terrace, and the neat lawn was enclosed by a tall hedge. A narrow shed must be the outside loo.

'Miss Lacey is fortunate to have such a punctilious household,' said Freddy. 'I know things were difficult when her parents died.'

Miss Harris smoothed a pillow. 'We don't stand on ceremony. Mr Burgess helps with domestic duties.'

'And Mrs Dalton's the cook?' said Hugo.

'There is no Mrs Dalton, sir. She left years ago.' Miss Harris studied her polished shoes. 'I do the cooking.'

'And Miss Lacey isn't setting up a doll shop,' said Freddy, nodding to show he understood.

'We don't want to be any trouble,' said Sophie.

'No trouble. It'll be nice to have company.' Miss Harris looked up. 'Would you mind eating in the kitchen with us?'

Freddy blinked, startled.

'Miss Lacey eats in her bedroom, doesn't like the dining room. It would greatly upset her if you took your meals there.'

That made no sense, but Sophie said hastily, 'Eating in the kitchen would be fine.'

'Dinner's at eight.' Miss Harris bustled downstairs.

'Eating in the kitchen!' Freddy shook his head.

Charlotte stared out the window and Hugo slipped off his jacket. His shirt sleeve had a red tidemark from Wells' bullet. 'On the upside, no need to dress up for dinner.'

In Marion's basement, the kitchen table was large enough to accommodate Mr Burgess, Miss Harris, and their guests. Charlotte sat on the floor, pretending to be a regular dog.

The room had shabby wooden cupboards and piled on a

scarred dresser was a stack of well-thumbed newspapers. Evidently, the kitchen was the heart of this home.

'We very much appreciate your hospitality.' Freddy helped himself to beef pie. 'Particularly given Miss Lacey's condition.'

'We're accustomed to her ways.' Mr Burgess' tone was frosty.

'I suppose you can't leave her alone?' said Hugo.

'I take her to the square when the weather's fine,' said Miss Harris.

'And we each have a half-day off,' said Mr Burgess. 'Once a week.'

'So, you can't go on a longer holiday?' Sophie asked the maid.

'One of us is always here.'

Mr Burgess poured himself water. 'The income from Miss Lacey's investments pays for our wages and the gardener, and it covers the upkeep of the house.'

The young butler's manner placated Sophie's instinct to be suspicious. There was nothing stopping him — or Miss Harris — stealing Marion's money and living high on the hog. But there was no wine with dinner, everyone drinking water or in Sophie's case, tea.

'I owe Miss Lacey's family a great deal.' Translation. Mr Burgess would be watching them, protecting his employer.

After dinner, Freddy led the way up to their bedrooms which were stuffy and humid, even with the window open. Sophie took off her vest-armour and Hugo helped her remove the corset. She put on the T-shirt from her carpet bag.

Charlotte stood patiently while Sophie unfastened the dog coat and removed Charlotte's vest. Above the back garden, the clouds had gone, and pink streaks were bright against the darkening sky.

'If Miss Harris has been working here for seven years,' said Hugo, 'she must have been around twelve when she started.'

Scullery maids in Shorten began work at that age. Sophie tried to imagine Bella at twelve. Whatever was happening in Shorten, she wouldn't be sent into domestic service.

'Mr Burgess is so young,' said Hugo. 'Presumably, recruited as a teenager.'

'He's nailed the stern-butler vibes.' Sophie set up Charlotte's cosy mystery book on the page-turning machine.

Freddy knocked on the half-open interconnecting door, wearing just his boxers, and came in. He moved the stool from under the dressing table, sat on it, and placed the pistol on the table. 'This feels different from the last time we were up against Wells.'

'And not in a good way.' Hugo settled himself on the edge of the bed. 'He's waiting for the right moment to pounce.'

'While we were wandering the streets, or in Grosvenor Square,' said Freddy, 'he could easily have ambushed us, aimed at our heads.' The vests only protected their core.

'Killing us all would be difficult, unless he got right up close,' said Hugo.

Charlotte glanced up from her book and Sophie grimaced, glad to be safe inside Marion's house. 'Freddy, what's with the gun?' She gestured at it.

'Wells knows we're not likely to sleep in the vests. My room looks over an internal courtyard. If he takes a pot shot, he'll aim at here from the garden.'

As Sophie snapped the window shut and swept the curtains closed, she imagined Bad Wells creeping across the lawn.

CHAPTER 15

A mile from Thornbridge House, Hattie Wells walked into her club on Albemarle Street. Her evening gown had a scoop neckline and short sleeves, though wearing a corset and obligatory petticoat, she welcomed the cooler temperature in the foyer.

In the lounge, she sat in a burgundy leather chair and ordered a brandy. The atmosphere in the club was always convivial, the faint scent of gentlemen's cigars welcoming her in. In every universe she visited, when work allowed, she met her friend here, different versions of him. It was nice to catch up, but this was never a casual chat. Each encounter was a precious opportunity to change his fate. Some versions listened.

Just before ten, Oscar Wilde sauntered in and acknowledged her with a nod. 'A vision to delight the heart.' Like most versions, he sounded English, not Irish, his native accent long discarded.

'You're a vision of loveliness too.' He was, from his polished Oxford shoes to the white bow tie, perfectly straight below his wing collar. The satin stripe along the outer seams of his trousers matched the silk-faced lapels of his black tail-coat. The tailcoat was open, showing off the white shirt and pique waistcoat.

He sat opposite her, and the waiter handed him a glass of 1874 Perrier-Jouët champagne. Oscar's favourite vintage. He was leaner than in the last universe, but his mouth had the same sensuous curves.

Oscar had a serene, confident manner, as if he hadn't a care, unlike her, yet theirs was a friendship forged from loss and mutual understanding. Years ago in his cups, he'd confided about his sisters' deaths in Ireland and Hattie had told him about her Daisy. How whooping cough had taken her sparkle and her energy, then her life.

Hattie had joined the Guild to alter the past and save her daughter, but the Guild prevented contact with close family, precisely to prevent such interventions. Saving Oscar's sisters had proved impossible too. Serving officers were monitored. She'd have been caught and executed.

'I know that look, Mrs Neal.'

Hattie never used her real name. 'I can't think what you mean.' Her tone was playful.

'You're plotting someone's downfall.'

'Not at all.' Though he knew homosexuality was illegal, Hattie quietly reminded him. He was surprised, but she continued, summarising his libel case and the criminal trial that would follow in six years. She'd recited it so often, she knew it by heart.

Curiosity, bemusement, and finally scepticism showed in his eyes, as it always did.

Hattie finished her brandy. 'You presume this is just a bizarre story—'

'More an unsubtle morality tale.'

'This has nothing to do with morality,' said Hattie. 'Fore-warned is forearmed.' In Oscar's case, the Guild's motto was entirely apt. 'When you sue your lover's father, you'll lose. It will obliterate your reputation, your coffers, and the hard labour in prison will wreck your health.' She paused for breath. 'Please remember this conversation when the Marquess of Queensberry delivers his poisonous note. He'll leave it for all to read.'

'What will it say?'

The more detail she could give him the better. 'For Oscar Wilde,' she whispered. 'Posing Sodomite.'

Oscar paled but recovered himself. 'Quite a calling card.'

'When you pick up the note, destroy it, then immediately go abroad. Rumours will swirl, do no harm.'

'I wasn't aware you were a fortune-teller.' He took a sip of champagne. 'Are you losing your wits?'

The light-hearted question didn't fool her. She'd rattled him and was glad. If he paid heed and avoided disgrace, the Guild would notice this timeline had altered, might track her down. It was worth the risk. Every act of rebellion was a chink of light, flaring in the dark, and this was hers. 'Best to travel to the continent the day you receive the note. If you must stay longer and meet your friends in the Café Royal, follow their advice.'

'Where will you be?'

'Away.' In March 1895, at the height of Oscar's success, she'd tried countless times to warn him, but advance warnings were more effective. Planted a seed of caution that grew. 'Fame and admiration bestow a false feeling of security.'

'There's one thing worse than being talked about, and that's not being talked about.'

Hattie sighed. 'A good witticism to include in your next novel.'

'It is.'

'Oscar, fame won't save you, it'll condemn you. Lengthen your jail sentence.'

He raised a sardonic eyebrow.

'Write down what I've said and refer back to it when you need to.' The written account of their conversation could tip the balance. 'Do it now.' Hattie handed him a blank journal and a pen from her evening bag.

Oscar wrote in it, his handwriting not reflecting the idle flamboyant he pretended to be. His letters were unfussy and diligent. He made to tear out the page.

'No, keep the journal.'

Oscar slid it into his jacket pocket and returned the pen. 'I'm dining with Mr Wells tonight. He's dead set against writing novels. I'm trying to persuade him to take an interest in plays, if only to review them. You should join us.'

Different versions of her were friends with Oscar in many universes. Physical proximity with any of them would kill her. 'I'd love to, but unfortunately I can't.'

His eyes twinkled. 'I think you live an exotic secret life, hidden from ordinary folk.'

'Don't tell Mr Wells about this conversation, or anyone else.'

He swirled the last of the champagne in his glass. 'All right.'

Hattie stood up and he did too.

He pushed his wavy hair from his face. 'I'm worried about you.'

'Regret, denial, or forgetfulness can change the past, alleviate the lesser sorts of pain. Don't let them ruin your future.'

'Would you mind if I used that, adapted it?'

'When you do, it'll sound utterly wonderful.' She kissed him on the cheek and left, hurrying as if she had an appointment. Had she said enough or too much?

Without access to the Guild's database, she'd never know.

CHAPTER 16

The next morning in Marion's house, Sophie was jerked awake by Charlotte barking. Charlotte was backing away from the window and from outside came a loud gunshot, followed by a clank. Birds screeched.

Sophie leaped out of bed in her T-shirt and knickers and joined Charlotte as far from the window as possible, pulling her close.

Bang.

Hugo jumped out of bed in his boxers, grabbed the pistol from the dresser, and flattened himself against the wall next to the window. He cautiously looked out and slumped in relief. 'It's Marion. She's firing from the terrace at metal targets.'

Freddy opened the connecting door and rushed into their room in his underwear. 'What's happening?'

'Marion's doing target practice,' said Hugo.

'That's all right then.' Freddy surveyed the garden.

'How is that *all right*?' Sophie stayed put with Charlotte. 'She's not … all there and wielding a loaded gun!'

Bang.

'In Shorten, my great aunt was an excellent shot,' said Freddy.

Hugo drove his hand through his tousled hair. 'No one's raising the alarm in surrounding houses. The neighbours must be used to it.'

Sophie approached the window with Charlotte. The sky was clear except for a grey band of mist drifting above roofs and chimneys. At the end of the garden were square metal targets arranged in a semicircle in a flower bed. The targets were tied to the top of wooden sticks and painted with flowers, mirroring the real plants growing around them: pale lemon primroses, pink tulips, and bright yellow daffodils.

Bang.

Hugo folded his arms. 'She's hitting all the targets.'

'When my great aunt was young, she was also known for her horsemanship,' said Freddy. 'She rode stallions and jumped six-foot fences side-saddle.'

Okay, impressive. Sophie had been obliged to ride side-saddle in Shorten. Hadn't gone well. 'Marion's too young to be a great aunt.'

'She won't be a great aunt until I'm born in 1904,' said Freddy. 'I mean, another version of me.'

Hugo pulled on his trousers. 'You'd think they'd have warned us.'

'We should wait before completing our toilette.' Freddy pointed at the garden. The outside loo was directly in the line of fire.

The kitchen was warm with hot breakfast smells. As they sat down, Sophie said, 'We were surprised Miss Lacey's shooting didn't upset the neighbours.'

'Miss Lacey's keen on her safety rules,' said Miss Harris.

'Which is fortunate,' said Mr Burgess, 'for us and for them.'

Hugo's mouth twitched, appreciating the butler's sense of humour. He poured tea into a bowl. Fortunately, the butler's attention was on his newspaper and Miss Harris was busy plating up.

'Miss Lacey learned to shoot up north,' said Miss Harris.

Freddy nodded. 'In Derbyshire.'

'Perhaps it reminds her of happier times during her childhood?' said Hugo. 'Hence the dolls?'

'Possibly,' said Miss Harris.

Sophie tucked into creamy scrambled eggs, the butter and milk rich on her tongue. 'Can anyone buy and use a firearm here?' The laws in this 19th century might be different from home.

'There's no law against it.' The butler turned to a new page in the paper. Going by the date on the front page, it had been delivered that morning.

Freddy gave a sausage to Charlotte. 'Would you mind if we stayed a few more days? Our business in town won't take long.'

The butler lowered the paper, in two minds.

'We'll be out during the day,' said Hugo.

The maid's eyes met Sophie's. 'Miss Lacey tires easily.'

'I can make myself useful.' Sophie stood up and went to the sink to wash up.

After a moment's stunned silence when Sophie feared the butler would keel over, Miss Harris said, 'It'll be nice to have some help.'

Miss Harris left the kitchen and a few minutes later returned with a tray of dirty crockery, half a meal still on the plate. 'I wish Miss Lacey would eat more. She picks at food like a sparrow.'

'Apart from outings to the park, does she ever leave the house?' asked Sophie.

Miss Harris hesitated. 'She reacts to unfamiliar surroundings … inappropriately.'

'Breakfast was splendid.' Freddy got to his feet. 'But we must be about our business.'

In the hall, Hugo said to him, 'Are your outfitters far? We can't afford a cab.'

'Savile Row.'

Hugo took out his map.

The shopping street at home was famous for upmarket clothes. 'Your outfitters wouldn't buy the walking stick from Gladys' friend,' said Sophie. 'Take in stolen goods.'

Freddy lifted his hat from the stand. 'We should check.'

Across the hall was the door to the drawing room and further along was another door. *Miss Lacey eats in her bedroom, doesn't like the dining room.* Curiosity getting the better of her, Sophie tried the second door. It wasn't locked. She ventured in with Charlotte.

The shape of a long table, chairs, and a sideboard could be discerned beneath white dustsheets. On the wall, a sheet covered a frame taller than Sophie.

Hugo and Freddy came in, holding their hats.

'Why would Marion loathe a room so much that she wouldn't set foot in it and wouldn't want it used?' Sophie walked over to the picture and lifted the sheet. It was an oil painting of a red-haired woman in a brown crinoline dress and a handsome man in a suit. The woman's expressive eyes homed in on Sophie and she let the sheet drop.

Charlotte whined, realising it was Marion's late parents, and Sophie stroked her. Everyone coped with grief in their own way, and this was Marion's. She hadn't destroyed the painting or shut it in the attic, but she couldn't bear to look at it.

Empathy flooded over Sophie. She drew a deep breath, willing it gone. A drain on energy and a distraction. The cylinder was still lost, and Bella was waiting, out of reach. Yet the empathy didn't subside, it grew worse. 'I could choose my moment, suggest to Marion that in at least one universe my parents are safe and so hers will be too.'

'She's childlike, so might believe you,' said Freddy. 'Would want to cross universes to find them.'

'And die trying.' Hugo's voice was melancholy.

'Worse, she might think you were mocking her,' said Freddy.

'She could withdraw more into her make-believe world,' said Hugo.

Sophie sighed. 'Okay. We should leave well alone.'

CHAPTER 17

*L*oitering in Marion's hall, Sophie debated whether to return the carpet bag to the bedroom. It was a nuisance to cart around but if something should prevent them returning, they'd lose the spare ammunition, not to mention Charlotte's page-turner. No, best to keep it with her—

'*Polly put the kettle on. We'll all have tea...*' The singing was coming from the drawing room.

'Before leaving, we should pay our respects,' said Freddy.

In the drawing room, the maid was adjusting dolls and cushions, and Marion was sitting in the same chair with a book on her lap. She stopped singing, her gaze lingering on Sophie. 'I love your brooch.'

'It's very old,' said Sophie. Or was it new? Gifted by a stallholder in Rome only weeks ago.

Freddy smiled at his great aunt. 'We must go into town and may return this afternoon. Is that alright?'

Marion jumped to her feet, still clutching the book. The cover featured a man in a shiny red suit, half standing up from a chair. The rest of the image was filled with gold and red text: *Beeton's Christmas Annual. A Study in Scarlet* by Arthur Conan Doyle. She dropped the book on a side table. 'I'll come with you! I haven't been out in ever so long.'

Miss Harris shook her head.

'Our business is very boring,' said Sophie.

'Where are you going?' Marion's delicate face was animated.

'A gentlemen's outfitters, so of limited interest.' Freddy straightened, using his full height to add authority. Unnecessary, as he was a foot taller than Marion.

'Harris, bring me all my outdoor shoes.'

The maid sighed and left with obvious reluctance. Sophie chewed her lip. Marion couldn't come with them. Forget 'inappropriate behaviour.' When Wells pounced, Marion mustn't be there.

Miss Harris returned with a trunk. She set it on the floor, moved a doll safely out of the way, and took out sturdy boots.

Marion pouted. 'I want different ones.'

'It will rain soon,' said Freddy. 'Unpleasant weather for walking.'

'Nonsense,' said Marion.

The maid lifted out another pair of black boots, then another pair, but Marion couldn't decide. Miss Harris pulled out cream boots from the bottom of the trunk. They had wonderfully pointed toes, delicate filigree patterns on the shoe part, and buttoned up past the ankle. If Sophie developed a shoe fetish, these would be first on her bucket list.

Marion clasped her hands. 'I shouldn't wear those.'

'You're still mostly in black,' said the maid. 'Those boots won't upset them.'

Miss Harris helped Marion put on the boots and Marion marched off into the hall.

'What did you mean?' Sophie asked the maid. 'Who might the cream boots upset?'

'Miss Lacey worries her parents will be sad if she stops wearing black.'

'How long do people wear mourning?' said Sophie.

Miss Harris' eyes widened, surprised she didn't know. 'For full mourning, women are veiled in public for ten months. After two more months, there's half-mourning, with touches of white on the collar or sleeves.' She paused. 'When I first arrived, I persuaded Miss Lacey to leave off the veil. She's stubborn about the rest.'

Out in the hall, Marion was pulling on dark gloves.

Mr Burgess hurried in from the kitchen, concern wrinkling his smooth brow.

Marion ignored him. 'Chop, chop. Or we'll be late.'

Miss Harris reluctantly fixed a black hat on Marion's head.

'It's about to rain,' said Freddy.

'Never fear.' Marion reached into the stand and extracted an ebony-handled umbrella.

Mr Burgess exchanged a worried glance with Miss Harris and Charlotte stood at the front door, her bulk creating a formidable obstacle.

'I don't feel well.' The maid held a dramatic hand to her temple and swayed.

'Oh my!' Freddy played along, guiding her into the drawing room.

Hugo and Sophie followed and to their relief, Marion came too. Sophie transferred dolls from a sofa to the floor, leaving space for the maid to lie down, and Miss Harris closed her eyes. The butler paused in the doorway, his face inscrutable.

'I'm alright,' said the maid. 'I just need to rest.'

Marion put her hands on her hips. 'Burgess, please ensure

she recovers.' She turned on her heel and brushed past him into the hall.

Sophie hurried after her. 'Miss Harris needs you.'

'Harris needs to improve her acting skills,' said Marion, fixing Sophie with a glare. 'Step aside.'

Freddy and Hugo hurried over, and Sophie shot them a despairing look.

The butler strode across the hall. 'Miss, we go back a long way—'

'I know.' Marion squared her shoulders.

Sophie fished out Charlotte's book from the carpet bag and held it up. 'This is ever so good.'

Marion's lips clamped in a stubborn line, and she advanced towards the front door.

The butler stepped forward but made no move to physically stop her. An awkward silence descended. They'd run out of socially acceptable options.

'We'll keep her safe,' said Freddy to the butler. 'You have my word.'

Marion tut-tutted.

'Just a short walk,' said Hugo.

Freddy's great aunt did a 'move' gesture to Charlotte. Sophie gave a resigned nod and Charlotte stepped aside.

'You're better behaved than your owners.' Marion patted her.

'I suppose you are family.' The butler's words grated like fingernails on a board as he opened the front door.

Marion rushed out and Freddy sprinted after her, holding his hat.

Sophie, Charlotte, and Hugo followed in a rush. Freddy caught up with Marion and distracted her, pointing at the blossom on an apple tree. Marion's servants were standing by the garden gate.

'Lovely day,' said Freddy. The smog was fainter, and the sun was shining.

'And no prospect of rain.' Marion's eyes were stony. 'Make haste to your tailors.'

Sophie had assumed Freddy's great aunt suffered from anxiety. That didn't fit with this iron resolve to accompany them. 'We should walk,' said Sophie, taking Marion's arm. Hopefully, she'd grow bored, and they could turn around.

Marion shrugged her off. 'Call a cab. We need a growler.'

'A what?' said Sophie.

'The bigger sort of cabs that seat up to five,' said Freddy. 'They're called growlers because of the sound they make on cobbled streets.'

Sophie's bracelet shone and rang, and the map loomed up — then vanished. She didn't have time to register the red dot's location.

As Marion squinted at her, puzzled, Freddy hailed a cab, and they clambered in. 'Jeeves and Fox,' he called to the cabbie. 'Savile Row.'

Marion stared out of the window and commented on skipping children, dirty-faced chimney sweeps, and women in fashionable fussy gowns. Sophie shut out her chatter, her mind on Bella and the cylinder. Then she pictured Wells waiting in a dark alley. He knew they'd be visiting Savile Row. Would be ready. Charlotte did her worried whimper.

'We don't want to be rude,' Freddy whispered.

'Politeness may be our undoing,' said Hugo. 'And Marion's.'

Sophie's bracelet chimed and flashed. The map was there for a second and she saw the road name. 'You were right, Freddy. Gladys' friend is in Savile Row.'

The dense traffic meant it took a while to get there. Sophie peered out of the cab window. Gentlemen's outfitters lined the street. No sign of the boyfriend with the cylinder, or Wells. But Wells could be watching from inside a shop.

The bracelet went off and the map appeared too briefly for Sophie to locate the cylinder. Hugo paid the driver through the roof-hatch and the driver unlocked the doors.

They got out and Marion gazed about like a child in a sweet shop.

Freddy led the way towards Jeeves and Fox. In the window was a single mannequin in a white-tie suit. The interior was all polished walnut furniture and dark wood panelling. How Sophie imagined a posh gentlemen's club would be.

'Good morning.' Freddy addressed a moustached man behind the counter, keeping on his hat.

Hugo had taken his off. He put it on again. This was a shop, so a public place. One of the few perks of being female and out and about in the 19th century was once your hat was on, it stayed on.

The assistant stared at Charlotte.

'We're searching for a stolen walking stick.' Freddy managed to sound annoyed and polite at the same time.

The assistant raised an eyebrow. 'A chap just tried to sell us it. I gave him short shrift.'

'What did the stick look like?' said Hugo.

'A nice green heart on the handle. Obviously stolen.'

'When the thief left, did he go right or left?' Sophie asked him.

'I'm afraid I didn't see.'

Marion ran her hand over a soft pullover displayed on a counter. 'Aren't we going to buy anything?'

'Perhaps later,' said Hugo, his tone gentle.

Outside the store, Freddy scanned the shopfronts. 'We should check every outfitter.'

They worked down the street. All had been approached and refused to take the walking stick.

'Last one.' Freddy stood in front of the most imposing store. 'Henry Poole was founded before the battle of Waterloo. Their suits are six times the price of Jeeves'. Their tailors invented the dinner jacket.' He turned to Hugo. 'You didn't know that?'

'I did not.'

'Ha!' Freddy went inside, and Sophie scurried after him, guiding Marion in with her.

Freddy was perky, maybe due to Wells not showing up. He asked about the walking stick.

The assistant shrugged. 'Nobody tried to sell it here.'

'If someone wanted to pass off dodgy goods, where would they go?' said Hugo.

'You might try Berwick Street Market.'

Out on the pavement, Hugo consulted his map. 'Berwick Street's in Soho. Not far.'

The bracelet pinged and Sophie's breath hitched. 'The dot's there.'

'To the market!' shouted Marion, so loudly that Sophie jumped. Freddy's great aunt could change from subdued to energised in a heartbeat. A concern at the best of times. And tracking down the cylinder, knowing Wells would attack…

The worst of times.

CHAPTER 18

The stalls in Berwick Street Market sold cheap food, second-hand clothes, and all sorts of tat. Shoppers dressed in variations of dreary brown huddled around a smelly sausage stall and a counter selling suspiciously fancy dinner plates. Some stallholders proclaimed their wares in sing-song London cockney, others were Irish, and many shoppers were conversing in an unfamiliar language.

'Is that German?' Sophie asked Hugo. If anyone would know, he would.

'I think it's Yiddish. If it's the same as home, Jewish people came here from Eastern Europe.'

Freddy hurried to a stall across the road. Walking sticks were gathered on a table in a jumbled-up pile. The cylinder wasn't there. 'Is there another stall that sells walking sticks?' he asked the stallholder.

The man shook his head.

Predictable. They were too late. Sophie's mental map had showed the dot here for a good five minutes, but then it had vanished, no longer outside.

Marion turned on the spot, whirling her closed umbrella in a circular motion, level with her waist. A passer-by side-stepped to avoid it.

'I'll carry your umbrella,' said Sophie.

'Why do you want it?' Marion's eyes narrowed.

Sophie acknowledged the perturbed shopper. 'In case it rains.' She tucked it under her arm and as she did, a flash of purple caught her eye down the street, bright in the sea of dull clothing.

Hugo addressed the stallholder. 'We're searching for a particular walking stick.' He described it.

'You with the police?' The man's accent was cockney.

'No,' said Freddy.

The man hesitated. 'The walking stick was yours?'

Sophie nodded. She patted Charlotte who was trying not to look as if she was listening.

'I just bought it,' said the stallholder, 'and sold it real quick.'

Freddy sighed.

'Did the buyer have a droopy moustache?' said Sophie.

'His moustache was clipped short.'

Okay, not Wells.

'Can you describe him more?' said Freddy.

The stallholder sucked his teeth. 'Dark hair, expensive suit.' He grinned. 'Quality. A bit like your good selves.'

Marion pulled at the umbrella under Sophie's arm and Sophie let her have it. Couldn't exactly fight for it in the street.

'He was the same height as you,' the stallholder told Hugo. His tone suggested he was enjoying himself. Owners of stolen goods asking questions should have been bad for business. Maybe it came with the gig. 'He had a foreign accent.'

'Yiddish?' asked Hugo.

'Don't think so.'

'Did he select the walking stick immediately or take his time?' said Freddy.

'Strange sort of question,' said the stallholder. 'But he made a beeline for your stick. Never bothered with the others.'

'Did he make any comment about the stick?' said Hugo.

The stallholder shrugged. 'Nope.'

They moved off through the market, Marion tapping the end of her umbrella on the pavement, humming to herself. Her companions were silent, lost in gloomy thoughts.

'At least the buyer wasn't Bad Wells,' said Freddy. Marion was ahead of them and couldn't hear.

Sophie willed the bracelet to ping. 'Whoever bought it must have left in a cab or be inside a bus.'

'The walking stick would have appeared much finer than the others,' said Hugo.

Freddy bit his lip. 'Or the buyer could have the gene? He saw the aluminium cylinder and was intrigued?'

'If that was the case, he'd surely have said something to the stallholder?' said Hugo. 'The cylinder would have looked weird in the middle of the stack.'

Freddy's great aunt dawdled in front of a shoe shop and Sophie slowed so she didn't bump into her. 'Could the buyer have *recognised* the cylinder?'

'I suppose he could have seen Nice Wells taking it to work,' said Hugo. 'That's quite a stretch.'

'Or the buyer could have crossed universes like us,' said Freddy, 'recognised it from ancient Rome.'

'Oh.' Hugo came to an abrupt halt. 'I know who might have bought it! He fits the stallholder's description. Though in our universe, there's no record of him visiting London…'

Hearing the excitement in his voice, Freddy and Charlotte stopped walking. So did Marion.

As usual, Sophie's husband was working through a

problem at lightning speed, leaving everyone including Sophie trailing behind. 'Care to enlighten us?'

'Nikola Tesla,' said Hugo, with a flourish.

Charlotte pricked up her ears.

'Gosh,' said Freddy.

'She sounds familiar,' said Sophie.

'Perhaps because of the Tesla car company,' said Hugo. 'But Nikola Tesla is male, not female. His first name is spelled with a k.'

'He's a hero of mine,' said Freddy. 'A wonderful inventor and engineer.'

'In twenty years from now, Tesla will predict we'll carry phones in our vest pockets,' said Hugo. 'Okay, he gets it wrong about vests. Completely out of fashion.' He paused. 'If it is him, we can check the newspapers for scientific workshops and demonstrations, easily track him down.'

Charlotte tilted her head, intrigued. She'd watched a documentary about Tesla or read about him. Marion resumed tapping her umbrella on the pavement and Hugo and Freddy glanced at her. Focused on Tesla, they'd forgotten she was there.

'It might not be him,' said Sophie. 'London's full of people with foreign accents.'

'It has to be Tesla. His prescience was so extraordinary, visiting the future must have informed his theories and inventions,' said Hugo. 'I should have realised before—'

Sophie's bracelet went off and the map was back. She swayed and grabbed Hugo to keep her balance. 'It's outside a place called the Langham.'

'Another swanky hotel,' said Hugo.

'So, whoever has it, they're enjoying the high life,' said Sophie. 'Does that fit with Tesla?'

Hugo nodded. 'At home, he lived in hotels, even when he lacked the means to pay.'

'That couldn't have continued for long,' said Freddy.

'Tesla offered one of his inventions as collateral for the debts,' said Hugo. 'I don't remember the details.'

'What a lovely bracelet,' said Marion, watching the ruby flashing. 'I'd like one.'

'The map's frozen.' Sophie blinked. 'No, it's working again.'

'What's the dot doing?' asked Freddy.

'It's moving away from the Langham, fast walking-pace,' said Sophie. 'Heading south.'

'Where to?' asked Hugo.

Sophie pressed her hand to her forehead. 'No idea.'

CHAPTER 19

They jumped into a cab. Freddy reached up and pulled the lever to open the driver's flap. 'I'll keep this open for directions.'

'Head down Regent Street.' Sophie put the carpet bag on the floor.

Charlotte pushed her muzzle against her mistress' skirt, seeking reassurance. Whenever the map appeared, chasing after the dot was too predictable. Made them easy targets for Bad Wells.

The cab sped off and Marion pressed her face against the window. 'I want to go home. Please inform the driver.' According to Miss Harris, Marion hadn't ventured further than Grosvenor Square in years, so Marion had a remarkable sense of direction.

'We'll go back to Thornbridge soon,' said Freddy. 'Unfortunately, there is something that must be attended to first. It's extremely important.'

Marion half turned, raising a delicate eyebrow. 'Your business is interesting.'

'We're hoping for uneventful,' said Hugo.

'If you see a chap with an oversized handlebar moustache,' said Freddy, 'be sure to tell us.'

Marion's attention was on the road again. 'Why?'

'We should explain,' Sophie whispered to Freddy. If Marion shared, no one would take her seriously and if she believed them, it might make her cautious.

Freddy closed the flap. 'A man called Wells is trying to kill us. He has a droopy moustache.'

'Very interesting business.' Marion sounded unfazed — and undaunted.

Hugo opened the flap.

'Go to St James.' Sophie held tight to the seat. The swaying cab and the mental map rotating as they changed direction were making her feel sick. They were fast catching up with the dot. 'Head to Spring Gardens.' But even as she spoke, the dot disappeared, and the map snapped off.

They climbed out of the cab. Spring Gardens had no trees, no grass, and no gardens. It was a commercial district with grubby office blocks. Smog hugged the buildings down to the ground.

Sophie stood beside the noisy road and peered at Hugo's map, comparing it to the map that had recently filled her mind.

Which part of the street had the dot been on when it disappeared? 'I think it was this side.'

The office block behind them had many floors and extended around the corner. Above the entrance was a sign: *London County Council.* Charlotte sniffed at it, nonplussed.

'Why would it be in there?' said Hugo, voicing Charlotte's confusion.

Sophie scanned the dreary façade. 'The bracelet may have followed a false signal.' If it had, they were stuffed.

'No harm in asking inside,' said Freddy.

The foyer had a hard floor and tatty reception counter. The air was institutionally musty, as if occasionally cleaned by reluctant employees.

Hugo kept on his hat. 'Is Mr Tesla here?'

The employee behind the counter flicked through a ledger. 'He's in a meeting.'

Hugo allowed himself a smug nod. Tesla was the buyer. 'When is it due to finish?'

'Meetings take a while.'

'Another hour?' persisted Hugo.

'Probably.' The man's lips curled upwards in a sneer. 'Please remove your circus dog.'

'Why?' Sophie sent the guy waves of hate.

'Against council policy.'

They filed out and stood in a huddle. Feeling vulnerable in this rundown district, everyone except Marion checked up and down the road for Wells.

Sophie's relief she couldn't see him was tinged with unease. 'What's Wells playing at?'

'Perhaps he's hoping if he waits long enough, we'll let our guard down?' Freddy's tone suggested he thought this unlikely.

'I was right about Tesla,' said Hugo.

Charlotte put up her paw, and he bent down for a high five. Marion watched them with a frown.

'This confirms the bracelet works.' Sophie didn't set down the carpet bag. The pavement was too grubby. 'What else do we know about Tesla?'

'The version in my universe worked for the Edison Electric Company in America,' said Freddy.

'The stallholder didn't say he was American.' Sophie

transferred her weight from one foot to the other. 'But with no TV or movies, he might not have recognised the accent?'

'Tesla's Serbian,' said Hugo. 'Emigrated to the US.'

'I guess we just wait,' said Sophie. 'Good that it's not raining.'

'I knew it wouldn't.' Marion absent-mindedly stroked Charlotte who happily acquiesced. Charlotte had warmed to Marion while everyone else was only focused on protecting her. Marion was curious about her surroundings, while also serenely detached, as if nothing was real. She hadn't wandered into the busy traffic yet. Didn't mean she wouldn't.

An urchin of around six ran past.

'Do you have children?' Marion asked Sophie.

Taken by surprise, Sophie lied. 'I don't.' The last thing she needed was a barrage of questions concerning Bella. She felt guilty enough, being so far away.

Freddy studied the pavement and Sophie did too. Why had she lied? Denied Bella existed? Fear of becoming upset? Not wanting to worry Marion? Sophie checked for Wells again. Stress? None of those excuses held up. Regret soured her throat.

A man with an angular face and neat moustache strode out of the council building, a leather folder under his arm. Sophie's bracelet chimed. The red dot on the mental map was large and close and blurry and the familiar headache kicked in with a painful thump.

'It's Tesla,' said Hugo. 'Looks the same as the online photos at home.'

Sophie strained to see past the map. He fitted the stall-holder's description. Posh suit, smart bow tie, and immaculately polished shoes. But he wasn't carrying the cylinder. Unease, then panic. 'The dot's right here.'

'No cylinder.' Freddy's voice cracked.

'The bracelet says otherwise.' The map came into focus, the red dot still huge.

Charlotte shook herself, as if flicking off raindrops.

Freddy stepped forward. 'Mr Tesla?'

'Yes?' The man didn't turn, his eyes on the traffic.

'My name is Mr Frederick Lacey. I have an interest in your work.' Freddy offered his hand and after a moment's hesitation, Tesla accepted the handshake.

'Would you permit us to buy you tea?' said Freddy.

'Why would you do that?' Tesla's accent had a faint, melodic edge.

'We have a proposition for you.' Freddy was winging it. The inventor had acquired the cylinder for a reason. Wouldn't just hand it over. But where was it?

'Afternoon tea at the Langham?' said Hugo. The dot had first appeared near the Langham, so that was likely Tesla's hotel. Was the cylinder there? Why was the map showing it here?

'The Langham would be convenient.' Tesla smiled at Charlotte, who stared back, assessing him.

'How far is it?' asked Marion.

'Only two miles,' said Tesla.

'These boots aren't comfortable for walking,' said Marion.

Tesla tipped his top hat respectfully towards her and Sophie. 'I'll meet you there.' He marched across the road.

Sophie's map readjusted. 'The dot's following him.'

Hugo flagged down another cab.

'You described Mr Tesla as an inventor,' said Marion, as they all clambered in. 'What's he invented?'

The cab moved off with a lurch. 'You must have read about them in the newspaper,' said Hugo.

Marion looked at her lap. 'I don't have time to read the paper.'

'Mr Tesla invented the induction motor,' said Freddy.

'What does that do?' asked Marion.

'Among other things,' said Freddy, 'it enables factories to manufacture items faster.'

'Oh.' Marion sounded disappointed.

'Tesla's inventions will change the world,' said Hugo.

Sophie moved closer to the window as they passed the inventor striding up the road. 'The dot's staying with him. Why?'

Freddy drummed his fingers on his knee. 'If he's examined the cylinder closely, it's possible that a tiny piece of metal could have attached itself to his clothing.'

Sophie's head was pounding, and she was struggling to think.

'He has an interesting accent,' said Marion.

Hugo nodded. 'Like Russian, only softer.'

Charlotte leaned against Sophie's legs. 'And he likes dogs.' An indication of good character, though not always.

'Tesla preferred animals to people,' said Hugo.

'Still no sign of Wells,' said Freddy. 'What's he up to?'

Marion crossed her ankles. 'Perhaps he's had a carriage accident?'

CHAPTER 20

Three hours before Tesla left the London council building, Hattie Wells was leaving Claridge's to prepare for the next Event. She visited the catering agency that supplied waitresses to the Langham and, posing as a hotel employee, cancelled one of the waitresses for that afternoon. After that, she went to the Langham, memorised the layout of the kitchens and dining room, and identified escape routes.

Back in her suite in Claridge's, she changed to practise her Krav Maga routine. What she'd learned with the Guild was part of her muscle memory, but she still practised every day. The 20th century martial art had saved her more times than she could count.

Agents trained in all weathers and in different clothes. Hattie had practised in men's trousers and a shirt, tunic and sandals, a heavy Elizabethan girdle, with layers of petticoats, and soldier's garb from various centuries. Today, she was wearing a spare corset and evening wear she kept for the purpose. Her profession required a high level of physical fitness, maintained by press-ups, squats, and running on the spot.

When she'd finished, she bathed, put on her housecoat, and rang the bellpull for tea. Usually the exercise calmed her, but her mind kept returning to the flawed itinerary. The original explanation— just error —was reassuring. Wherever the client had obtained it, the itinerary had been incorrectly filed or named and didn't apply to this timeline. The second explanation — this timeline had been corrupted — was more likely with every botched event.

Corrupted timelines were rare, irrecoverable, doomed to collapse. Fortunately, timelines, like stars, took aeons to die.

If the client had known this timeline was corrupted, and concealed it, the deception would be grounds for ending the contract with immediate effect. But that was unlikely. Monitoring timelines required vast resources.

She should make haste to complete this commission, as the itinerary would be progressively less accurate. The time divergence at the Grosvenor Square Event had jumped to more than forty minutes. Instead of going there after lunch, the targets had left Claridge's without ordering. Hattie had followed in a cab, learning nothing of value, just that the targets were searching for someone.

Her plan to remove the artefact from Mrs Alveston's suite had initially gone smoothly. Hattie had been discreet, recruiting a burglar she'd encountered on a previous job. He'd asked at hotel reception about the walking stick and subsequently, in the foyer, Hattie had overheard one of the targets chatting with housekeeping, identifying Mrs Alveston. After that, gossiping with a group of ladies about wealthy guests had easily given up the name of the woman's suite, and she'd sent the burglar to fetch the artefact.

But while Hattie was waiting outside Mrs Alveston's

rooms, a ruckus had forced her to intervene and by then, her burglar was dead. The elderly Mrs Alveston had managed to stab him in the neck with a letter opener, and the blade had found his jugular vein. Mrs Alveston had clutched at Hattie, asked for help — and could identify her. So, Hattie had used the heart-stopper. Untimely deaths that would set off an anomalies alert in the Guild command centre. Too minor to merit any action.

The police here would declare it a botched robbery. The burglar had a criminal record that fitted. Yet two people were dead and all for nothing. The artefact hadn't been in the suite.

The targets must have discovered the bodies only minutes after she'd left. What possible reason could they have for being there? Unless … the targets and the artefact were connected, not separate jobs.

Later, from The Corner Suite, Hattie had watched the targets walking down Davies Street, proceeding south beside Claridge's. A second generous window overlooked the side road.

The male targets had stayed close to the woman, alert and protective. The three could be siblings, or lovers. The ones with the same surname could be married. Not that it mattered. After the failed ambush at Marble Arch, they knew they were being hunted, should have been lying low. And there was something odd about the dog. Sniffing, but also scanning the streets, its head turning from side to side.

Hattie had assumed the client was a wealthy private collector with a personal grudge, though given the targets had Guild armour, they might be professionals. Stealing historical artefacts to order? Could the client be a crime syndicate, keen to eliminate competitors? No. The syndicates dispensed their own justice, didn't need Hattie Wells.

A knock on the door signalled a maid delivering tea. After she'd gone, Hattie settled herself on the sofa and took a thoughtful sip. She'd never had to concern herself with a client's identity. They always paid. And she never investigated targets' backgrounds. Knowledge brought empathy, and empathy would slow her hand, make her sloppy. But too much was going awry with this job. Had she missed some detail about the artefact?

She reread the letter. *Retrieve and return historical artefact to Coutts Bank in your home universe. Storage box number to follow.* There was no detail to miss. She'd been spoiled in the Guild. Pre-mission documents had included sketches or photographs, place of manufacture, materials, functions, and evidenced history.

Retrieve and return... Guild wording. Hattie chewed her lower lip. Could the client be the Guild? While she'd been serving, there'd been talk of urgent off-the-books jobs assigned to discredited agents. Would explain the exorbitant fee and might explain the flawed itinerary. Cobbled together remotely, outside of protocols...

But off-the-books agents didn't steal historical artefacts, only cutting-edge technology. Perhaps the inclusion of 'historical' in the letter was there to cover the Guild's back if it fell into the wrong hands?

Hattie gave a heartfelt sigh. The next Event. Given the unreliable timings, best she arrive a good hour early. At least the previous locations had been accurate, and the setting was suited to her skills. Not dealing with the dog would technically be a breach of contract. She didn't hurt animals. If the client was the Guild, they'd know that.

She changed into a servant's black dress, then chose a blonde wig from a selection and put it on, ensuring it entirely covered her own hair. Into a carpet bag she placed a white apron, rolled up to avoid creasing, and a frilly waitress' hat. She also needed spectacles. Hattie's eyes were her most attractive feature, and too memorable. Tapping the spectacles' rim appeared to alter the colour of the wearer's eyes. She selected an unremarkable brown colour, secured the spectacles in their case, and packed them beside a well-cushioned poison bottle.

CHAPTER 21

*S*ophie ignored her headache and the mental map, and looked around the Langham's dining room, feeling for the pistol in her pocket. She didn't expect Wells to start a fire fight here but checking for him was an ingrained habit. As per usual, her bag — and the spare ammo — had been whisked off to a cloakroom with the top hats.

'We shouldn't order yet,' said Hugo, as they were shown to a table with place mats engraved with entwined cream letters, T and L. 'Given the choice of meeting strangers or staying in the comfort of his hotel room, Tesla might not show, but if he does, I'll take notes.' He'd picked up writing paper and a pen in the foyer. Beside the hotel logo on the pad was the royal warrant, indicating that Queen Victoria and her family patronised the hotel. Afternoon tea would be expensive.

'The dot's outside the Langham, near the entrance.' The map in Sophie's mind switched off. The headache would ease soon.

A moment later, Tesla came in. He'd chosen the tea with strangers option, after all.

Freddy and Hugo stood up and shook hands with him. 'May I present Mr and Mrs Harrington, and Miss Lacey?' said Freddy.

Sophie and Marion acknowledged Tesla, and Charlotte studied him, intrigued. When he sat down, Charlotte settled by his feet. He slid his folder onto his lap.

When Freddy offered to order cakes, scones, and sandwiches, Tesla said, 'I'll just have a cup of tea, thank you. Sugar accelerates aging.'

What a horrid idea. If true, Sophie would be forty in no time. Would she trade more years for never eating chocolate cake? No.

'We'll all just have tea,' said Hugo, glad they could save their cash.

Tesla scowled at them. His eyes were a lighter brown than his hair and moustache which were almost black. 'Did Edison send you?'

'Your employer?' said Freddy.

'I've parted ways with Edison.'

'We're here on our own account,' said Hugo.

'You have an interest in electrification?'

Hugo tapped his notepad with his pen. 'Among other things.'

Tesla had walked here at a brisk pace, but his short hair was neat, as if he'd recently combed it. This man couldn't be more different than the stereotype of a genius inventor.

Marion was playing with a teaspoon, turning it one way, then the other. Hugo and Freddy were wired, in awe of Tesla, and Charlotte's golden eyes were fixed on him. Sophie was simply nervy. How could they convince him to give up the cylinder?

Tesla patted Charlotte and she let him. Good. His attitude to dogs could establish a connection, build trust. Only then should they bring up the walking stick. Start off gently.

Sophie cast around for a canine topic. 'Expensive hotels are surprisingly tolerant of dogs.'

'They tolerate the most exotic animals,' said Marion. 'A maharaja from India staying at Brown's has a monkey.'

'Brown's?' asked Sophie.

'Another luxury hotel,' said Hugo.

'They're less tolerant of babes in arms,' said Marion. 'I suppose they annoy the guests.'

'Indeed.' Tesla's attention was apparently on the spotless tablecloth.

There'd been no babies in the café, and they hadn't seen any in Claridge's or here. Presumably, toddlers from wealthy families stayed at home with their nannies. Sophie imagined her daughter in this swanky place. Bella would point her finger and say—

'We're searching for a metal object that can be mistaken for a walking stick,' said Freddy.

Tesla's head jerked up and his lips thinned. 'What did you say?'

So much for going in gently. They'd been pretty sure he'd bought the cylinder, and his reaction confirmed it.

'Most people see it as a wooden walking stick,' said Sophie. No point in being subtle now. 'That's why it was for sale in Berwick Street Market.'

'You were following me?' Tesla narrowed his eyes.

'Apologies, yes,' said Sophie. She wasn't going to tell him about the tracking bracelet.

Tesla's expression shut down. 'I pass by the market on my walks.'

Hugo nodded. 'A healthy habit.' He could yet save the day, row back from their initial ham-fisted approach.

'I walk ten miles every morning,' said Tesla. 'It clears the mind.'

'The cylinder must have looked peculiar on the stall,' said

Freddy, his tone low and respectful. 'Compared to the walking sticks.'

Tesla shrugged. 'All sorts of goods are traded in that market. It intrigued me. To reduce the risk of damaging it, I took a cab back to my hotel.'

Sophie clasped her hands in her lap. That explained why the map had vanished.

Tesla took a ball from his pocket. The bottom was flat, the lower half grey and the upper half transparent, and Sophie recognised it instantly. He'd removed the cover from the top of the cylinder. That's how the bracelet had tracked him. Sophie's breath caught in her throat. Had he broken it?

'That's part of it, how it really is?' Hugo leaned forward.

A horrible stab of alarm and Sophie stifled a gasp. Hugo could see it. The illusion of the walking staff wasn't working. What else no longer worked? The buttons? If the reset button couldn't end Janus, they couldn't travel safely in his ship to Shorten and to Bella. Another crossing in Juno was their last option — which they might not survive.

Freddy made a squeak sound that turned into a cough. 'Was it difficult to remove?' He managed to sound mildly curious.

'In the cab back from the street market, I easily twisted it off, like a lid on a jar.'

'Have you taken the rest of it apart?' said Hugo, struggling to keep his voice neutral.

'That would require considerable time and effort. The case is welded.'

'It's fragile.' Sophie's words came out more accusatory than she'd intended.

Tesla raised an eyebrow. 'This resembles glass, but I don't believe it is.'

In ancient Rome, when Sophie had opened the transparent cover, she'd had zero interest in its manufacture. 'It may be a type of plastic.'

Tesla squinted at her, baffled. When was plastic invented?

Freddy steepled his fingers. 'We would love to see the whole object.'

Tesla stood up, his folder dropping off his lap. He picked it up. 'You are from Edison. Out to ruin me.'

'We're not from your old company,' said Hugo. 'Please hear us out.'

'The main body of the cylinder is an unusual type of aluminium,' said Freddy.

'How do you know?' said Tesla. 'Have you tested it?'

Freddy folded his arms. 'We've no wish to test it or patent it for commercial gain.'

'Then why do you want it?' Tesla sat down, though he still looked wary.

'We should tell him the truth,' said Hugo. 'He's travelled like us.'

Down by Tesla's feet, Charlotte did her little nod. 'Okay.' Sophie drew a calming breath. 'We need the cylinder to reach our baby daughter.'

Tesla wrinkled his brow, confused.

'There's a ship that can take us to her,' said Freddy. 'Unfortunately, the creature in charge of it is a malevolent god who terrorises passengers. The cylinder can summon him, then end him. Once he's dead, the ship's automatic systems will ensure our safety.'

Marion was watching him, listening intently.

'This is why we've travelled in time,' said Hugo, 'as you have.'

Tesla burst out laughing. 'What utter garbage.' Then he grinned, revealing even white teeth. 'But entertaining.'

Freddy and Hugo couldn't hide their surprise. Neither could Charlotte.

If he hadn't seen the device summoning Janus in Rome, how did he recognise it in the market? 'Why did you buy the cylinder?' asked Sophie.

'The casing was an unfamiliar metal. May prove useful.' Tesla placed his folder on the table. 'Your far-fetched tale was welcome. It's been a long and unproductive day.'

'Your board meeting wasn't fruitful?' said Freddy.

'It was not. The streetcars in Pittsburgh will soon be powered by electricity. Your … trams, as you call them, will continue to be pulled by horses, with all their problems.'

'What problems?' said Marion.

'The animals are expensive to feed and to house, and their manure pollutes your streets.' Tesla sighed. 'Perhaps the French will be more receptive.'

'I know you don't believe us,' said Freddy, 'but we'd be very grateful if you could consider giving us the cylinder.'

'Out of the question.' Tesla's voice was hard.

'We'll pay a substantial sum,' bluffed Freddy.

'Good day to you.' Tesla stood up and stashed his folder under his arm.

'You're not staying for tea?' said Marion.

Tesla gave her a curt farewell bow and strode away.

Freddy let out a weary sigh, and Sophie put her hand over his. 'Tesla goes for long walks in the mornings,' she said. 'While he's out, I'll blag my way into his room when it's being cleaned.'

Hugo's lips tightened. 'He might take it with him.'

'All of this may be for nothing,' said Freddy. 'The cleverest man on the planet may have broken it.'

'Summoning an evil god sounds dangerous.' Marion had a playful glint in her eye.

Right. Like Tesla, she thought their tale make-believe.

'Initially, we planned to transport the walking stick to a

safer time and place where Janus is summoned by other travellers,' said Hugo. 'End him there.'

'But our current mode of travel is too risky to repeatedly search for a suitable location,' said Freddy. 'There are too many universes.'

Understatement. Juno had told them there were 2.5 billion versions of their home universe. Freddy's universe had that many, so did countless others.

'There's no way to identify a suitable universe in advance,' said Hugo. 'Even if we survived all the crossings, the process could take the rest of our lives.'

Freddy made a dismissive huffing noise. 'It would take thousands of years. Perhaps millions.'

'So, we have to summon Janus with the cylinder,' said Sophie. 'He's stopped *us* summoning him, not the cylinder.'

'And summoning him is so deranged, he might not anticipate it,' said Freddy. 'Give us wriggle room.'

A lot hinged on Freddy's 'wriggle room.' His belief that as Janus interfered with time and space, the consequences would become impossible to control. Even a god couldn't retain every detail of every timeline, all at once.

'We only need a split second after summoning him to press the reset button,' said Sophie. 'Janus is restrained from harming travellers by his ship.'

'Does that restraint apply outside his ship?' asked Marion.

A dart of fear. 'We don't know,' said Sophie. Tesla hadn't believed them, hadn't picked holes in their plan. Yet despite thinking it hogwash, Marion was dissecting it.

'It's funny,' said Marion. 'Killing the Roman god relies on you having time after summoning him, but he's master of time.'

'Funny's not the word I'd use,' said Hugo.

'There's another flaw in your tale,' said Marion.

'Go on,' asked Sophie. They'd been living with this quest for so long, they might be missing something obvious.

Marion's stare was reproachful. 'You told me you didn't have children.'

An inconsistency, not a flaw. 'I'm sorry. I lied because I couldn't bear to talk about her. Occasionally, it's too painful.'

Marion nodded. 'I don't like sad stories.'

A waitress arrived with a laden tray. The cups, teapot, and hot water jug had extravagantly curved white handles. Most of the porcelain was white, adorned sparingly with dark blue ferns and flowers. The nob on the teapot lid was fashioned in the shape of a blue and white sparrow. The waitress had brought four cups and saucers. Must have seen Tesla leave.

'This tea set is lovely,' said Marion. Charlotte did a single, loud bark and diners looked up, startled.

Bitter almonds. Bad. A woman's voice spoke inside Sophie's mind, and she jumped. Something up with the bracelet? Sophie pulled up her sleeve. The oval ruby was silent, inert, and the voice repeated. *Bitter almonds. Bad.* The voice was urgent — and frightened.

Marion leaped from her seat and barged hard into the waitress. She sent the waitress flying and the woman landed in an undignified sprawl. The waitress' glasses fell off and she clumsily put them on before struggling to her feet.

Freddy stood up and hurried forward. 'Apologies. Our guest isn't right in the head.'

The waitress turned and walked stiffly away, rubbing her hip.

Marion glared at Freddy and returned to her seat. 'Something's not right,' she said.

Freddy sat down and Hugo picked up the teapot.

The voice inside Sophie's brain grew so loud it hurt. She pressed her palms against her temples. *Bitter almonds. Bad.*

'What's wrong?' said Hugo.

Charlotte pawed at Sophie's skirt, her eyes wide and pleading. The next moment, Charlotte bit down on the end of the tablecloth and pulled. Freddy viewed Charlotte with alarm and put both hands on the table to stop the cloth sliding, taking the crockery with it.

The voice… It wasn't possible but who else could it be? 'I don't know how or why. Charlotte's talking to me,' Sophie said in a rush. 'She's saying bitter almonds, bad.'

Hugo gasped and slammed down the teapot, and Charlotte released the tablecloth. 'I think Charlotte can smell poison,' whispered Hugo. 'It must be in the tea or hot water jug. Cyanide dissolves in hot liquids.'

Horror flashed across Freddy's face. 'Oh, my.'

Sophie hugged Charlotte. 'How can you talk to me?' she whispered. Charlotte just stared back. She didn't know.

'We shouldn't involve the police.' Hugo got to his feet. 'Claridge's and now the Langham.'

'We can't leave this crockery here,' said Sophie. 'If Charlotte's right…'

Charlotte cleared her throat, affronted.

'Speak to me,' whispered Sophie.

Charlotte gave an almost imperceptible shake of her head. Other diners were watching them. Charlotte didn't want to speak or maybe couldn't?

'We must dispose of the jug and teapot,' announced Marion at full volume, her order carrying across the room.

CHAPTER 22

Outside the Langham, Sophie scanned the street for Wells and the blonde waitress. Had the woman been an accomplice, or an innocent duped into helping him? She squinted at the hotel porters. The crockery might contain poison, but they were still stealing it. The porters weren't moving, showing no interest.

There was a small drain a few paces away, the square metal grill flush with the pavement. Sophie went to pour in the hot water and Freddy stayed her hand. 'Slowly,' he said. 'Don't let any of it splash.'

Standing beside Charlotte, Marion watched, horrified and fascinated. Sophie ensured the lip of the jug was through the grill and carefully poured out the contents. She waited for the jug to stop dripping before straightening and stepping back with it.

Hugo strode out of the hotel with the carpet bag and top hats. 'Nearly a shilling for three cups of tea.' In Shorten in the 1920s, two half pints had cost five pence. He set the bag down. 'I asked a waiter about the waitress, pretended we wanted to tip her. The guy was surprised. Said he'd told her off for being slow.'

Freddy put the teapot spout into the drain and tipped the pot, holding onto the sparrow-lid until the last dregs were gone.

'We must wash our hands.' Sophie flexed her fingers. 'Is cyanide lethal forever?'

'The poison stops working after a few hours,' said Marion. 'The murderer has to administer it quickly.'

Everyone looked at her in surprise and some alarm. An in-depth knowledge of the properties of cyanide surely wasn't normal. Marion enjoyed shooting. Was the study of poisons another hobby?

Marion registered their expressions and set her mouth. 'It was in *The Times*.'

'I thought you didn't read the paper,' said Freddy.

'Harris reads me the interesting bits.'

'We should throw the crockery in the Thames.' Hugo shuddered.

'How far to the river?' said Sophie.

'Two miles.' Hugo gestured at the busy street. 'We can't risk contaminating a cab.'

Marion tightened her hold on her umbrella. 'The exercise will do me good.'

The more she got to know Freddy's great aunt, the more Sophie liked her.

As they set off, Freddy glanced back at the hotel. 'I don't think the waitress poisoned the tea. If she had, she'd have been nervous. But when she was knocked to the floor, she was shocked and annoyed.' He turned to Marion. 'I owe you an apology. I shouldn't have said you weren't right in the head. It's just … you haven't ventured out recently.'

Marion shrugged.

'How did you realise about the poison?' Sophie asked her.

'I didn't. The waitress' boots were wrong.'

'In what way?' said Hugo.

'They had a kitten heel and fastened with good buttons,' said Marion. 'Servant's boots are flat with laces.'

Sophie gave Marion an appreciative nod. Move over Sherlock.

Charlotte grimaced, maybe remembering the scent of the poison. Sophie hugged her. 'Thank you.' She hoped Charlotte's response would sound in her mind. 'Talk to me.' After the initial shock, Sophie longed to hear her voice. Charlotte shook her head.

'Her terror when she smelled the cyanide could have triggered a temporary ability,' said Freddy. 'The builder in medieval Georgia mentioned that some individuals with the gene communicate telepathically.'

Sophie nodded. When the woman in Georgia had spoken inside Sophie's mind, it had been creepy, but Charlotte's voice had been consistent with her resourceful character, precious and comforting.

'Charlotte's cognitive abilities have increased as she's absorbed more knowledge,' said Hugo. 'Perhaps that played a part?'

'According to the builder, it improves with practice,' said Sophie.

'I couldn't communicate telepathically in Georgia.' Freddy sighed. 'I wish I'd heard Charlotte today.'

'This might be a one-off?' said Hugo.

'I hope not.' Sophie planted a kiss on Charlotte's brow.

They walked towards Regent Street. 'My dolls only speak when they're in the mood,' said Marion. 'They're all different.'

'Describe Charlotte's voice,' said Freddy.

Sophie considered. 'Feminine and authoritative.' Charlotte acquired a spring in her step.

Moored on the Thames were houseboats, and on the bank, men were hunched on garden chairs, their fishing lines like long fingers stretching over the water. Further out, pleasure boats glided past, dark steam from their chimneys folding into the grey mist higher in the sky. The air was fresher.

Charlotte drank from the river, and Sophie peered down into the water. 'This is surprisingly clean.'

'That's down to a new sewage system,' said Hugo. 'A guy called Bazalgette devised it.'

'Mr Bazalgette's famous,' said Marion.

Hugo's general knowledge was truly awesome. Sophie kissed him.

'We should go further along,' said Freddy.

They passed more houseboats and walked under a bridge. Although she was holding the poisoned jug, the summer scents of grass and water and happy chatter from passers-by relaxed Sophie's tight shoulders.

'If it's the same as home,' said Freddy, 'the current should take the crockery out to sea.'

'How do you know?' asked Sophie.

'From watching the Oxford and Cambridge boat race. Every year, I studied the crews and how the current might affect each team.' Freddy shielded his eyes against the sun. 'I bet three years in a row and lost every time.'

Sophie filled the jug from the river to ensure it sank and gave it to Hugo. 'You can throw further than me.'

He threw it and the jug landed with a plop and bobbed on its side. After long seconds, it finally dipped and disappeared. Freddy dunked the teapot until it was full, then hurled it. After a long float on the surface, that sank too.

Sophie knelt on the bank and rubbed her hands together in the water. 'We need soap.'

'Harrods has nice soap in their lavatories.' Marion pointed at her boots. 'My feet hurt.'

They plodded to the road and Freddy flagged down yet another cab.

Once they were all inside, Hugo rummaged in his jacket pocket. 'We're running out of money.'

'I'll pay,' said Marion.

They soon arrived at Harrods. 'We appreciate you paying for the cab,' said Hugo, reminding Marion she'd offered.

She looked blank. 'I don't have any cash.'

Charlotte eyed Hugo, her furry face worried. Did she realise they could end up in jail if they couldn't pay?

'We've got enough.' Hugo counted out the fare. 'But one more cab ride and we're down to the last sovereign.'

In Harrods department store, Marion led the way past glass cabinets of gleaming jewellery, heading for the toilets. She evidently remembered the layout.

'When were you last here?' Sophie asked her.

'Many years ago, at Christmas.'

'Will you visit Shorten this December?' said Freddy.

'I will not. Lady Lacey disapproves of me. Thinks I'm flighty.'

Sophie assumed Marion was confused. Anne would gather her in… No, Marion wasn't talking about Anne, Freddy's mother. She was referring to his paternal grandmother. If Anne travelled from the 1980s to the version of Shorten in this universe, she'd arrive in November 1893, four years from now, when the current Lady Lacey was in charge. The fine hairs on Sophie's forearm rose in goosebumps. On Anne's account, that lady of the Manor hadn't been nice but how wonderful it would be to meet the young Anne! Might be weird for Freddy, though.

Sophie went with Marion and Charlotte into the ladies'

loo. Some customers had dogs, cradled in their arms or on leads. None of the dogs were as large as Charlotte, and a few customers stared. Sophie thoroughly cleaned the handle of the carpet bag, then her hands. Marion hadn't handled the crockery, but she'd touched the waitress, so Sophie persuaded her to wash her hands too. Charlotte sat quietly by the sinks.

Back in the main store, they met up with Freddy and Hugo, and Marion walked purposefully past a glass partition into another department. She tapped her brolly on the floor. 'Come on, Mrs Harrington,' she said. 'Keep up.'

Charlotte was staying close, on alert for Wells, and Sophie kept her eyes peeled. The enormity of what had nearly happened hit her anew and her legs were shaky.

'Chop, chop,' said Marion. 'Much to do.'

Sophie trailed after her. Death by poisoning would have been horrible, but if there was a hell, it would also involve endless, pointless shopping.

'Marion's issues make her unpredictable and that's good,' said Hugo. 'Harrods might not be on Janus' itinerary, so Wells won't know about it.'

'But isn't Marion's unpredictability … predictable?' said Sophie.

Hugo grimaced.

Marion homed in on a table displaying a pair of green and silver shoes. They were suede, with pointed toes and a high heel. Printed on a notice was *Price On Request*. If you had to ask, you couldn't afford them. She picked up a shoe, held it by the heel, and twirled it like a celebratory flag.

A shop assistant rushed over. 'Just in from Paris, madam.'

'Do you have a Harrods account?' Freddy asked Marion.

She gestured vaguely at other shoes on display. 'I have sound credit. Endless amounts.'

Freddy turned to the assistant. 'Please confirm Miss Lacey's credit.'

The assistant hurried off.

'How do they know she can pay?' asked Sophie.

'Their accounts department will keep a list of approved customers,' said Freddy.

'She may have credit,' said Hugo, 'but this could empty her bank account.' He gently extracted the shoe from Marion and returned it to the table. Marion did an annoyed huff.

Distract her. 'Let's see the rest of the store.' Though Sophie tried to sound keen, Freddy knew her too well.

He glanced at her. 'I'd forgotten you don't enjoy shopping. An unusual trait in your sex.'

In front of the jewellery counter, a group of women were gesturing and comparing necklaces. Their cut-glass accents were like an excited flock of geese.

Hugo cringed. 'There should be a collective noun for animated, wealthy women.'

'A chatter?' suggested Sophie.

'A cacophony?' said Freddy.

A woman at the rear of the group yawned, covering her mouth with her gloved hand. Her elaborate pink gown matched her hat, and her neat, plaited hair bun emphasised her graceful neck and round face.

Marion yawned in sympathy. 'I'm ready to go home.'

Sophie gave silent thanks to this universe, took her arm, and scurried to the exit.

Seated in yet another cab, Marion beamed. 'This has been the *best* day.'

Sophie stroked Charlotte and made herself smile back, though her heart wasn't in it, reliving Charlotte's terror. *Bitter almonds. Bad.* 'I wonder where Wells got the poison?'

'All apothecaries sell it.' Marion's tone was conspiratorial.

'Last week, a lady was hanged for poisoning her second husband. She was caught because she'd poisoned the first one.'

She paused, anticipating avid interest, but Sophie's mind was on their narrow escape. 'Freddy, you thought the waitress didn't know about the poison. She was best placed to pour it in.'

'She had good cheekbones,' said Marion.

'Wells must have dispensed the poison in the kitchens.' Freddy hugged himself. 'Would only take a moment.'

'An unfamiliar guy wandering around would surely have been called out?' said Sophie.

'He could have pretended to be a new member of staff,' said Hugo.

The swaying of the cab was making Sophie feel sick, or that could be remembering the cyanide. 'Wells would have needed to identify which tea tray was coming to us. Known the setup of the tables.' Years ago, in the school holidays, she'd worked as a waitress.

'And once the tea was ready,' said Freddy, 'brought it out straight away.'

'The waiter told me he'd chided the waitress for being slow,' said Hugo. 'She could have been adding the poison.'

From now on, blue and white crockery would give Sophie the creeps. 'A willing accomplice?'

'But why wasn't she nervous?' said Freddy.

'Ha!' said Marion. 'Perhaps she'd done it before.'

Back at Thornbridge, Miss Harris tearfully hugged Marion as if she'd returned from a war, and Mr Burgess had to remove something from his eye.

There was only one bathroom. After Marion, her guests took it in turn to wash, then retired for a siesta.

Lying on the bed, Hugo rearranged the pillow behind him. 'Wells didn't know Charlotte could tell us about the poison.'

'I'm not sure Charlotte knew herself,' said Sophie, 'until it happened.'

Charlotte did her solemn nod.

Hugo reached down and patted her. 'We assumed the shooter in Marble Arch was a man.'

Freddy paused in the doorway to their room. 'Wells is a man.'

Charlotte shook her head.

'You think Wells is female?' Sophie asked Charlotte. 'Why?'

Charlotte gave a low whine, frustrated she couldn't speak.

'I didn't see the shooter,' said Hugo.

Sophie tried to picture the figure in the arch, but they'd been in shadow, hidden. 'Why would this Wells be female?'

'The possibility should have occurred to me after we met Nice Wells,' said Hugo. 'Given how many parallel universes there are, there must be countless variations. How do the variations develop?'

'How do you mean?' said Sophie.

'The process in the womb, when an individual is formed.'

Where was he going with this? 'Give us the version for dummies,' said Sophie.

'How a foetus develops depends on the genetic inheritance from the parents,' said Hugo, 'alongside other factors.'

'Like what the mother eats,' said Sophie. She'd eaten for England when she'd been pregnant with Bella. The longing for her daughter surged up in a stronger ache.

'And what's happening around the mother, beyond her

control,' said Hugo. 'Women who suffer extreme stress pass that down the generations.'

'If they tell their family.' Freddy gazed out at the garden.

'It's more than that. The trauma leaves a chemical mark on the mother's genes, passed to her baby and then on to the descendants. I'm oversimplifying, but the point is the environmental stress can cross over, become a genetic legacy too.'

Freddy turned from the window and Sophie stared at Hugo.

'Why didn't you mention this before?' Her voice was shrill. When Bella was conceived, her parents had been trapped in a bear pit in medieval Georgia. Shortly after that, Sophie had been shot with an arrow laced with wolfbane.

'The stress analysed in the research study lasted for years,' said Hugo, 'not weeks.'

Sophie drew a relieved breath. Bella shouldn't be affected. They'd returned safely to modern London within days.

'The iniquity of the fathers is visited upon the children unto the third and fourth generation,' said Freddy, quoting the bible.

'I always thought that weirdly vindictive.' With her father being a pastor, Sophie had grown up with theology. 'What's this got to do with female versions of Wells?'

'Babies can be born with both male and female genitalia but mostly, gender selection is binary,' said Hugo. 'Male or female. So, why wouldn't half the versions of Wells be female?'

'We encountered men in Rome because Janus selected them,' said Sophie, working it out. 'Versions most likely to kill us.'

'Horses for courses,' said Hugo. 'A female version might be most suited to London in 1889.'

'Goodness,' said Freddy. 'You're saying—'

'That waitress may not have been an accomplice,' said Hugo. 'She could have been Wells.'

Sophie gasped. She hadn't seen the resemblance, but she hadn't been looking for one.

'We can't be certain,' said Freddy.

Sophie sat on the bed. Spotting Wells in time to defend themselves had just got twice as hard.

CHAPTER 24

*H*attie Wells left the Langham and headed to a rougher part of London. As the small cab deftly manoeuvred around bigger traffic, she removed the blonde wig and glasses, and stashed them in the carpet bag.

She'd been taken by surprise by the madwoman, and Tesla. His name was in the itinerary for tomorrow, not today. It was opportune he'd gone early. Poisoning him would have caused a major rupture in this timeline.

What happened next had been baffling. Hattie had returned to the hotel kitchens, nursing her sore hip, and waited for a commotion to erupt in the dining room as the targets consumed the poisoned tea. Instead, the targets left, safe and sound, taking the tainted teapot and jug with them.

The dog had smelled the cyanide but couldn't have told its owners. Obviously. So, how had the targets known?

Strychnine would have delivered a nastier, slower death. Appropriate for a single target, preferably someone who deserved it. Though cyanide showed up in post-mortems, in the right quantity it provided a quick, kinder end. Hattie set her mouth. Academic now.

The next Event was tomorrow. *08.35. Artefact. Tesla's Tower Suite. The Langham.* Better suited to a professional thief, not an assassin.

The cab driver opened the ceiling flap and called out, 'Elephant and Castle.'

Hattie paid him the inflated fare. 'Please wait. I'll be ten minutes.' He gave her a surly nod. Cabbies didn't like this district.

She paid him extra and ignored the racket from buses and carts and the pong of uncollected horse manure. At least her servant's ankle-length skirt didn't drag through the dirt.

A road surrounded the Elephant and Castle public house on three sides. On the pub's third storey were the names of beers in pale letters, including *Imperial Stout*, and above that was the pub's name. Years ago, there'd been a forge here and Indian elephant ivory had been used to make knife handles.

On the roof was a statue of an elephant with a howdah seat on its back. The howdah with a canopy had a vague resemblance to a castle. Matching everything else on these streets, the statue was filthy with soot.

Hattie walked alongside the pub. It never opened before six in the evening, barely turned a profit. The workshops made up for that.

By the pub, the alley widened into a courtyard, with the first workshop up ahead, its shutters open. Seamstresses were making fine garments destined for upmarket shops in plain sight. Beyond the workshop was an office, stables, and a maintenance yard for cabs. The place appeared ordinary, but the cabs were built for speed and the clothes produced here were ... special.

In the courtyard, sitting at a workbench, a woman was squinting through an eye glass, fixing fake gems into a cheap necklace with a metal tool. Setting baubles into clasping prongs without damaging either was skilled work. A sketch of the genuine necklace close at hand ensured the worthless jewellery would look identical. Hattie strode past and didn't greet the woman, not wanting to distract her.

She walked through the workshop to the office, the heels of her boots tapping on the concrete floor. The toe and base were lined with a substance yet to be invented. Wafer thin and harder than diamonds.

Mary Carr stood up from her desk by the window, her plain skirt and jacket enlivened by a shiny chatelaine belt. Mary's chatelaine had sewing tools like the seamstresses, and also held pens and keys, reminding Hattie of happier times, when the most lethal object she'd carried had been scissors.

'You're a sight for sore eyes,' said Mary. Her accent was broad cockney, though when required she could speak as good as royalty.

'How are you?'

'Well enough.' Mary had a healthy bloom in her cheeks.

'Business good?'

'Yeh.' Mary's business was shoplifting, and the female gang she led was so well run, they'd never been caught. They called themselves hoisters. Everyone else called them the Forty Elephants, after the pub. Perhaps there'd once been forty in the gang, but Mary was choosy. 'Today, we did Harrods. Just got back.'

'It went smoothly?'

Mary grinned. 'Like clockwork.'

'You used the crush method?' Four or five women would crush together in a store, some distracting staff while others hid clothes and other items about their person. The women joked that when their pockets were full, they were as big as real elephants.

'Doing a ringer next week,' said Mary. The Forty Elephants went window shopping around expensive jewellers, then drew meticulous sketches from memory to make worthless, replicated trinkets. A genuine piece of jewellery would be pocketed in a shop, while the copy was returned to the counter. Mary's bookcase was overflowing with all the sketches.

'You need more shelves.' Hattie folded her arms. 'I don't know how you get away with it.'

'Fooling 'em with fancy clobber always works.' On their thieving trips, the gang dressed up as toffs.

Mary smoothed a mousy curl on her hair bun. 'I worry sometimes it's too easy.' She wore a diamond ring on every finger, giving a razor edge to her punches. 'Never had to take on the bobbies.'

Hattie caught the regret in her voice. Mary relished violence. But the police, nicknamed bobbies after Sir Robert 'Bobbie' Peel who'd founded them, remained unaware of the Forty Elephants.

'You 'ere for new clothes?'

'No, not staying long. I've brought more Velcro.' Hattie pulled a sheet from her bag.

Velcro was perfect for sealing hidden pockets. The girls sewed it into bloomers, dresses, coats, muffs, even hats. On Hattie's last visit, the workshop had made her skirts and jackets with Velcro fastenings, allowing her to dress and undress in seconds. Hattie had no need of a maid, and she could change outfits in a trice, wrong-footing targets.

Mary had never asked why Hattie required the outfits, didn't know that Velcro wouldn't be invented until the 20th century, or that Hattie travelled in time. Mary assumed she was just a resourceful criminal — like her.

'I've a hoist that needs your special talents,' said Hattie. 'Requires a ringer.'

'Usual rates?'

'Better.'

Mary threw her a shrewd look. 'Now, that makes me nervous.'

She was wise beyond her years. Hattie had come across her on a Guild job. They'd been friends ever since.

'We do well 'cause we're careful.' The gang never wore stolen clothes, sold them on. The resulting cash bought legitimate classy outfits to wear while shoplifting. 'I don't need high-stakes jobs.' Mary put her hands on her hips. 'Spell out the risk.'

'No more than normal. My client has more money than sense. The item's a wooden stick with a carved handle.'

Mary frowned. 'Sounds like nothing.'

'It has sentimental value.' The lie tripped off Hattie's tongue, smooth and plausible. Historical artefacts fetched mind-boggling sums.

'When do you want it done?'

'Tomorrow morning, from a hotel suite while the owner's at breakfast.'

'Have you got a sketch for the ringer?'

Hattie inwardly cursed. She should have taken the sketch from the other Wells' cousin. 'I'm afraid not. Once you have it, could you finish a ringer in a few hours and replace it?'

'Describe it more. What sort of wood?'

Hattie had no idea how the artefact would appear to Mary up close, or to anyone without the rare gene. 'I haven't any more details.'

'Don't worry, once we have it, Julie will make a replica real quick. She's new, but there's nothing she can't turn her hand to.'

A day after being nearly poisoned in the Langham, Hugo changed their last sovereign for cash, and they reluctantly returned there. Sophie had left the carpet bag in Thornbridge as Marion had lent her a small, draw-string handbag, decorated with delicate beads and lace. Just the right size for storing bullets.

They'd left the house before Marion was awake. Rude, but for the best. Needing to keep her safe brought additional stress.

Sophie hurried past the hotel doormen. 'You'd think someone would have noticed us taking the crockery, told them not to let us in.'

'Good hotels are tolerant of eccentricity.' Freddy strode over to reception.

This was the safest opportunity to steal the cylinder from Tesla's room. Hopefully, he'd be downstairs eating breakfast.

'I'm here to see Mr Tesla.' Freddy exuded the confident air of a person of consequence.

'Mr Tesla's staying in The Tower Suite, sir. He may be at breakfast. Is he expecting you?'

'He is.' Freddy took off his top hat and strode towards the dining room.

Hugo removed his hat and hurried after him. Sophie and Charlotte hurried too.

They passed a grand staircase and an ornate glass lift. 'I didn't realise hotels had lifts?' Sophie said to Hugo. 'Are they like modern ones?'

'Pretty much. Hydraulic.'

Freddy paused by the dining room entrance. 'He's there and the cylinder isn't.' He stepped back. 'Though the transparent cover could be in his pocket.'

With the cover missing and the illusion of the walking stick disabled, the rest of the cylinder might not work at all. Only one way to find out. Sophie's breathing quickened. Hopefully, 19th century chambermaids wouldn't question well-to-do guests.

But crossing the foyer, they froze. The lift was open and standing on the threshold was a woman carrying the cylinder. It was tucked under her arm, and she was gripping the top — and the reattached cover — with her other hand.

Freddy gulped. 'Hugo, do you see the walking stick?'

He nodded.

Relief washed over Sophie, sweet and energising. The woman's face was obscured by a lattice veil, part of a green hat that matched her gown. She stepped into the foyer, put the base on the floor and limped, using the cylinder as a walking stick. In the lift, she'd been clutching it like a precious prize. Did she know what it was?

She was heading for the exit, and Charlotte did her battle growl. 'This doesn't need a public fight.' Sophie patted the pistol in her pocket.

Hugo took Charlotte's lead. 'Without seeing the real thing, I may damage it, if we have to wrestle it off her.'

Sophie rushed forward with Freddy. They easily

passed the woman before she reached the exit and turned to face her. Sophie recognised her through the veil. The yawning customer from the jewellery department in Harrods.

'Excuse me,' said Sophie, politely.

The woman's grip tensed on the cylinder. 'I'm in rather a hurry.'

'We won't detain you for long,' said Freddy. 'You've picked up our walking stick by mistake.'

The woman carefully laid down the cylinder on its side. What was she doing? Why was she putting it on the floor? In one swift movement, the woman straightened, and punched Freddy in the face. The blow was delivered in an upward sweep, catching his chin. Taken by surprise, Freddy toppled backwards.

Sophie gasped, and the woman punched out at her. She'd instinctively stepped away, so the swipe barely connected, but the force of it made her reel. Before Sophie could stop her, the woman grabbed the cylinder and ran out the exit. Hugo dropped Charlotte's lead, and Charlotte sprinted, so fast she was almost a blur. Sophie couldn't move, disorientated. Her mind was filled with the map, the scarlet dot huge and close-up.

Hugo caught Sophie's arm, steadying her, and the map vanished. They rushed outside.

Charlotte was pacing on the pavement, eyeing the cabs leaving and arriving like a caged animal. Sophie's jaw was aching. She touched her chin, and her palm turned red and sticky.

'It's just a scratch.' Hugo hugged Charlotte, who looked downcast and was shaking her head. 'Freddy's hurt. Come on.'

Back in the foyer, the man from reception was addressing guests. 'Remain calm. I've called the hotel nurse.'

'He's with us,' said Hugo. They struggled through the guests who were gathered in a huddle around Freddy.

He was sitting in an armchair holding his chin, his fingers bloody. A doorman was standing next to him, and Charlotte planted herself on his other side, her eyes shuttered.

'Your instinct was right,' Sophie whispered to her. 'We shouldn't have stopped you taking her on in the foyer.'

'Nasty,' said the doorman. 'Injured by something sharp.'

A nurse approached wearing a crisp white apron, embroidered with the hotel logo, T L. When she saw Freddy, her brow lined with concern. She rummaged in a sturdy doctor's bag and took out a Milton bottle of disinfectant and a bowl. 'Please fill this with water.' She gave the doorman the bowl and he scurried off.

Sophie felt her own chin. 'How can a punch do this?'

'She must have had a knuckleduster. Metal with sharp edges that fits over your fingers.' Hugo clenched his fist to demonstrate.

With growing rage, Sophie relived how the woman had hit Freddy. That woman had known exactly what pain she was inflicting. The anger spluttered out, replaced by worry about Freddy.

The nurse examined the inside of his mouth. 'No damage beyond the lip.' She mixed Milton disinfectant into the bowl of water, then applied it with a cloth. Freddy stiffened and winced. The nurse rolled out a bandage and covered the wounds, tying off the bandage on top of his head. 'You should shave off your beard. Get some air to these cuts.'

Sophie moved closer. The bandage was already tinging red. 'He surely needs stitches?'

'Harley Street isn't far,' said the nurse.

Harley Street was famous for its doctors, but Freddy needed the Victorian equivalent of Accident and Emergency. 'Where's the nearest hospital?' Sophie asked her.

'Public hospitals harbour infection. He doesn't want to contract lockjaw.'

What was lockjaw?

'Are you residents?' The nurse returned the unused bandage to her bag. 'I'll visit every day.'

'Thank you,' said Hugo. 'Unfortunately, we're not.'

'What's lockjaw?' Sophie asked the nurse.

'Muscle stiffness of the jaw and neck, causing breathing and heart problems.' She straightened. 'It's a life-threatening condition.'

'Tetanus,' Hugo muttered, recognising the symptoms.

Freddy gestured for a pen. Pens and paper were near to hand on side tables. Sophie grabbed one of each and handed them over. He wrote, 'CHASE,' scarlet blood from his fingers smearing the paper and the cream Langham logo.

CHAPTER 26

They took a cab to Thornbridge, and Marion ushered Freddy upstairs, clucking like a mother hen. He sat on his bed, wincing and checking the bandage protecting his chin.

'What on earth happened?' said Marion.

Hugo hesitated. 'We were robbed. A woman took our walking stick.'

'You haven't got a walking stick,' said Marion.

'We'd just bought it,' said Sophie. Stick to the truth as much as possible. Didn't want to contradict themselves. 'When we confronted the thief, she lashed out and cut his face.'

'She?' Marion sounded half-incredulous, half-angry. 'Was it the waitress?'

'A different woman,' said Sophie. 'Do you remember the customer in the jewellery department of Harrods, the one who was yawning?'

'Short, with mousy hair.'

'That's the one,' said Sophie.

Marion shook her head. 'What's the world coming to?'

'This bandage is horrible.' Freddy was imitating a ventriloquist, barely moving his lips.

Charlotte pawed at Sophie's carpet bag.

Sophie took out the carry case from Juno and selected a packet of plasters. She couldn't read the builders' writing, but based on the image on the front, they were steri-strips. Juno's bandages and plasters contained a powerful substance to stop infection.

'We need to shave off his beard,' Hugo said to Marion.

'I'll fetch Mr Burgess.' She hurried out.

Miss Harris came in with a bowl of water, soap, and a towel. Sophie washed her hands and while Hugo washed his, she undid the safety pin and gently peeled away Freddy's bandage. It was stuck to the wounds and his beard and though she was as gentle as possible, he yelped.

Marion returned with the butler who had a tray of shaving implements.

'If I may suggest, this is an occasion for dry shaving,' said Mr Burgess, channelling Jeeves from the Bertie Wooster stories. 'Perfection is not required.' As he set about his task, Freddy clenched his fists, his knuckles white.

Once the beard was gone, the butler left with the shaving stuff, and Miss Harris applied a cloth soaked in Milton disinfectant. After that, she patted the area around the wounds dry with another cloth.

'You'll feel better once we've patched you up,' said Sophie, hoping he would. Hugo pressed the gashes closed while she applied the steri-strips, sealing them.

'The sticky bandages are unusual,' said Marion. 'Where did you get them?'

'America,' lied Sophie. When were steri-strips invented?

The cuts sealed shut, they stepped back to check their handiwork. 'With any luck, you won't have a scar,' said Sophie.

Miss Harris was cleaning a curved metal tube. Apart from being silver-plated, it resembled an alarming tool that a surgeon would use in an operating theatre.

'What does that do?' Sophie asked her.

'Allows invalids to drink.'

Sophie dug out two codeine pills from the carpet bag. Marion held a glass of water steady while the maid kept the bottom of the tube inside it and angled the top of the tube into Freddy's mouth. He swallowed the painkillers and drank all the water.

'Thank you,' he mumbled.

'This has been quite a palaver,' said Miss Harris to Marion. 'You should lie down for a bit.'

'Not now.'

The maid had mentioned that she tired easily. Sophie shot the maid an apologetic glance. 'We're sorry to bring this trouble here.'

Marion folded her arms. 'This is the best place to be. Guarded by Britannia.'

'Sorry?' said Sophie.

'You mean the gargoyle by the front door?' Hugo asked Marion.

'She watches over us.'

'It's a lovely carving,' said Hugo.

Marion beamed. 'My old guardian gave it to me.'

Sophie nodded. After Marion lost her parents, her guardian must have been a pivotal figure.

'When did the guardianship end?' said Hugo.

'On my 21st birthday.'

'How about that lie-down?' persisted Miss Harris.

Marion avoided her eyes. 'I'm not tired.'

The maid turned on her heel. 'I'll go help Cook prepare lunch.'

She left to assist the imaginary cook, and Charlotte lay beside Freddy's bed.

'I'm glad you're not tired,' said Hugo to Marion. 'This has knocked us for six.'

'Me in particular,' muttered Freddy.

Hugo studied his shoes. 'Sorry, poor choice of words.'

'My ears are ringing and my chin hurts.' Freddy spoke with difficulty. 'Floored by a lady.'

Marion tilted her head. 'I wonder why she stole your walking stick? She was bored in Harrods. Paid no attention to the jewellery. Only her friends were doing that.'

The woman hadn't been bored when she'd stepped out of the Langham lift. Her lips had been set in a determined line.

'Is the walking stick part of your interesting business?' said Marion.

Freddy gave a slight nod.

Sophie came to a decision. They'd already shared a lot with Marion. In for a penny… 'The thief stole the cylinder from a hotel guest.'

'Cylinder?' said Marion.

'Most people see it as a walking stick,' said Hugo. 'A few individuals see a metal cylinder.'

'It's magic?' Marion pouted. 'You're teasing me.'

'We're not,' said Sophie. 'It's advanced science.'

'Individuals who see the cylinder have slightly different biology,' said Hugo. 'We call it a gene. And if that woman has the gene, she could be Wells.'

Marion wrinkled her nose. 'You said Wells was a man with a droopy moustache.'

'He still might be,' said Sophie. 'Or Wells could be the waitress or this other woman.'

Charlotte flicked her eyes towards Sophie. Frustrated they didn't know?

'It's unlikely…' Freddy mangled the words. 'But the waitress and the thief may both have the gene.'

If so, either could be Wells. Would a female Wells resemble the male version? Brothers and sisters looked similar, though not always. 'If Wells is female, my money's on the woman from Harrods,' said Sophie. A well-off lady wearing a knuckleduster on her punching hand was unusual in most times.

'If she is, Janus must have tasked her to find the cylinder, as well as killing us,' said Hugo.

'To destroy it,' mumbled Freddy.

'There's an even worse scenario,' said Hugo.

Charlotte gawped at him. So did Sophie. 'What could be worse than losing our last chance to reach Bella?'

'Wells using the cylinder to summon Janus out of his ship,' said Hugo. 'Permanently.'

Fear sped up Sophie's heartbeat. Janus tormented his passengers. 'Freed from his ship, who knows what he'd do—'

'How can you fight a creature who probes your mind?' Freddy sat properly on the bed and drew up his knees.

'Why is he evil?' said Marion.

Sometimes, the simplest questions had no answers.

Hugo hesitated. 'He learned from us.'

'I'm not evil.' Marion bristled. 'Are you evil?'

'Janus has accessed his passengers' minds for centuries. Not just their personal memories. Knowledge of their species. He's evaluated the consequences of billions, perhaps trillions of choices. How doing the right thing can bring an individual little reward and risk horrible consequences. So, he focuses on transactional decisions, devoid of morality, that benefit him.'

Sophie cast around to lighten the mood. 'Evil hasn't won at home.'

Hugo raised an eyebrow. 'Our little bit of it, the west.'

'Okay, other countries…' Sophie tailed off. Recently, she'd found it hard to listen to the news.

Hugo's eyes held a melancholy Sophie hadn't seen before. Awesome general knowledge wasn't all positive, not if your brain stored terrible stuff.

Sophie's thoughts turned back to the thief and her mood lifted. 'If Wells meant to summon Janus, she'd have done it by now.'

Hugo huffed. 'We don't have all the facts. It may be that Janus has planned his theatrical arrival for a specific day and time.'

'But why is she trying to kill us?' said Sophie. 'If she intends to summon Janus, he'd easily snuff us out.'

'She's following his instructions, and he craves entertainment,' said Hugo. 'Pain and fear and struggle.'

Marion squinted at him and Sophie cringed. Sometimes, she hated it when Hugo was right.

Ping. The map loomed up in Sophie's mind. She lurched over to Freddy's bed and sat on the edge. 'The dot's on the other side of London, behind another hotel … the Elephant and Castle.'

'If it's where I'm thinking of, that's not a hotel,' said Hugo. 'It's a pub in South London.'

'I've never been to South London,' said Marion.

The map was glitching, switching on and off. 'The cylinder's coming out of the pub, and straight away going inside again.'

Hugo hurried into the adjoining bedroom and returned with his map. 'There might be more than one pub called the Elephant and Castle.'

Sophie sighed. 'The map's gone.'

Hugo touched his printed map with his forefinger. 'Was the dot here, south of the river?'

'Yes, not far from Southwark Cathedral.' Sophie rubbed

her temples to ease the ache that came with the mental map. 'I'm guessing she saw Tesla with the cylinder, thought it valuable, and she's selling it in the pub. She'll be confused when she realises everyone else sees a walking stick.' The headache was easing. 'Maybe she's not Wells? Just a thief who happens to have the gene?'

'A *violent* thief,' mumbled Freddy.

'I can't believe she'd have taken it to the Elephant and Castle herself,' said Hugo. 'She wasn't dressed for that district.'

'How do they dress there?' asked Marion.

'Basic, working clothes,' said Hugo. 'Our thief would have looked like Queen Victoria visiting a slum.'

Uncomfortable image. Sophie stood up. 'The bracelet's still tracking the cylinder and it's not broken. Best we check out this pub.'

Freddy got to his feet and swayed, and Sophie steadied him before slowly pushing him back onto the bed. She put her hand over his. 'You should rest.'

Hugo stiffened, standing straighter. 'No need for a top hat.'

Sophie chewed her lip, wishing she could dress down. Charlotte jumped to her feet and Sophie stroked her. 'Stay here. You'd make us more conspicuous.' Charlotte's dog coat covering her armour was stylish, but even pampered dogs here only wore collars.

Charlotte harrumphed.

A new Charlotte sound. Sophie kissed her brow. 'We won't be long.'

CHAPTER 27

Sophie flagged down a cab.

'We should go by bus,' said Hugo.

'That would take too long. We need to get there before it's sold on.'

Hugo sighed, followed her into the cab, and opened the flap. 'Elephant and Castle, please,' he told the cabbie.

'You what?' yelled the cabbie.

'It's south of the river,' said Hugo.

'I don't go south of the river.'

'Three and a half miles,' said Hugo. 'A return trip so, seven miles.'

'What will be the fare?' asked Sophie, hoping the prospect of extra cash for the longer journey would persuade him.

'A shilling and eight pence one way, but for south of the river, it's double.'

Hugo scowled. 'Double for the way back too?'

'Plus waiting time.'

'Too much,' said Hugo. 'Please let us out.'

The cabbie released the doors.

Down the street, there were plenty of buses, most of them

run by the London Omnibus Company. The name was painted on the side. 'There's no numbers,' said Hugo. 'Let's hope the routes are vaguely the same.' Hugo had grown up in London.

They eventually found a bus stop where the destinations ended at Westminster Bridge. Hugo pointed. 'This will take us halfway.'

A bus soon arrived, and the fare was tuppence each.

In Westminster, they crossed the bridge. It was the same as home, except the lamp posts were gas. The cast-iron arches were painted green, and the style was gothic revival like the House of Commons. Two policemen strode past, and Hugo lowered his voice. 'Tesla will have called the police, assumed we stole the walking stick.' His lips tightened, maybe imagining himself in a Victorian prison.

South of the river, they boarded another bus to South-wark. Every time the bus stopped, they took on ever more down-at-heel passengers. On the road, there were no more carriages, and fewer buses. When they got out at Southwark, a youth leaning against a lamp post, dressed in a scruffy suit and cap, did a sarcastic whistle.

Yes, Sophie was as overdressed as Queen Victoria but without the security detail. 'We should have brought Char-lotte. Wouldn't have drawn more attention and would have been safer.' She checked to ensure no one was watching and slipped the pistol to Hugo. 'You're a better shot than me.'

'It's not far.' He'd checked the map on the bus.

The air tasted gritty and smog obscured the road, a darker shade of grey, almost brown. They had to breathe it in.

They hurried past run-down shops and terraced houses, ignoring curious stares from other pedestrians. Sophie's skirt trailed over the pavement, collecting dirt.

Scruffy children ran out of an alley and surrounded them.

The oldest ones couldn't have been more than eight. They pressed in close, hyenas mobbing their prey, and Sophie's breath hitched. Get a grip. They're only a few years older than Bella.

Hugo took the pistol from his pocket. The children weren't surprised, respect registering in their eyes. They scattered.

Feral kids didn't bode well. Sophie quickened her pace. 'Do you think they're based at the pub, in a pick-pocketing gang like in *Oliver Twist*?'

'I'm more worried about Wells,' said Hugo. 'She knows about our armour. We've lost the element of surprise.'

Sophie tried to picture the figure who'd attacked them at Marble Arch. They hadn't seen any police since they'd crossed the river. Despite being suspected of Tesla's theft, she'd feel better for seeing them. 'Did you ever go to South London at home?' Sophie hadn't.

'I did, just not this bit. I went to the East End too. Isobel used to be obsessed with Jack the Ripper. That started her interest in medicine.' Isobel was Hugo's sister. 'We took the Jack the Ripper street tour. Following a guide around Whitechapel, visiting the sites where he'd killed his victims, was disturbing, even so long after the murders.'

She'd forgotten about Jack the Ripper. 'Is he around now?'

'The last murder was in 1888, last year.' Hugo paused. 'It may be different in this London. I hope he's been caught.'

Sophie moved closer to Hugo.

They turned a corner and there was the pub. A filthy, three-storey building with a statue of an elephant on the roof.

They crossed the street, dodging carts, the clang of metal wheels on the cobbles ringing in their ears. With no constable regulating the traffic, you crossed at your own risk. Sophie shut her mouth against a strong manure smell.

The pub was closed, and the pavement in front deserted. The entrance door had a small round hole in the centre, as if someone had fired a bullet into it, and the windows were so grubby you couldn't see in. Sophie cleared a patch with her finger. 'There's a bar and chairs and tables, but not the kind of place any version of Wells would hang out in.'

'Many versions, many lives.' Hugo peered through the clear bit. 'A good place to sell stolen stuff.'

'The dot was right by the pub,' said Sophie. They made their way cautiously along the side of the building and came to an alley. 'Down here.'

The alley led to the rear of the pub, to a courtyard and a workshop. Women were sitting in rows, sewing. A few glanced up, unfazed by strangers approaching.

They moved closer. The women were working with beautiful fabrics.

'We're searching for a walking stick,' said Sophie to the nearest woman. 'Have you seen one?'

She didn't stop sewing. 'Why would it be 'ere?'

To their left, the backdoor of the pub was ajar.

Hugo patted his pocket. 'I'll go first.'

They paused on the threshold, waiting to adjust to the gloom. The grate in a fireplace was swept and empty, the lounge deserted. Sophie breathed in the smell of stale beer.

'Let's do a quick search.' She squatted behind the bar, eyeing cupboards and drawers. All too small to hold the cylinder.

Sophie straightened — and stopped breathing. A man with a shaved head was standing in the back doorway, silhouetted by the sunshine outside. His white sleeveless vest, tucked into black trousers, clung to his body, showing off his six-pack. Sophie darted towards Hugo, who was near the window.

'Who the hell are you?' The man went to the bar and picked up a beer glass.

'We're meeting a lady,' said Hugo, managing to sound relaxed.

'Pub's closed.' The guy looked like he boxed for a living.

'She suggested the Elephant and Castle,' said Sophie, following Hugo's lead. The original thief in the Langham may never have come near this pub but if she had, the bloke might know her.

'This lady has a name?'

'Um, we haven't been formally introduced,' said Hugo.

'She's shorter than me,' said Sophie. 'Round face, mousy hair.'

'Describes most of the women in London.'

'She can punch as good as a man,' said Sophie. 'Can't be too many women who can do that?'

To her surprise, the guy laughed. 'I can think of plenty.' He flexed his arm, holding the beer glass. 'Now 'op it.'

Hugo was making no move to grab the pistol from his trouser pocket, and his eyes flicked to the door. He put up his hands in a cooperative gesture and they both scuffled backwards and out into the courtyard.

Another man was in front of the workshop, his muscular arms folded. Shared his mate's boxing hobby.

Hugo grabbed Sophie's hand. They scurried fast along the alley and broke into a sprint when they reached the street. Though Sophie's corset was pressing hard into her ribs, she kept running, only stopping when the pub was out of sight. She'd barely caught her breath when Hugo pulled her on, half running, half trotting. When they joined the bus queue, he was still checking behind them. Those men had spooked her, but they'd spooked Hugo more.

Once they were on the bus, heading to Westminster

Bridge, Hugo turned to her. 'If they'd gone for us, we wouldn't have stood a chance.'

'Why didn't you use the pistol?' she whispered.

Hugo squeezed her hand, his palm sticky with sweat. 'When every instinct screams at me to run, I listen.'

CHAPTER 28

The day after the confrontation at the Elephant and Castle pub, they still had no viable plan to retrieve the cylinder. Freddy suggested threatening the landlord with the pistol to extract answers, but they couldn't be certain he knew about the cylinder. What if it had been quietly stashed in the pub by a customer? And the landlord had caught them snooping. Enough to provoke most people, let alone such a hostile man. Even if Freddy and Charlotte pinned him down while Sophie and Hugo searched the higher storeys, that would take a while, increasing the risk that more of the landlord's mates might turn up.

Sophie argued they should ask the police to search the premises, but Hugo thought they'd be fobbed off or, worse, get jailed for stealing the cylinder from Tesla. Charlotte agreed with Hugo.

As Sophie plodded towards the kitchen for breakfast, her shoulders drooped. 'The cylinder's lost to us and creating a safe way to Bella is lost with it. Back to Juno.' The ship would land in Freddy's universe. Would they live long enough to disembark?

Hugo gave her a tired glance. 'If we survive the crossing, I'll stay a few weeks in Shorten, then take my chances in Juno again.'

The old misery filled Sophie, and she couldn't look at him. They were soulmates, yet he wasn't prepared to spend the rest of his life with her in Shorten, 'in limbo' as he called it. He'd explained how he felt long ago. *This version of me has only one life and I'd like to seize it. Have a regular life at home.*

Sophie stumbled on the stairs and Freddy steadied her. 'I don't feel strong,' he said, 'so you need to be.' Thanks to Juno's steri-strips, his chin had almost healed, though his split lip was still sore, and wasn't helping morale.

Charlotte tilted her head, fixing her mistress with a resolute stare.

She wasn't giving up. Her mistress shouldn't — not yet. 'Hugo, the walking stick illusion is posh, right? It'll be sold on, taken out of the pub. Then we can snatch it.'

Hugo said nothing, unconvinced.

In the kitchen, Mr Burgess didn't acknowledge them, engrossed in the paper. He always read *The Times* over breakfast, occasionally reading aloud news that caught his eye. He was grumpy about Charlotte, and she settled as far away as possible.

Miss Harris was cooking at the stove, and Sophie grabbed an apron. The servants were fine with her helping but had politely declined when Hugo and Freddy had offered. Why was a mystery. Misplaced pride? Gender issues?

'*Claridge's Botched Burglary Solved,*' read the butler. '*Mr Robert Farley, a convicted felon, broke into Mrs Alveston's hotel room and died as she tried to defend herself. Mrs Alveston suffered a fatal heart attack, brought on by the ordeal.*'

Sophie paused stirring scrambled eggs. The memory of the young man holding the letter opener and Mrs Alveston clutching her chest was all too vivid. The police had gone with the obvious and presumably, a lot of the time, that was right. Yet it didn't feel right.

'Terrible,' said Miss Harris, 'and in such a posh hotel.'

They hadn't shared with the servants, or with Marion, how they'd been there for the aftermath.

When the maid left the kitchen to help Marion dress and the butler went off to check household accounts, Hugo said, 'We should pay a visit to Tesla.'

Freddy raised an eyebrow. 'So, he can escort us to the nearest police station?' He gestured at the paper. 'Yesterday, a twelve-year-old was sentenced to six months' hard labour for stealing bread.'

They'd meant to steal the cylinder. Just been beaten to it. Charlotte met Sophie's eyes. What happened to prisoners' dogs?

'If we can convince Tesla we didn't take the walking stick,' said Hugo, 'he might help us get it back.'

'How?' Sophie started on the washing up.

'He's very clever,' said Hugo.

'Even if nothing comes of it, we should talk with him before we leave,' said Freddy.

Sophie scrubbed at a dirty pan. 'We should sneak out before Marion comes down.'

'What an honour to speak with him again,' said Freddy.

Sophie sighed. 'You're hopeless fanboys.'

Freddy made a face. 'Fanboys?'

An hour later in the Langham, Freddy and Hugo took off their hats and climbed the hotel's grand staircase to Tesla's suite. Though not expecting a gunfight, Sophie had the pistol in her pocket — just in case. She reluctantly followed with

Charlotte who had a spring in her step. Tesla was bound to be hostile, yet Charlotte wanted to see him.

The stairs were broad and shallow, winding anti-clockwise, and entirely deserted. Most guests used the lift. The balustrade was embellished with TL in exquisite latticework on the inside and outside, so guests riding in the glass-walled lift could admire it. Charlotte had wanted to take the elevator, not worried it could be a portal, but none of the others were keen.

The Tower Suite, as the name suggested, was in a tower, approached by a short flight of stairs. Sophie knocked, taking the lead. Tesla's chivalry might temper his annoyance if he saw her first.

He opened the door, saw them, and made to shut it.

Sophie inserted her boot into the gap. 'We're sorry to disturb you. We know who stole the cylinder.'

'I'm busy,' said Tesla. 'Go away.'

Hugo and Freddy pushed open the door and elbowed past Tesla into a sitting room. Charlotte followed them and Sophie stepped in last. 'Sorry about this,' she said, closing the door behind her.

'Outrageous,' said Tesla. 'Get out.'

Barging in would reinforce his view they were thieves and charlatans. Sophie leaned against the door. It was done now.

Tesla's sitting room was circular, furnished with deep sofas, a walnut coffee table, and a desk covered with neat piles of paperwork.

Freddy tightened his hold on the rim of his hat. 'A female thief took it to South London.'

'We can give you her description,' said Hugo, 'to help the police.'

Tesla set his mouth. 'The cylinder hasn't been stolen. This

is a pathetic attempt to make me reveal where it's kept, so *you* can steal it.'

'The cylinder was stolen days ago,' said Sophie. 'We saw her with it.'

'We tried to detain her, but she punched me with a knuckleduster.' Freddy pointed at his battered chin.

'A lady did that?' said Tesla, his eyebrows raised.

Freddy shuffled his feet.

Tesla peered at him. 'What are those pieces of paper?'

'They work as stitches,' said Freddy.

Play to his curiosity. 'They're called steri-strips,' said Sophie. 'They've yet to be invented.'

Tesla grabbed a sharp-bladed letter opener from the desk. 'If you rush me, you'll get this in the guts.'

They all backed away from him, including Charlotte, and Tesla shot her a sharp look. 'Is your dog from a circus?'

'Yes,' lied Sophie, keen to dampen his interest in Charlotte. Tesla was drawn to animals and was also a showman. One hint about Charlotte's true nature and he'd want to test her in public like his inventions.

'We'll keep our distance,' said Hugo. 'If you check for the cylinder, you'll find it's gone.'

Tesla fished a key from his pocket. He strode into his bedroom and unlocked a wardrobe, opened it — and nearly fell over. 'A walking stick.' Still gripping the letter opener, he lifted it up with his left hand.

'That's not the cylinder,' said Freddy, stating the obvious.

'To me, it's the same,' said Hugo.

Sophie held her breath. She'd never seen the walking stick. It was solid and polished and beautiful. 'The thief switched it. Made a replica of the illusion.'

'I have the only key.' Tesla's eyes flicked from the stick to Sophie and back again, his brow puckered in confusion.

'She must have picked the lock,' said Hugo.

Tesla returned to the sitting room and rested the base of the walking stick on the floor.

'When did you last check on it?' said Freddy.

'Not since I put it in the wardrobe. On Friday.'

Today was Tuesday. 'The thief must have got in here twice,' said Sophie. 'Once to steal it and once to substitute the replica.'

'The same weight as the cylinder.' Tesla laid it on the floor. 'Who would do this, and why?'

Without being asked, Sophie sat on the nearest sofa. 'Whoever made the replica must have done it fast, had the materials to hand. I'm thinking that woman could have stolen it to order.'

Keeping hold of the letter opener, Tesla stared at the walking stick. 'Remind me how you believe the cylinder would end Janus.'

Freddy settled in an armchair and talked about the reset button, and Tesla interrupted.

'Machines can't be changed or repaired by switching them off and on.'

'To work, the cylinder may rely on a computer chip,' said Hugo, sitting beside Sophie.

'A tiny wafer of semiconducting material with an embedded electronic circuit,' explained Freddy. 'It contains microscopic components called transistors that send out data signals. Over time, the signal can become degraded or fail. By turning a machine off and on, you take the chip back to its original state, clearing the problem.'

Tesla's jaw dropped, but he recovered quickly. 'Why can't other people see the cylinder?'

Hugo laid out a simple history of DNA and how those with the gene had inherited it from the builders. 'I don't have the gene.'

After Freddy shared how they tracked the cylinder with

the bracelet, Sophie explained why Wells was trying to kill them. Now he had the complete picture, Tesla might spot a useful detail they'd missed.

'How many years have you spent concocting this tale?' he said.

Sophie ground her teeth. 'You're supposed to be a genius. Why would we have swung by just to entertain you?'

Hugo shifted in his seat. 'If we end Janus, you'll have a safe way to visit alternate pasts and futures.'

'When you say "alternate," you mean there isn't one past and one future?' Only now was Tesla's curiosity stronger than his cynicism.

'There may be infinite numbers of parallel universes where time passes at different rates,' said Freddy. 'So, yes, an infinite number of pasts and futures.'

'Interesting.' Tesla sounded cautious. Understandably. That sort of info would have floored a regular person.

'Perhaps a breakthrough that happens in the 21st century might convince you of our trustworthiness,' said Freddy. 'Continuing the work of George Cantor.'

'I know of him,' said Tesla.

'Two scientists, Malliaris and Shelah, will prove that two different variants of infinity are the same size. If you give me paper and a pen, I can show you.'

Tesla pointed to blank paper and a fountain pen on his desk, and Freddy pulled up a wooden Windsor chair and scribbled. The writing looked like gibberish, but when Freddy finished, Tesla accepted the jottings and studied them for a long ten minutes.

Finally, he rested his head back against the leather upholstery of his wing armchair. 'Say I believe you. The cylinder is in the hands of … undesirables.'

'And we only have one pistol.' Sophie took it from her pocket.

Tesla shrank down in his chair, and she hastily put it away.

'You could easily have forced me to reveal the hiding place.' Tesla put the letter opener on a side table.

'It's just for self-defence,' said Hugo. 'I wish we didn't need it.'

Tesla paused, evaluating each of them in turn before tapping the sheet of paper. 'Please join me for dinner at nine. Westinghouse will pay.'

'Westinghouse?' asked Sophie.

'My employer.'

'On our last visit, dining here was … unpleasant,' said Freddy. 'Would you mind eating at Claridge's?'

CHAPTER 29

That evening, Sophie crept down the stairs in Thornbridge, Charlotte padding beside her. Freddy and Hugo silently followed. They were halfway across the hall when the door to the drawing room opened.

Marion stepped out, dressed in a black crepe dress with a scoop neckline. A jet pendant flattered her pale skin and, courtesy of Miss Harris, her red hair was piled up in an artful array of curls. She gave them a stern stare.

They furtively cast around for the servants.

'Harris is mending a petticoat and Burgess is busy with correspondence,' said Marion, answering their unspoken question. She smiled, delivering the killer blow. 'Surely guests could invite their host out to dinner?'

After an embarrassed silence, Freddy said, 'Absolutely.' He drew out the word as if he were being strangled.

'We're walking to Claridge's,' said Sophie, hoping that would put her off.

'No matter.' Marion poked her foot out from under her skirt, displaying flat pumps, topped with a bow.

Hugo took his notebook and pencil from his jacket

pocket, tore out a page, and wrote, *Miss Lacey's with us, at Claridge's. Won't be late back.* He secured the note under the dogs figurine on the console table.

~

Gas lamps in Claridge's foyer softened the edges of sofas and tables and flattered the guests, gentle light playing on the flounces of gowns and on faces. In a few years, when electric light arrived, it would be more efficient, but gaslight was kinder.

'We're half an hour early.' Freddy sat down near the entrance and self-consciously touched his chin, still decorated with steri-strips. 'I hate not being appropriately dressed.' Other guests were in formal evening wear, the women in gowns, the men in white tie.

'I don't care,' said Sophie. Body armour, corset, and a full-length bustle outfit was good enough.

By Freddy's chair, Charlotte sat straighter, tensing up. Her eyes flicked towards the hotel entrance. Sophie gasped. The thief who'd punched Freddy was crossing the foyer, the train of her heavy turquoise gown gliding behind her. She was heading for the lift.

Freddy stood up. 'Give me the pistol.'

'She'll spot you a mile off,' said Sophie. His steri-strips were too conspicuous. She checked the gun in her pocket.

'I'll come with you,' said Hugo.

'If she comes down to the foyer without us,' said Sophie to Charlotte, 'detain her.' Yes, asking Charlotte to attack the woman was a bit extreme, but how else could they hold and interrogate her?

'Please stay and help Freddy,' Sophie said to Marion, who was on her feet.

Marion reluctantly sat down.

The thief went into the lift, along with one other guest, and the lift boy dragged a concertina inner door closed. The external doors shut, and the elevator moved upwards. Hugo and Sophie climbed the staircase beside it, keeping their heads down as the lift moved ahead of them. Sophie was on Hugo's far side, hoping the thief wouldn't recognise her through the lift's glass walls. It didn't help that she was wearing the same gown and hat.

The lift stopped on the first floor and the other guest got out. Hugo and Sophie hurried on to the next floor. The lift passed them, and they pressed on up the stairs. The bottom of the elevator above them wasn't glass, the occupants lost to sight, but the thief was now alone with the lift boy, heading for the top floor and the expensive suites.

They paused climbing the stairs so the thief wouldn't see them when she came out.

The lift halted above their heads, and a few seconds later descended. They ran up the remaining stairs.

Out in the corridor, the thief was hurrying off at a good pace to their right. Sophie turned to face Hugo and kissed him, concealing her face in case the woman turned around.

The thief knocked on a door and it instantly opened. 'Come in.' A female voice. The thief disappeared inside.

Sophie stared down the corridor. 'Could it have been a maid that answered the door?'

Hugo shook his head. 'A maid would have been more formal, called the visitor madam.'

Back down in the hotel foyer, Hugo picked up a booklet from reception. They re-joined Freddy, Marion, and Charlotte, and Hugo flicked through the pages.

'That's where she went.' Hugo pointed at a drawing of an

elegant sitting room with picture windows. *'The Corner Suite is located at the far left and front of the hotel,'* he read aloud. *'Affords delightful views in two directions.'*

'Let's take a leap of logic,' said Sophie. 'What if the woman in The Corner Suite is Wells?'

'Why would the women be connected?' said Freddy.

'The walking stick connects them,' said Hugo.

Marion was animated, enjoying the puzzle. 'Could the lady in the Corner Suite be the waitress?'

'Or we're wrong about Wells being a lady,' said Freddy, 'and both women are accomplices.'

Sophie jumped up from her seat. 'I've an idea how we can find out.' She strolled over to reception. Behind the counter, the young man's expression registered disapproval that she wasn't wearing evening dress, though he was quick to mask it. 'A friend of ours is staying in The Corner Suite. Miss Wells.'

The guy thumbed through a ledger. 'You're mistaken, madam. Mrs Neal has that suite.'

Sophie thanked him and walked back across the foyer. 'A Mrs Neal is staying there.'

'I wonder…' said Hugo. 'Neal was Wells' mother's maiden name.' Was there literally nothing Hugo didn't know — and remember — about their adversary?

'You're aware coincidence is tricky,' said Freddy. 'Neal is a common name.'

Tesla came into the foyer and walked towards them. As Freddy and Hugo stood up, Tesla turned to the ladies and did a mini bow. 'Enchanted to see you again.'

Marion blushed.

'I hope I'll live long enough to see women ruling the world,' said Tesla.

Random. Was he drunk?

'Very funny,' said Marion.

Tesla shrugged. 'It's one of my more controversial theories.'

Okay, not drunk. Enlightened.

'Women will soon have the vote, and our country will have female prime ministers,' said Hugo, 'but not for a century.'

Tesla nodded, pleased.

Good. If they flattered him with the truth, they might cement his trust.

They went to the dining room and once they were seated, Tesla ordered sweet sherry for everyone, apart from Charlotte, who looked put out.

Sophie picked up a menu. The French text was dense and small, designed to glamorise the cuisine and embarrass non-linguists.

'This menu is similar to the Ritz,' said Hugo.

Freddy glanced up. 'You remember from all that time ago? I don't remember it at all.'

'I'll order what I did in 1925,' said Sophie. 'Oeuf Poche Florentine.' The pastry tart starter, with sauteed spinach and a poached egg in cheesy sauce had been yummy.

'You can't mean 1925,' said Marion. 'That's a long way off.'

'Yes,' said Sophie. 'My mistake.'

Tesla caught her eye. 'If you are charlatans, you're accomplished ones.'

'You speak French?' Marion asked Tesla. When he'd ordered the drinks, he'd pronounced 'aperitif' with a French twang.

'I do.'

'I believe you're fluent in seven languages,' said Hugo, politely, 'as well as your first language, Serbo-Croat.'

Tesla raised a dark eyebrow, surprised. Charlotte, sitting on the floor between Sophie and Hugo, raised her own furry eyebrow, seriously impressed. Like her mistress, she'd struggled to learn a second language, never mind more.

Freddy had spoken fluent Latin in Rome and Sophie's mind wandered to Bella. Would she inherit her father's talent?

'Mr Tesla, you're currently well known,' said Hugo, 'and your inventions will make you far more famous in the future.'

'You exaggerate.'

'Not really,' said Freddy.

'If you are time travellers, you must be made of stern stuff,' said Tesla. 'Hardy adventurers.'

He said hardy adventurers with a flourish. Was he being sarcastic?

Everyone chose a starter and a main except for Tesla, who just requested tomato soup.

'Are you not hungry?' Marion asked him, her smile tempering the rather blunt question.

'I don't usually eat dinner. Controlling my diet keeps my brain keen.'

'Like the walking?' said Sophie.

'Indeed.' Tesla ordered a bottle of red wine.

As the waiter uncorked it, Marion giggled. 'Goodness.'

'Alcohol is a veritable elixir of life, improves health and lengthens our lifespan,' said Tesla, apparently serious.

'Here's to that,' said Freddy, finishing his sherry.

'One should avoid tea, coffee, tobacco and meat,' said Tesla. 'They irritate the stomach.'

'I'm with you on the tobacco and meat,' said Sophie, 'but not the tea and coffee.'

'Few people agree with me.' Tesla sighed. 'I'm leaving London soon. It may be useful to exchange correspondence.' He slid a dark cream card across the table, the same size as a modern business card. On the top was printed *Westinghouse*

Electric & Manufacturing Company, and underneath in smaller letters was *Pittsburgh, Pennsylvania*. Under that was *Turbines, Generators, Motors*.

Marion gave a gracious nod, and Hugo wrote Marion's address in his notebook. He tugged out the page and handed it to Tesla. 'This is only temporary.'

A line appeared between Tesla's brows.

'A version of my home in Derbyshire exists here,' said Freddy, 'but letters won't reach me.'

Sophie tried to picture Shorten Manor, so many versions, in countless worlds, the images dancing and fading. The sheer scale of parallel universes was unimaginable.

The starters arrived and Marion made patterns in her soup with her spoon.

'If your tall tale is true,' said Tesla, 'seeing mankind's future would be irresistible, if terrifying.'

'That sums it up,' said Hugo.

'However, the prospect is theoretical,' said Tesla, 'the cylinder tangible.'

'The thief is in this hotel right now,' said Sophie. 'She's visiting another suite, maybe meeting with Wells. We could go there and negotiate.'

Hugo set his mouth. 'If Mrs Neal is Wells, she'll be armed. In a confined space, her futuristic pistol could finish us off in a spray of bullets.'

Sophie stifled a shudder. Hadn't thought of that. Pity they hadn't got invisible body armour to cover their heads.

Tesla eyed Freddy's steri-strips. 'Despite the possibility that testing the cylinder's casing could improve Westinghouse's machines, I'm reluctant to confront either woman. However, if hardy adventurers like yourselves were to secure the cylinder, Westinghouse would pay handsomely.' He fastidiously wiped his lips with a napkin.

Freddy raised his chin. 'You know we need the cylinder to

reach our daughter. No amount of money is more important than that. Can you think of a way to help us?'

Tesla stood up. 'I'm afraid not.'

In bed in Thornbridge with Hugo, Sophie rested her head on his chest. 'Why would Tesla think we'd choose money over Bella?'

'Hmm?'

'He's supposed to be so clever.'

'No idea.'

'You were in such a mad rush just now. You took me by surprise,' whispered Sophie. He'd made love in a silent frenzy, carrying her with him, but something was wrong. 'What's the matter?'

He hesitated. 'We don't know what tomorrow will bring.'

They never knew. Whatever was wrong, when he was ready, he'd tell her.

CHAPTER 30

*H*attie Wells opened the door of her suite to Mary Carr. Mary's expensive evening gown tastefully flattered her hourglass figure.

'Come in.' Hattie shut the door. 'Any problems?' She was only making conversation. Mary was the best thief she'd ever met. And she'd met quite a few.

'Nothing I couldn't 'andle.' Mary sat on the sofa by the fireplace, her posture perfect. 'A bloke in the Langham accosted me, asking about your walking stick. Got a Mary-punch for his trouble.'

'Describe him.'

'Tall and handsome.'

Hattie pictured the targets. 'Dark or fair hair?'

'Fair, and he was with a blonde woman.'

Hattie removed the top from a crystal decanter. 'Sherry?'

Mary nodded. 'Your walking stick's safe, stashed in the pub. Just as well. This afternoon, the same lady and a different bloke came snooping.'

Hattie handed her the sherry in a dainty glass. 'They followed you?'

'Must 'ave. I can't see how. I got clean away.'

Hattie poured a drink for herself. The targets had Guild armour so might have security bands. Would explain how they knew the artefact was at the pub. Could the targets be ex-agents, like her? That was possible, if unlikely. When she'd left the Guild, her armour and security band had been reallocated, but she'd taken her ship with its spare heart-stopper. More than most disgraced agents managed. Perhaps the targets were serving and had gone rogue? If the Guild was the client that would make sense.

'They nosed about the pub,' said Mary. 'Didn't take nothing.'

'Where's the stick stored?'

'In the upstairs office in a trunk. It's more than just a stick, Hattie. Nice quality.'

Hattie sipped, trying to piece together this puzzle. Why had the targets searched the pub? Their security bands should have led them straight to the artefact in the office. And bands also tracked other travellers. She had no blocking device, yet the targets hadn't tracked her.

Perhaps the targets had older, unreliable bands? But that would mean they weren't serving agents. She sighed. Going round in circles.

Mary coughed. 'We agreed fifty guineas.'

She drove a hard bargain. An agent's annual salary. Hattie unlocked a desk drawer and counted out crisp banknotes. Mary stuffed them in her evening bag without counting them.

Hattie topped up their glasses. 'I have a job for Len.'

Mary paused drinking her sherry. 'You know I don't get involved in his business, and he don't with mine.' The men had protection and betting scams. The women's shoplifting was more lucrative.

'This won't affect the Forty Elephants. Tomorrow morning, that couple will snoop around the pub again, with another man. They need to disappear.'

Mary shook her head. 'Len wants to lie low after the last dog and duck.' Dog and duck was rhyming slang for a ruck or a shoot-out.

'Firearms won't cut it,' said Hattie. 'I appreciate this sounds far-fetched. They wear metal under their clothes. Bullets bounce off.'

'Eh?'

'This will require close-up work and your cousin's legendary cleaning skills. There'll be a dog as well, but it's off-limits.'

'Len said they were toffs—'

'No one will miss them. My payment will keep the McDonald gang in clover for years.' And Len was greedy.

Mary downed her sherry. 'Eighty guineas, half in advance.'

CHAPTER 31

The next morning in Thornbridge, walking into the kitchen, Freddy touched his chin in amazement. Four days after the thief's savage punch, the steri-strips had fallen off while he'd slept. The wounds had healed.

'You can grow your beard again,' said Hugo.

Freddy touched his bruised lip. 'At the start, beards are so scruffy.'

His chin's miraculous healing was a welcome surprise. Double down on it. 'When Clarissa sees you, it'll be a cool beard,' said Sophie, 'and Bella won't notice.'

It was the butler's half-day off and after breakfast he left, and the maid went to help Marion dress.

Hugo and Freddy washed up and Sophie bagged *The Times*. Ignoring the front page with its adverts for soap and cure-alls, she turned to the first inside page and the news. *Dockers Threaten to Strike*. Underneath the headline was a sepia photo of men on a quay with a huge ship behind them. Their faces reminded her of her great great grandfather. He'd been a docker. His photo was somewhere in her parents' house. He'd looked as hard as nails, like them.

Ping. The bracelet flashed and Sophie jumped to her feet. 'The map's back.'

Freddy whirled around from the sink. 'Where's the cylinder?'

'Outside the Elephant and Castle. It's in the courtyard. Not moving.'

'Don't even think about it.' Hugo's stare was uncompromising. 'The landlord would kill us.'

'We need more firepower,' said Sophie. This decision had been brewing since they'd fled from the pub. Hugo was right about the landlord, but they had to do something. Anything would be better than starving to death in Juno, never seeing Bella again.

'There's lots of firepower right here.' Freddy ran upstairs and soon returned, his expression glum. 'The maid says my great aunt loves her firearms like children, and we can't have them.'

'I'm sure we can persuade Marion,' said Sophie. A bigger problem would be ensuring she didn't come with them. This was their fight, not hers. She met Freddy's eyes, seeing her own determination there. Was this too reckless, just a different sort of giving up? The final scene from *Angel*, the old TV spin-off from *Buffy*, came into her mind, so strongly, it briefly blotted out the map and the dot. Old friends meeting their fate, going out fighting. She and Hugo and Freddy were tired, relentlessly chasing the cylinder…

Charlotte nuzzled into Sophie's skirt.

'If Wells knows we're tracking it,' said Hugo, 'she could have moved it outside to lure us into a trap.'

That had occurred to her before. Sophie waited for him to talk them out of this. He'd been scared witless in the pub.

Hugo did his crooked smile. '*If* we can borrow Marion's guns, I'm up for it. We're out of options.'

Sophie hugged him, blinking away tears. Where would she be without him?

Charlotte leaned more insistently against her mistress. In two minds? 'You could keep Marion company?' said Sophie. Charlotte shook her head.

They trudged up to the hall, Sophie taking the treads slowly, disorientated by the map. She tugged her hat from the stand and pinned it on. The men might get away without hats. If she went hatless, even in South London, people would stare. 'Oh! The map's gone.'

Marion came down from her room. She was wearing a new mourning outfit, with a v-shaped beaded panel on the jacket. Like her other skirt, there were four layers of flounces below the bustle. Victorian mourning conventions were a puzzle. Miserable black and lavish styling.

'More interesting business?' said Marion, her attention on Sophie's hat.

'Not interesting,' said Freddy. 'Unpleasant and dangerous.'

Marion's eyes sparkled. 'I'll help.'

Freddy set his mouth. 'Please remain here.'

Sophie hurried off to fetch the borrowed bag with the spare ammo.

Five minutes later, back in the hall, Miss Harris was standing beside Marion, a worried line between her brows. 'The doctor said to avoid excitement.' Her tone was kind but firm.

Charlotte loomed large near the front door, blocking it.

Freddy addressed his great aunt. 'I have an unusual request. Could we borrow some guns?'

Marion showed no surprise. 'Harris, bring me my gun bag.'

Under protest, the maid fetched it. Marion didn't hand it over. Instead, she sat on the stairs. 'Fetch my walking boots.'

Miss Harris took her time fetching the boots and while she laboriously fastened them on Marion's feet, Hugo said, 'We're visiting a rough part of London.'

'It'll be boring,' said Sophie, hoping it would be.

Marion stood up and folded her arms. 'I'll be the judge of that.'

'Honestly, it's too dangerous.' Sophie pulled out the pistol from her pocket. 'We insist you stay home.'

The maid backed across the room. 'Goodness.'

Marion glared. 'Are you going to shoot me?'

'No… Of course, not.' Sophie returned the pistol to her pocket, her shoulders sagging. She was out of ideas.

Marion plonked her hat on. Nothing frightened her, which could only put her in harm's way.

Charlotte hadn't moved from the front door, but Marion simply brushed past, and Charlotte didn't react, uncertain what to do.

'Chop, chop.' Marion opened the door and rushed out.

Miss Harris gulped. 'Please bring her home safe.'

'We'll protect her with our lives.' Sophie mentally crossed her fingers. It shouldn't come to that. They were armed to the teeth.

Out on the pavement, Marion held the gun bag in both hands. 'You've forgotten your hats,' she told Hugo and Freddy.

'Are you sure you want to accompany us?' Freddy's voice was gentle, pleading.

'I'll be more help than hindrance, I promise.'

Resigned, they headed towards the main road by Hyde Park and took the bus to Westminster Bridge. South of the river, they caught the second bus. Sophie gave the pistol to Freddy. He was the best shot.

'This is exciting.' Marion surveyed their fellow passengers as if they were exotic birds.

'If by some miracle we find the walking stick,' said Hugo, 'we're under no obligation to tell Tesla.'

'Agreed,' said Freddy, his gaze on Marion. 'We have enough complications to deal with.'

The Elephant and Castle pub loomed ahead of them, hazy brown in the smog. They crossed the busy road, Sophie gripping Marion's arm.

'Any sign of trouble, we leave,' said Sophie.

'Of course.' But Marion's eyes betrayed her excitement.

Freddy led the way past the pub's closed front door. The hole in it was evidently a permanent feature. The alley was quiet, and in the courtyard, though the workshop shutters were open, not a soul was there.

'It's not Sunday.' Freddy squinted against the sun. 'Not a church day.'

'Marion, stay with me,' said Sophie. 'The cylinder didn't move far before it disappeared. Could be in the workshop.'

A piece of cloth blew into the courtyard and Sophie jumped. Nothing. A gust of wind. She followed Freddy through a doorway, still holding onto Marion. Hugo unclipped Charlotte's lead.

Fabric was strewn along the workbenches and the sewing machines all had thread in them. A half-eaten apple had been left on a plate.

'This is like the Mary Celeste,' said Hugo. 'The ship was found in the middle of the ocean with ample provisions, no damage, and no one onboard.'

'Creepy.' Sophie shivered. The workshop was cooler than outside.

Charlotte did a deep sniff and shook her head.

'There are other people nearby?' Freddy asked her.

A curt nod.

Hugo stiffened. 'Do you know where?'

Charlotte gestured to the left with her front paw towards the pub.

Freddy went further into the workshop. 'Just a quick search in here.'

Sophie opened a drawer in a sideboard, revealing thread, needles and thimbles. By the sideboard, a long table was piled high with rolls of green and turquoise taffeta.

Marion ran her fingers over the fabric. 'Lovely.'

An interior door led to an office and Charlotte trotted in, confident it was deserted, so they all followed.

A tall cupboard was crammed with blank receipts, and a bookcase held pencil drawings of fashionable outfits and jewellery. A lone desk was bare except for an inkpot. In the drawers was blotting paper, and a few fountain pens. Entirely what you'd expect.

Beyond the office was a maintenance yard that reeked of grease and petrol and housed a two-person cab. The driver's seat was pitted with holes and a door was missing. To the side were welding tools, spare parts, a pile of wood, and paint cans. Could the replica walking stick have been made here?

Next to the maintenance yard was a stable block. Most of the building stored cabs but three glossy-maned horses in stalls whinnied as they approached. Hugo looked around, his eyes nervy. 'Not completely deserted.'

The traffic, a few yards distant, was the only sound.

Sophie touched the outline of Bella's key-rattle under her jacket, hoping the familiar shape would lessen the creepy feeling. 'It's not here—'

Charlotte barked and pointed back to the courtyard. She tensed, assumed her battle-stance, ready to charge.

Sophie's stomach dropped.

Hugo touched Charlotte's collar. 'Wait. First, assess the threat.'

They crept past the cab, through the office, and then the workshop. When they had sight of the courtyard, they came to an abrupt halt.

The landlord and his friend were there, armed with machetes. The blades were polished, reflecting the dirty smog in the sky. Behind them, ten men blocked the gap to the alley. They carried their knives with an arrogant confidence, and cricket bats rested on their shoulders, casual promises of pain.

Inside the workshop, the office door slammed. A key clicked in the lock.

No escape. No way out.

They were going to die.

Despair surged through Sophie. She'd never cradle her child again.

Marion walked into the courtyard. Sophie moved instinctively, planting herself in front of her. So did Freddy, Hugo, and Charlotte. An unspoken pact.

The landlord swept his machete in an arc and smiled. He was enjoying the thought of inflicting horrific injuries. Sophie's legs turned to jelly.

'Dear God,' murmured Freddy.

'We don't want any trouble.' Hugo's voice was calm. His actor's voice.

Sophie couldn't speak. Her throat had closed. Marion bent to rummage in her gun bag, her bustle stuck out like a pecking bird. She was humming as if this were a parlour game. Sophie scrabbled for bullets in her own bag, her hands shaking.

Charlotte growled, about to leap. 'Keep behind us.' Sophie's voice was low, for Charlotte's ears. 'They'll cut you to pieces.'

'Let us leave,' said Hugo, stalling.

The landlord laughed. 'Think you can get off that easily? Are you that stupid?'

Sophie's eyes skittered to the pub. The door was shut, probably bolted. The only route out was through the men.

The landlord advanced, swinging his machete, and the others moved with him, a slow, ominous rhythm. Predators circling prey. A youth at the edge of the group was whistling, a tuneless, jarring sound that scraped at Sophie's raw nerves.

A click. Freddy had cocked his pistol. But there were too many—

A gunshot and the landlord jerked backwards with a grunt, stumbling, still holding the machete. Sophie gasped, confused. Freddy hadn't fired. Her eyes darted, searching for the shooter.

Marion. She had a pistol in each hand. One was smoking, dark twirls winding into the air. 'Surrender your weapons,' she said, her voice imperious. 'The police are on their way and Mr Doyle has a warrant to search the premises.' She nodded at Hugo.

Mr Doyle?

The jaunty whistling faltered, and the men hesitated, doubt flitting across their faces.

The landlord snarled, 'I don't see no police. She's bluffing.' He clutched his wounded shoulder. 'Go.' His men surged forward, yelling obscenities.

Marion didn't flinch. She tossed a pistol to Hugo and shoved another into Sophie's hand.

Hugo fired point-blank. The first man dropped like a bundle of wet laundry.

Sophie aimed her pistol. At the same moment, a cricket bat swung at her head. She ducked just in time, reeling, the breath snatched from her lungs. Bangs, murderous yells, screaming…

The bat swung again but mid-swing, the man slid sideways.

Bang. Then silence.

Sophie had space to move, time to take stock. Five of the men were down, cursing and groaning. The others raised their hands.

Freddy and Hugo's bullets must have found their mark, as had Marion's. Sophie was panting with relief, as if she'd been running, and her brain was clearing. She kept her weight evenly balanced on both her feet and levelled her pistol, clasping it with two hands. As instructed, Charlotte was behind her mistress, snarling her frustration.

'Drop your weapons,' said Freddy, his tone ringing with authority.

Knives, cricket bats, and machetes fell with a clatter.

'We're going to collect them,' said Sophie. 'If anybody moves a finger, I'll shoot.' Okay, she hadn't shot anyone, but she could.

The landlord twisted on the ground and reached for his machete, murder in his eyes. Marion kicked it beyond his reach. The wounded men continued swearing and moaning.

Hugo and Freddy laid the men's weapons in front of the workshop. Sophie and Marion kept their pistols in position.

'All of you who can, move to near the pub,' said Hugo. The uninjured men shuffled across the courtyard.

Sophie steadied her breathing, fighting the urge to run. Get more info. 'Have any of you seen a fancy walking stick? Heart-shaped handle, green and gold.'

Some of them squinted at her, others shook their heads. 'I ain't seen no walking stick,' muttered the landlord.

Keeping the gun up, Sophie's hands were trembling. If he was bluffing, they wouldn't have another chance, but the men seemed genuinely nonplussed. It would take hours to check the whole pub—

Distant whistles.

'The police,' said Freddy.

Passers-by must have heard the gunshots and alerted them. 'We should ask the police to search the pub,' said Sophie.

Hugo gestured at the injured thugs. 'No. They'll arrest us. Let's go.'

Marion returned one of her pistols to the gun bag. Pointing the other, she hurried towards the groaning men and continued past them. The train of her skirt glided over a man's face, leaving a trail of grime from the courtyard, and he spluttered and swore.

Charlotte bounded around the injured men, so fast they couldn't grab her. Sophie returned the reserve ammunition to her handbag, and keeping the pistol as steady as she could, scurried to the alley, giving the men a wide berth. Hugo and Freddy did the same.

Marion was waiting by the road. 'Make haste, my dears,' she said, as if they were late for tea. The sound of insistent whistles was louder.

Though the road was as busy as ever, they dashed on, not waiting for a lull in the traffic. They pelted down the street to the bus stop.

There was no queue and no sign of a bus.

'Keep going,' said Hugo.

Sophie struggled to keep up, her heart banging against her corset. She had yet to master running in period costume. Likely never would.

The street curved left, and they sprinted by terraced houses that were dark with soot. Five minutes later, the road straightened, cutting through scrubland, and they passed a building site with a sign. *Opening 1890. Elephant and Castle Underground Station.*

Hugo stopped running and doubled over, catching his breath. 'Would have been handy but we're a year too early.'

Freddy glanced over his shoulder. 'They're not following us. Not yet.'

'The police will wish to speak to them,' said Marion.

Sophie marvelled at her matter-of-fact tone. If the landlord's men weren't chasing them, the police soon would be.

Hugo took the map from his jacket pocket and hastily unfolded it, tearing the paper on a fold. 'We need to retrace our steps. We've overshot the turning to the Thames and the bridge.'

They set off again, scanning the road through the grubby mist. Once over the street, they turned into another.

Tormented by a stitch, Sophie slowed and held her side. 'If the landlord doesn't know about the cylinder, somebody else must have bought it from our thief and stored it in the pub.'

'Perhaps someone employed there?' said Hugo. 'Stored it in a safe place to sell on later?'

A glum line marred Freddy's brow. 'I hope not. It may not be moved for years.'

Charlotte was keeping close to her mistress. 'You did good, not fighting,' said Sophie. Charlotte gave a soft grunt. Her way of saying she'd found it difficult. The confrontation in the courtyard repeated in Sophie's mind. 'Marion, you were awesome.'

Marion beamed, revealing a pretty dimple on her cheek.

'Why did you call me Mr Doyle?' Hugo asked her.

'After a novelist. You're how I picture his clever detective, Mr Holmes.'

Hugo raised his eyebrows.

'They won't find us now,' said Marion.

Sophie glanced up the street. 'Wells can.' This hike would be on Janus' itinerary.

CHAPTER 33

Unable to find a bus going north, they walked towards the river. No one was following them, and Sophie and Hugo returned their pistols to Marion's gun bag. The smog grew thinner and eventually, up ahead, Westminster Bridge emerged through the gloom.

A group of burly men strode onto the street. Freddy checked the pistol in his pocket, but the men barely glanced in their direction. Two were carrying a cloth banner hoisted up on poles. On the banner, embroidered in large letters, was *The Dockers' Tanner*. Others carried placards and saucepans.

'Good luck to you,' shouted Marion, and the men responded with a cheery wave. Though their clothes were shabby, they strolled with a swagger.

'You know them?' asked Sophie.

'Not personally,' said Marion. 'Without their labour, we'd have no tea from India and no sugar to sweeten it.'

'What's the docker's tanner?' said Freddy.

'It's what they want to be paid,' said Marion. 'A tanner an hour.'

'How much is a tanner?' said Hugo.

'Sixpence.' Marion peered at him, surprised he didn't know.

Soon, more dockers came onto the road, stopping the traffic.

'The police will arrive soon,' said Marion.

Sophie exhaled, uneasy. Of course they would.

Hugo looked back down the street, then at the bridge. 'Let's get across the river.'

Sophie attached Charlotte's lead and Charlotte gave her a grumpy stare, fed up with maintaining appearances. They kept pace with the marchers, mingling with them. Respectable pedestrians didn't run.

Ahead of the marchers, a dozen black cabs clattered onto the road and flanked the entrance to the bridge. They had no windows. Constables spilled out of the cabs, hurried onto the bridge, and lined up on both sides. The silver buttons on their jackets and the badges on their helmets glinted in the hazy sunshine.

A tall man with a bushy beard joined the front of the march. He was older than most of the dockers. His three-piece suit contrasted oddly with his straw hat, the sort you'd wear on a day out in the park.

He led the way onto the bridge, the dockers banging their saucepans in a raucous, clanging rhythm. The first officer on the bridge acknowledged Sophie and Marion, his expression respectful. 'If we keep walking,' Sophie whispered to Hugo, 'we'll be fine.'

Hugo put his arm through hers. 'Wells won't try anything. Not with the guard of honour.'

'This takes me back,' said Sophie. 'I used to go on marches right here, in a different universe.'

'Let me guess?' Freddy patted Charlotte. 'For animal rights.'

A docker began singing and the others joined in. A

familiar tune with unfamiliar words.

'Sing a song of sixpence,
Dockers on the strike.
Guinea pigs are hungry as the greedy pike.
Till the docks are opened,
Burns for us will speak.
Courage, lads, and you will win,
Well within the week!'

Marion sang along in a strong soprano, her delicate face flushed with enthusiasm.

'Who's Burns?' Hugo asked her.

She pointed at the tall man at the head of the march. 'He speaks for the dockers.' When the song finished, she waved her pistol in the air.

Sophie hadn't realised she was still holding it. Nearby marchers turned their heads, alarmed, and the next instant, a policeman launched forward and wrestled Marion to the ground.

'Release me at once!' shouted Marion, pinned under the officer. She clutched at her ankle as he rolled off her.

The officer confiscated her pistol and hauled her to her feet.

Marion winced and Charlotte growled.

'The policeman's just doing his job,' whispered Sophie. She raised her voice. 'The lady means no harm.'

The officer snapped handcuffs around Marion's wrists. 'Madam, I'm arresting you for a breach of the peace.'

Marion looked affronted. 'I've turned my ankle.'

Freddy picked up the gun bag.

'You all together?' asked the constable.

Sophie hesitated. What if the police knew about the courtyard fight, had their descriptions—

'You're all under arrest.'

Another policeman stepped forward. He fastened handcuffs on Sophie's wrists. Somehow, she kept hold of Charlotte's lead.

'Officer, I must protest,' said Freddy, as other officers cuffed him and Hugo.

The police manhandled them back across the bridge and the dockers jeered and catcalled. The constable who'd arrested Marion had given up on her walking and was carrying her over his shoulder. She was so slight and small, she could have been a child.

'I've never arrested a woman in mourning weeds before,' he said to his colleague. He unloaded Marion roughly into a window-less cab. Charlotte reluctantly jumped in and everyone else was bundled inside.

Sophie glimpsed hard benches before the rear door shut, plunging them into total darkness. She shuffled to the front of the compartment and sat down, keeping Charlotte nearby. The cab smelled strongly of disinfectant, like a cleaned-up crime scene. Sophie tried to loosen her jacket collar. Sweat was running between her breasts under her corset.

'A breach of the peace is a minor offence,' said Freddy.

'What about the gun bag?' said Sophie. Once the police opened it…

'I'll tell them it's my brother's, that I use his pistols to practise at home.' Marion sounded entirely unconcerned.

The police wouldn't buy that. They were stuffed. 'How's your ankle?' Sophie asked her, half-worried, half-exasperated.

'It hurts.'

The police cab moved off at speed, swaying, and Sophie cuddled Charlotte, trying not to panic. Charlotte's heart was beating fast. 'Don't worry,' she said. 'We'll explain at the station, and they'll let us go.' Charlotte snorted, unconvinced.

'Perhaps us getting arrested wasn't on Janus' itinerary?' said Freddy.

'It certainly wasn't on mine,' Hugo replied.

Hugo's sense of humour was intact, and that buoyed Sophie up. But as the cab rattled on, claustrophobia set in, and she fought to control her breathing. Someone touched her arm, and she squeezed their hand. The darkness was so total, her eyes might as well have been shut.

'Think about something comforting,' said Hugo.

Sophie pictured the old dining room in Shorten Manor with its portraits of Freddy's ancestors. She imagined Anne and Clarissa at the table, and Bella in the highchair, messily eating, sprinkling crumbs on the royal blue carpet. When she saw Bella again, she might be a tidy eater, sitting in a regular chair… If she ever saw her again. Don't dwell on that.

The carriage lurched to a stop. The back door was wrenched open, and they stumbled out, blinking against the bright sunshine. Sophie's eyes adjusted. They were still on the bridge. Had they been driven round in a circle? No, this was a different bridge. Grey granite, and chunkier.

Two officers herded them onto a pier and into a tatty, one-storey building. *Waterloo Police Station* was signed in plain black letters.

The reception area was as hot as the police cab and reeked of body odour and sweat. A woman in a shiny bustle skirt and a jacket that showed off too much cleavage was hitting an officer with her fists as he dragged her along. Sophie wiped her damp brow with the back of her hand.

The officer who'd arrested Marion pushed her towards a desk.

The sergeant sighed. 'What have we here?'

'This lady waved a pistol at the dockers' march. Could have set off a riot.'

'Name?'

Marion shifted her weight onto her good leg. 'Miss Marion Lacey.'

A different officer approached. 'I'll take your bag, sir.'

Freddy handed over the gun bag and the policeman opened it. 'These guns yours?'

'Um—'

'They're Mr Robert Lacey's.' Marion gave the officer a serene stare. 'He's in the National Rifle Association.'

The NRA? Wasn't that an American thing? To Sophie's surprise, the policeman just nodded. He wrote *Mr Robert Lacey* on a luggage label, attached it to the bag's handle, and squeezed the bag into a metal cage crammed with prisoners' belongings.

Sophie handed over her small bag with the ammo. 'Robert Lacey.' The officer gave the contents a cursory glance before attaching a label and consigning it to the cage.

The sergeant assessed Marion and her companions with a weary air. 'You can pay bail?'

'Absolutely,' said Marion. She pointed at Sophie. 'Mrs Harrington's brooch is valuable.'

'It's not real gold.' Sophie's lie sounded regretful. No way was she handing over the brooch from Rome.

Unfazed, Marion said, 'Please contact my butler, Mr Burgess. Thornbridge, 41 Park Street.'

The sergeant scribbled in his book. He eyed Charlotte. 'Put them in cell five.'

The cells were in a row, with bars like cages. As they were herded down the smelly passage, prisoners shouted vulgar abuse from the other cells, mostly at Marion and Sophie. They were corralled into cell five which had a bench, a rectangular pillow made of wood, and a chamber pot. The bars clanged shut behind them and an officer locked them in.

The bench only had room for two people to sit on, but the floor was clean. Hugo and Freddy settled themselves on the concrete with Charlotte, who rested her head on Hugo's lap.

'Can I see your ankle?' Sophie asked Marion.

Marion lifted her skirt, and Sophie knelt to unbutton Marion's right boot.

When the boot was off, Marion exhaled in relief. 'Thank you.'

Sophie sat on the bench beside her. 'We should take it in turns to sleep on here. It may be days before the sergeant contacts Mr Burgess, or he might forget.'

'Mr Burgess will pay bail,' said Marion. 'Then the police will release us.'

'I'm sorry to ask,' said Freddy. 'Have you been arrested before?'

Marion shrugged. 'My favourite novels have people being arrested, so I understand what happens.'

Sophie didn't remember much police procedure in the Sherlock Holmes TV series. Maybe the books were different?

Hugo put his head in his hands. 'The longer we're here, the bigger the risk the police will connect us to the fight in South London.'

Marion stared at the chamber pot. 'I want my gun bag.'

Freddy sighed. 'It'll be returned in due course.'

Sophie was glad the bag was secured away. Freddy's great aunt might try and shoot her way out and they'd be in even more trouble. 'Is your brother really in the NRA?'

'He dislikes sports, including shooting.' Marion did a mock guilty face. 'I made that up.' She rocked slightly, as if in deep thought. 'Women can't join the NRA.' Her tone was wistful. 'Apart from the queen.'

Sophie pictured Queen Victoria on a rifle range. Beyond bizarre.

Hugo stood up and peered through the bars. He stepped back as a constable approached and unlocked the door. With him was a woman in an overall, carrying a tray of bowls.

She placed the tray on the floor of the cell, strode away, and the constable relocked the door.

Besides a water bowl, there were other bowls containing grey porridge. Marion gestured at them. 'This must be stirabout. It has to be stirred while it's cooked.' She lifted a bowl, tasted a spoonful and spat it out. 'Apologies.' She plonked down the bowl for Charlotte. 'You can have it, dear.'

Charlotte sniffed and screwed up her face. Lately, she'd become fussy about food. Hugo pushed a tiny amount onto a spoon and tasted it. 'Oatmeal,' he said, as if he were a contestant on a cooking show. He returned the spoon to the tray. 'I'm watching my weight.'

Freddy made no move to eat, but Sophie was curious. She tried a mushy sliver. Lukewarm and musty, it smeared down her throat, leaving a slimy aftertaste. She scooped up water to rinse her mouth.

'How long can they keep us here?' asked Hugo.

'A day or so.' Marion didn't sound sure.

The stirabout in the bowls was glistening with grease and Sophie could still taste it on her tongue. Whether it was a day or a week, she'd rather starve.

CHAPTER 34

Hattie Wells hurried towards the queue of cabs outside Claridge's. The early morning smog had softened into mist, and the sun danced merrily on the cabs and horses, but Hattie's mind was on a different universe — home. Now the targets had been dealt with, she could fetch the artefact from the pub and return to her ship. It wasn't far. The locals wandered by it and through it, none the wiser.

In front of her, a man was staring at the cabs, debating whether to hail one. He turned around and despite his grey beard and top hat, she recognised him. Agent 49. Their eyes locked. He pulled out a heart-stopper and it was flashing. Hattie grabbed up her skirt and kicked out hard at his knee. The special substance in her boot delivered extra force and he went down with a groan, his hat rolling into the gutter.

He lay awkwardly on the pavement, still holding the flashing heart-stopper. Hattie snatched at it to turn it off, but she was too slow. A concerned hotel doorman ran forwards, straight into the heart-stopper's radius. He keeled over, clutching his chest.

Hattie switched off the heart-stopper and knelt beside the agent. 'I'm on a Guild job,' she hissed. 'Off the books.' His eyes widened. She thrust the now harmless heart-stopper into his jacket pocket and helped him sit up. She'd avoided death by seconds. That wasn't his fault. Field agents weren't privy to off-the-books jobs.

Drivers were jumping from their cabs and running towards the unfortunate doorman, and Hattie hauled the agent to his feet. She handed him his hat.

The agent shifted his weight from the leg Hattie had kicked. 'I didn't agree with your trial.' He grunted in pain. 'You're many things but you aren't a liar.'

Hattie bit back a sarcastic reply. She'd saved an agent and compromised a timeline. Though deserving of a serious reprimand, the Guild had dismissed her. The agent's eyes were hooded and the line between his brows more marked. 'You look terrible.'

'The last assignment went bad. Lost all my field equipment.'

His heart-stopper must be the spare from his ship. Fortunately for him, his translator device was still intact, faithfully translating his native medieval French into English.

'The corrupted timeline folded. I barely got out.'

Hattie frowned. Why would the Guild send an agent into a timeline at the end of its life cycle?

He hesitated. 'Alison didn't make it.'

By convention, only dead agents were referred to by name. 'I'm so sorry.'

His lips thinned. 'We're in trouble.'

'What's going on?'

'I can't discuss the details … watch yourself.'

He'd accepted she was working for the Guild, but being a protocols man, he wouldn't confide in a disgraced former agent.

The cabbies were in a huddle beside the late doorman. Hattie walked over to them and said quietly, 'Who's is the cab at the front? I'm afraid I need to leave.'

One of the cabbies returned to the cab. Hattie climbed in, the doors locked, and she opened the flap. 'Elephant and Castle, please.'

'The fare's double.'

'I know.' Hattie's hat had been knocked sideways and as the cab moved, she adjusted it, thinking about Agent 49. They'd never been partnered on an assignment, but they'd been on speaking terms. She'd last seen him eighteen months ago, on her final day with the Guild.

Losing Alison would have been traumatic, yet he'd surely lost countless colleagues over the centuries. Why was he so rattled? Must be down to this 'trouble.'

Hattie slowed her breathing. Calm down. In, out. In out.

CHAPTER 35

Just before noon, a constable opened cell five in Waterloo police station. 'Bail money's paid.'

Charlotte leaped to her feet. 'Thank God,' said Freddy, helping Marion stand up. Her injured ankle had ballooned.

Marion was too short to walk with her arm around his or Hugo's shoulders for support, so Sophie helped her limp towards reception. There was only one catcall from a prisoner as they passed by. The other cells were empty, the occupants freed or consigned to court.

Mr Burgess strode up, carrying the gun bag and an ebony cane. 'The police letter mentioned your injured ankle.' He glared at Freddy, no doubt blaming him for what had happened.

Marion accepted the stick. 'You've saved us.'

Everyone was beyond relieved. Sleeping in that cell had left them stiff and aching and bleary-eyed, except for Charlotte who'd slept soundly all night. The previous evening, when Charlotte had used the chamber pot, Marion had clapped her hands in delight, declaring her the cleverest dog in England. After that, Marion had recited from memory scenes from *A Study In Scarlet*, including a bizarre storyline involving Mormons in America. It had helped pass the time.

'I've brought sufficient funds for a cab,' said Mr Burgess.

Outside the station, they made their way slowly off Waterloo Bridge, and the butler flagged down a cab. As they set off, Hugo asked, 'How much was the bail money?'

'Six pence each,' said Mr Burgess. 'Two shillings in total.'

Back at Thornbridge, Miss Harris fussed over Marion, getting her settled in the drawing room, and the butler left to fetch a doctor. Sophie hung her hat on the stand and went with everyone else to the kitchen.

She filled a pan with water to make tea. 'When Marion offered up my brooch to pay bail, I assumed the bail amount was a lot.'

'I had no idea how much it would be.' Freddy scratched his chin. After a couple of days trying to grow his beard, the result was scrappy, like he'd forgotten to shave.

Sophie put a frying pan on the stove. 'Hey, we saved ourselves two shillings.' She transferred bacon into the pan.

'We haven't,' said Hugo. 'I repaid Mr Burgess, plus more for the cab.'

Freddy cut bread, applied a thick layer of butter, and gave a slice to Charlotte.

Sophie finished cooking breakfast and as she tucked into scrambled eggs and toast, she read *The Times*. Charlotte jumped onto the seat beside her. The first news story was headlined *Dockers March to Parliament*, but Charlotte plonked her paw on the page opposite, pointing to another headline: *Four Dead in South London*. The accompanying sepia photo showed bodies lying in a street and in the background, a building with a dark door. The door had a small hole in the middle. A lurch of recognition. The pub. They hadn't killed anyone!

Sophie scanned the article. 'There's a violent turf war going on in South London.'

The others looked up from their meals.

She read aloud. '*The McDonalds regard the Elephant and Castle public house and the surrounding area as their territory. The men lost their lives in a clash with the New Cut gang.*'

Hugo swore under his breath.

'There's more. *The Home Secretary, Sir Samuel Montagu, said in Parliament on Tuesday that the police didn't intervene because all the criminals carry firearms. From now on, the police will act.*'

'Does it say when the gang fight happened?' asked Hugo.

'Monday, 8th July.' Nausea rose in Sophie's throat. 'Two days before the McDonalds ambushed us in the courtyard.' She gulped down some water.

'Might explain why they didn't have firearms,' said Freddy. 'The thugs didn't want the sound of gunshots alerting the police.'

Not just thugs. Organised crime.

Sophie laid the paper flat on the table. If they'd known who they were dealing with, they'd never have ventured anywhere near that pub. She pushed aside her breakfast plate, her mind full of Bella.

Freddy stared at the crime photo, his mouth a grim line. 'The cylinder might as well be on Mars.'

Buck him up. 'It could still be sold on.' Sophie sounded convincingly confident.

Mr Burgess came into the kitchen and Charlotte hastily sprang off her chair. The butler held out a cream envelope. 'Mr Lacey, I'm presuming this is meant for you.'

Freddy took it. 'It's addressed to The Hardy Adventurers. Post-marked this morning, from the Langham.'

Charlotte's ears pricked up.

Freddy opened the letter. '*Dear Hardy Adventurers, after consideration, I would welcome further discussion.*'

Was Tesla entertaining second thoughts about helping them? Maybe he hadn't seen the paper today, didn't know about the turf war.

'*Let us dine at Claridge's at seven, courtesy of Westinghouse,*' read Freddy. '*Yours very sincerely, N. T.*'

CHAPTER 36

Hattie Wells entered the workshop with a spring in her step. 'Good morning.'

'You've got some cheek, coming 'ere,' said a seamstress.

Hattie pushed away a sinking feeling. 'I beg your pardon?'

'Len got a bullet in his shoulder and men are laid up like the Duke of Kent.'

'Duke of Kent?'

The seamstress set her mouth. 'Bent. Bashed up bad. Miracle no one bought it.'

Hattie hurried to the office.

Mary stood up from the desk, her face hard. 'You left out an important detail.'

'I told you everything I knew.'

'They was armed. All of 'em was armed.'

Hattie flinched. 'If I'd known, I'd have said.'

'Len wants double.'

Of course he did. She shouldn't allow this to sour relations with Mary, or Len. 'Double it is.' Hattie opened her drawstring bag and counted out banknotes. 'I'll wire the rest.'

She'd always paid promptly, though this was the first time she'd used her own money. Before, she'd used the Guild's.

A little girl skipped in, saw Hattie and did a bob curtsey. Her white pinafore was grubby, but her hair was curled in perfect ringlets and her eyes were as sharp as Mary's. She was holding a clump of blue thread.

Mary planted a kiss on her daughter's brow. 'She's a good 'un.'

'How old are you?' asked Hattie, her voice softening.

'Six.'

The child was as confident as a new penny, and the same age as Hattie's own daughter, Daisy. But Daisy would be six forever. Hattie forced herself back to the task in hand. 'I presume the woman and the others escaped?'

Mary nodded. 'There was another lady as well. Red hair. Bold as brass.'

The madwoman who'd been with the targets in the Langham. Delegating this task hadn't only been costly in terms of money. Hattie still had to deal with the targets, would have to delay taking the artefact. While she was here, she should check it was secure. She'd paid the cab more than enough to wait. 'Can I see the walking stick?'

Mary led the way through the workshop and into the pub. Her chatelaine clinked as she walked up the rackety staircase. Using a key from the chatelaine, she unlocked a door and Hattie followed her inside. A dusty desk and book-shelves, and obscuring most of the floor, a ship's cargo trunk.

'Safe as 'ouses.' Mary unlocked the trunk with a different key and lifted the lid with a creak. Inside was a MacDonald tartan blanket, blue and green with narrow red lines. The McDonalds had no traceable connection with the famous Scottish clan, but Len fancied they did.

Hattie leaned into the trunk and pulled aside the blanket to reveal a long metal cylinder. At one end was a ball, half transparent, serving as a protective cover. Underneath the cover were three raised buttons. Grey, matching the main casing. The buttons were well spaced, set out as a triangle. There'd been an artefact like this in the Guild Museum. So, an historical relic, in line with the client's letter. Hattie sucked her teeth. Not new Empire equipment, consistent with an off-the-books job. The Guild wasn't the client.

Mary bent and tugged a sheet of paper from under the cylinder. She tutted. 'Julie should have filed this with the office.' Mary unfolded it. 'Lovely.'

It was lovely. A walking stick drawn with great skill, detailing the varied wood grains in the shaft. The heart-shaped handle was green and the decoration in the middle, resembling the letter T, was yellow, mimicking gold. The air in Hattie's lungs evaporated and she struggled to breathe. 'Can I have a closer look?'

Mary handed it over.

There was no mistaking the illusion. The sketch was identical to the one in the museum. The colour picture had been displayed beside what was supposed to be the last surviving artefact from the famous festivals that had lauded Janus in Rome. Though only a madman would use it to summon Janus, freeing him from his ship, it was protected by arcane levels of protection.

But the artefact in the museum wasn't the last. This was another one. The room spun.

Mary took her arm. 'Are you alright, love? You've come over all pale.'

'Just a headache.' Hattie briefly closed her eyes, horror and regret squeezing her heart. Why did the client want the artefact? Either the client was insane or... The person who'd sent the letter, who'd paid her, was an intermediary. The next thought was so horrific, her brain could hardly form the words. Could the client be Janus himself? The question repeated in her mind.

Janus had been desperate to escape his prison for millennia. Once she'd delivered the artefact to the bank at home, the intermediary would use it to summon him.

Her hand shook as she gave back the sketch. The presentient Janus had been created by technology but when he'd been summoned from his ship, he'd been a biological creature with weight and mass. That Janus had been a puppet, programmed to entertain, not maim and kill. The sentient Janus without his shackles… Too horrible to imagine.

With the need for money, for security, she'd ignored instinct and common sense. If a job paid a king's ransom, of course there'd be a catch. How could she have been so stupid? She'd vowed this job would be her last, and it would be. Janus would make sure of that.

Mary relocked the trunk, then the office.

On the stairs, Hattie stumbled, dread churning her stomach.

Mary turned around. 'You need a sherry. That'll perk you up.'

'Thank you, no.' Hattie forced a smile. 'More work to do.'

Outside the pub, the cab was waiting. Hattie got in, her legs shaking as if she'd been struck down by ague. She collapsed on the seat, bile rising in her throat. Janus' flawed upgrade, triggering his sentience, had been a detail in a Guild history lesson. The Guild had no dealings with him. Why would it? Yes, Janus preyed on unwary travellers but trapped in his ship, he posed no wider threat.

Hattie put her head in her hands. Janus must have somehow bribed a passenger to write the letter and send her the money. She pulled the letter from her bag and re-read it with fresh eyes. A jolt of recognition. The shape of the letters, the meticulous copperplate style, was like hers because it *was* hers. Or to be more precise, another version of her. A different Wells had written this and come to her home universe to deliver it.

There was no shortage of travellers' tales about Janus. Landing underwater, just long enough so they didn't drown. Probing passengers' minds for atavistic fears, then selecting destinations where they'd endure them...

Hattie held onto the seat as the cab rattled and swayed. Janus would know that she'd discovered he was the client. After all, he could see the past and the future, and the present in all universes. Which begged the question: why was his itinerary so flawed? At the very first Event, she'd failed because a crucial fact had been omitted: the targets' armour.

What did Agent 49 say? *We're in trouble.* She'd assumed something was up with the Guild. Perhaps it was worse than that?

If Janus was sending assassins to other universes, there would be layers of consequences, untold ripples of chaos... She could hand over his letter to the Guild. It might assist. No. It wouldn't matter that she hadn't known Janus was behind the contract. No freelance jobs. No exceptions. She shuddered, remembering the execution of a retired agent. Not gratuitously painful, though still cruel.

When Hattie first joined the Guild, she hadn't cared if she lived or died, so had acquired a spurious reputation for bravery. Now she feared dying. Whether or not she completed this contract, she hadn't got long. Janus would send someone skilled with poison or firearms, or his own whispers to passengers would reach the Guild. All roads led to the noose.

How were the targets involved in this? She'd never heard of Janus sending passengers to end those who'd annoyed him. Wasn't that prevented by his original programming? And why did he want these targets dead? Yes, they'd somehow secured Guild armour and security bands on their travels but were otherwise unremarkable. Yet they couldn't be...

She stared out of the cab window, not seeing the street. It wasn't the targets that were special. It was what they were searching for. They meant to destroy the artefact, keep Janus in his prison. She'd save them the trouble. Historical artefacts were vulnerable to water. She'd soak it in Mary's bath.

As Hattie stood up to open the driver's flap to tell him to turn around, she was distracted by the cab ceiling. It was glinting. A spider's web, sparkling with all the colours of the rainbow, had attached itself. The sounds of the street outside and the rattling of the cab faded, banished by the web. A vision of creation, perfect, magnificent. Pulsating in time with her heart, it flowed out to her, nourished her, entwining with her soul.

She reached out to touch it. Before her finger made contact, it vanished, and the bliss that had addled her brain vanished with it. The noise from the street and cab was back, and Hattie blinked, disorientated. She trawled her memory, recalling a long-ago lecture at the Guild. The web was an early sign of a corrupted universe. A crack in space and time. If she'd touched it, she'd have disappeared to God knows where, reduced to subatomic specks. She sat down with a bump. Stay calm. Corrupted universes didn't fold in on themselves for aeons. The life cycles of timelines were unimaginably vast.

Hattie gathered her wits, her thoughts returning to Janus. With such an inaccurate itinerary, Janus might not notice everything she did here, but the artefact was central to this. The instant it was destroyed, Janus would know. She should return to the pub tomorrow, armed with the cyanide bottle.

End the artefact, then herself. Deny Janus his revenge. His lackeys couldn't torture a corpse.

She clasped her hands together. No, there was a better way. If she could bring the artefact to the targets, they would destroy it.

And they would bear the consequences.

At nine in the evening, Sophie walked with Charlotte into the grand dining room of Claridge's. She was still knackered. A bath and a few hours' kip hadn't made up for the previous night in jail. Fortunately, Marion's ankle wasn't broken. The doctor had diagnosed a nasty sprain.

Freddy and Hugo handed their hats to the waiter. The hotel diners were all couples, except for Tesla and, on a closer table, a woman dressed in full mourning, a black veil concealing her face. She was holding a cup under her veil to drink. Sophie checked the pistol in her pocket. That outfit was a perfect disguise for an assassin.

They approached Tesla and he gestured for them to sit down. Charlotte sniffed and pulled on her lead, and Sophie guided her to Tesla. After some hesitation, Charlotte lay down, facing out from the table.

Tesla ordered four sherries. 'You look … tired.'

'We had a run-in with the police,' said Hugo.

'Long story short, the cylinder's still in South London and organised crime is guarding it,' said Sophie. 'They attacked us with knives and cricket bats and machetes. We were lucky to escape.'

'The McDonald's gang?' Tesla swallowed. 'The ones in the paper?'

'The very same,' said Hugo.

'Miss Lacey sends her regards,' said Freddy. 'I'm afraid she sprained her ankle during her arrest.'

Tesla gasped. 'I hope she recovers soon.' He was shocked, not going through the motions of sympathy.

'We were surprised to receive your letter,' said Sophie. 'Do you have a plan to retrieve the cylinder?'

'The authorities fear the McDonalds.' Tesla drank his sherry. 'The cylinder is not so intriguing that I'd risk crossing them.'

'Yet you've kindly invited us to dine,' said Freddy.

'I remain to be convinced by your extravagant story, but I have no children, took insufficient account of your desperation to be reunited with your daughter. I retain an open mind and any information I can glean may prove useful.'

Freddy picked up the menu. 'Retrieving the cylinder here is impossible so we must try and return in Juno to my home. You might not be barred from travelling in Janus' ship. If you go to ancient Rome, say, 92 AD, you may be able to steal the cylinder.'

Three years before they'd tried to. 'Or you could visit the future?' said Sophie. 'Find other metals?'

Tesla looked solemn. 'You talked about Marble Arch and another place in England where I could … call this ship. Are there similar locations in America?'

'There might be,' said Hugo, 'though finding them would be tricky.'

The waiter set out a water jug and glasses. Tesla chose a starter, and everyone else ordered a main course.

'The cylinder breaks if it comes into contact with water,' said Freddy, his gaze on the jug.

Tesla raised a dark eyebrow. 'An unfortunate flaw.'

Sophie thought back to Rome. A tiny amount of moisture had broken the cylinder. Other technology had been more robust. Maybe more modern? Their language translators had been unaffected by steam in the Roman baths—

Charlotte growled.

A man with greying hair and a whiskery beard was limping towards them. As he passed the woman in mourning, she glanced up.

Hugo and Freddy jumped to their feet, shocked, and Sophie gasped. This was the man who'd followed them in Rome — who'd thrown their cylinder into the Tiber. He looked different with the beard and in Victorian evening wear, and his sallow complexion suggested he hadn't slept in a week.

Sophie gave him a level stare. 'I wondered when the time police would show up.'

Freddy remained on his feet. 'We're on your database.' He'd speculated to the others that the time police held records going back centuries, incorporating countless timelines. 'How did you anticipate which variant of 666 we'd choose?'

The man drew a deep breath. 'That's classified.'

More growling came from Charlotte, low and persistent, and Sophie gave her a reassuring pat. Yes, this man had destroyed the cylinder in Rome, but when Sophie had fallen in the river there, he'd dragged her out, and his partner had resuscitated her.

'May I present Mr Tesla?' Freddy was reverting to old-fashioned manners to smooth feathers and learn info. Unlikely that would sway the tight-lipped time traveller.

Tesla was on his feet now. 'Would you care to join us?' He

seemed curious despite the traveller's reticence, or maybe because of it.

A waiter hurried up with another chair and the traveller lowered himself into it, wincing as he stretched out his leg.

'You're injured,' said Hugo.

'I missed a step on some stairs.'

'Where's your partner?' asked Sophie. The girl in Rome had been around her age.

The traveller's expression clouded, and he didn't answer. He rested his hand on the tablecloth and his jacket sleeve rode up.

'You're not wearing your security band?' Sophie gestured at his wrist. Among other functions, his bracelet prevented him being tracked while tracking others with the gene.

The traveller shrugged. Okay, whatever had happened to his partner or his bracelet, he wasn't sharing.

The main courses and Tesla's soup arrived.

Freddy unfolded a napkin on his lap. 'Are you a police officer?'

'Of sorts.'

'Why all the cloak and dagger stuff?' Hugo asked.

'What do you mean?' The traveller shifted in his seat. 'Wrong universe for that.'

Okay, the guy had taken the cloak and dagger cliché literally. He had a slight accent, suggesting he was speaking via a translator device, like they'd used in Rome. When his translator had broken in the river Tiber, Sophie had heard him briefly speak in his native language. 'Are you French?'

The traveller's features shuttered.

Hugo sighed. 'Why do you have to be so mysterious?'

'It's the nature of my work.'

'You're familiar with the cylinder's functions?' asked Freddy.

'I am.' The traveller addressed Tesla. 'You of all people must know this cannot end well.'

Tesla narrowed his eyes. 'To what do you refer?'

'Their pursuit of the artefact.' The traveller's expression hardened.

'I've only just met them,' said Tesla. 'How can I predict their endeavour's success or failure?'

'Once Nikola Tesla has all the facts, the odds of success and failure will be easy to assess. Even as a boy, you could complete integral calculus in your head.'

'Who told you that?' Tesla's eyes narrowed more.

'Some individuals merit close attention.'

Tesla sat back in his chair, wrong-footed.

Sophie put down her cutlery, her appetite gone. The traveller would do all he could to stop them creating a secure way to Bella. He'd destroyed the cylinder in Rome and intended to destroy the cylinder here. But his database wasn't perfect. Or he'd have burgled Nice Wells weeks ago and left the cylinder out in the rain.

'Mr Lacey, I'm here to offer you safe passage,' said the traveller. 'I'll transport you to your home universe, together with Mr and Mrs Harrington.'

Charlotte did a sceptical grunt.

'And the hound of course,' added the traveller. 'My offer is sincere.'

'To my Shorten?' said Freddy. 'How?'

'I have my own vessel.'

'Why would you do that?' said Sophie.

'It provides an optimal outcome. You will be reunited with your family and furthermore, timelines can be restored and innocents protected.' The traveller fidgeted, stretching his leg. 'Many will be saved from a terrible death.'

'Scare stories about the end of the world aren't facts,' said Hugo.

'You misunderstand,' said the traveller. 'The end of worlds, not one world.'

Freddy folded his arms. 'Expand.'

'You don't need a lecture on theoretical physics, Mr Lacey. You've already pondered the consequences of Janus interfering with time.'

Freddy swallowed.

'This comes down to whether we can trust you,' said Sophie. 'Why are you offering to take us to Shorten?'

'As I told you, safe passage.'

'Precisely, why do you want to help us?' said Hugo.

The traveller hesitated. 'There is a remote possibility that you could end Janus, and that cannot happen.'

The woman in mourning knocked over something on her table and a waiter dashed to clear it up.

'If we made Janus' ship safe, it wouldn't just benefit us,' said Sophie. 'His passengers would travel without fear, experience other times and cultures. That would be—'

'Catastrophic,' said the traveller. 'Individuals would visit universes for the most trivial reasons. An interest in exotic fashion, to watch a battle, or search for a lost dog.'

Under the table, Charlotte whined, and Sophie was speechless. If a lost dog wasn't a good reason to cross universes, what about a lost child?

Freddy's lips narrowed into a bitter line. 'What is trivial to one person can be monumental to another.'

'Individuals with the best intentions corrupt timelines. Those who topple the powerful, bring about anarchy. Those who save a beloved individual from misery, condemn others to worse. Then there are those who enrich themselves and kill millions in wars and pointless conquest. The list is long.' He paused. 'You surely understand the complexity of restoring the status quo, even for a single timeline?'

'Is it possible to reverse the damage?' said Freddy.

'After collecting data for millennia, we can restore what we regard as sufficient.' The traveller's reply was smooth, as if reciting a stock phrase.

Sophie noted the word 'we.' Was the time police a small, determined band or a huge organisation? No point in asking. He wouldn't tell them.

'Your passage to Shorten is of immeasurable importance,' he said. 'The benefit to you and yours is a fortunate side-effect.'

Hugo's lips twisted. 'A side-effect. So, this isn't kindness. Your concern is protecting timelines, not us.'

'Altering timelines is a crime. Offenders must be dealt with.'

'With so many timelines,' said Sophie, 'how do you monitor them?' In medieval Georgia, she'd altered a timeline. Understatement. Wiped out an army.

There was no response from the traveller.

'I don't think you know for certain what taking us to Shorten would achieve,' said Freddy.

As a waiter cleared their dinner plates, Sophie struggled to stay calm. Charlotte was pressing against her legs beneath the table and Tesla was watching the traveller, a new line furrowing his brow. Hugo's and Freddy's faces were tight and drawn.

The traveller leaned forward in his chair. 'I've done many crossings with versions of you. However, on this occasion, probability is in unusual flux.'

'You sound like Janus,' said Hugo. 'Are you working with him?'

'Janus uses other creatures. He doesn't work with them.'

Hugo pushed his fringe off his forehead. 'If we ended Janus, his cosmic meddling would die with him.'

Time seemed to slow. The woman in mourning stirred

her coffee, the clink of the spoon mingling with the genteel hum of diners' chatter.

'Janus' safe ship would cause a chaos that would be impossible to police.' The traveller cleared his throat. 'Unlike Juno, in my ship the odds of you reaching your home universe alive are almost a hundred per cent.'

This was too good to be true.

A waiter walked past to clear a nearby table. The woman in mourning was leaving.

'We'll need to consider,' said Sophie, glancing at Freddy.

'Let us meet tomorrow evening,' said the traveller. 'At seven, in the foyer here.' He stood up. 'Mr Tesla, please persuade them to adopt the wisest course.'

The traveller didn't wait for an answer, turning on his heel and limping out of the dining room.

'Shall we retire to the lounge?' said Tesla. 'The ambience there is more relaxed.'

They followed Tesla out into the corridor and into a room with leather armchairs, dark walls, and expensive spirits. Men were smoking cigars and smoke wafted in a smelly mist, mimicking the smog in the street outside.

Only Tesla ordered alcohol. 'The mysterious stranger clearly values my opinion.' He accepted a glass of brandy from a waiter.

'He was trying to manipulate us,' said Hugo. 'Playing mind games.'

Tesla tapped his long fingers on the arm of his chair.

'Did you believe him when he said that other versions of us have accepted safe passage?' Sophie asked Freddy.

'I'm unsure.'

'Everything he told us could be rubbish,' said Sophie. 'We still don't know what his deal is.'

'Deal?' said Tesla. 'Is he offering a business contract?'

'No,' said Hugo. 'Is he a good guy or a bad guy?'

'Do you think we should accept his offer?' Freddy asked Tesla.

'I would.' He frowned. 'But I'm not you.'

On the walk from Claridge's, streetlamps shone hazily through the dark, leaving shadows that hid anything a few yards away. Charlotte was keeping close to the streetlamps.

Sophie tried to make sense of what had happened. 'The time police's database must be independent of Janus. The traveller was emphatic he had no dealings with him.'

Freddy scratched at the stubble on his chin. 'He chose his words carefully, didn't say the wider consequences of going with him were certain. Does that suggest he's honest?'

'It's what he didn't say that worries me,' said Sophie. 'When you asked how he followed us, he clammed up.'

Freddy nodded. 'And what clever timing. We can't retrieve the cylinder, so our only options are to wait for who knows how long for it to be sold on, or return to Shorten in Juno. And that's when he approaches us.'

Hugo was unusually quiet as Sophie considered the implications. The traveller had offered safe passage at the time and place they were most likely to accept. Yes, they were being played, though the offer could still be genuine. And yet… 'If we take his offer,' said Sophie, 'it's so … final.'

'Why has he given us so little time to decide?' said Freddy.

A tell-tale sign of a scam. 'What if we go with him,' said Sophie, 'and a week later, the cylinder here is sold on?'

They turned a corner, passing another streetlamp, and it illuminated their faces in an eery glow. Hugo's features were set, shuttered.

Back in Thornbridge, Freddy flopped into the cream armchair in Hugo and Sophie's bedroom. 'We need to decide once and for all whether we accept the traveller's offer, or I won't sleep.'

'I'm beyond tired,' said Sophie. 'I can't think straight.'

'Sleep will knit up the ravelled sleeve of care,' said Hugo, misquoting Shakespeare. He sat on the bed and took off his shoes.

Freddy stood up and sighed. 'You may be right.' He went off into his room.

Lying in bed an hour later, Sophie was still awake. 'Are you asleep?' she whispered to Hugo.

'Freddy and Charlotte are.' Soft snoring was coming from the connecting bedroom, and from Charlotte on the floor. 'The traveller's offer is too convenient, and we'd never get the walking stick.'

Sophie stared at the ceiling. 'It would be crazy to dismiss it out of hand. Guaranteed safe passage to Shorten…'

'It's not guaranteed. He shared no evidence to support his pitch and getting anything out of him is tortuous.'

Sophie turned on her side, snuggling up to Hugo, but he stiffened under her touch.

Dismayed, she drew away. 'What's the matter?'

CHAPTER 38

Silence, and it stretched out until she couldn't stand it. 'Hugo, talk to me.'

He sighed into the darkness. 'Finding the cylinder, reaching Bella, uses up every part of you. There's nothing left for me.'

What was he talking about? They were madly in love. Unease spread through her and the bedspread covering them seemed heavier. She and Hugo were bound together. Indivisible. *Nothing left for me.* Had she been too focused on Bella and the cylinder? Unintentionally shutting him out? And the traveller's offer had bowled her over.

But why was Hugo saying this now? Only yesterday they'd made love as if every moment was their last. 'We're okay. Right here, we—'

'I don't mean the physical stuff.'

Sophie closed her eyes. Whatever was wrong, she needed to sort this. 'You've risked your life coming here. You didn't have to. That's constantly in the back of my mind.'

'Risking my life… I'm used to it.' He snorted. 'Playing your sidekick in Shorten, that would be unbearable.'

Hugo staying with her in Shorten had always been too big an ask. What was a safe, long life worth without him? Yes, Bella was woven into her soul, but so was he.

'You and Freddy are in a private bubble of obsession and I'm a spectator.'

The words hit her like a blow. 'That's not true.'

'All the way from Claridge's, you agonised with Freddy over the traveller's offer. Not once did you consider what would happen to … us.'

'We were just weighing up the pros and cons.' Sophie blinked, fighting off tears. 'And our relationship doesn't concern Freddy.'

'You can't disentangle him. He wants you to choose Bella over me.'

Sophie's insides clenched. 'This is the traveller, isn't it? Trying to divide us?'

'He's succeeded.'

Her heart sank. 'Hugo, you should have called me out on this before.'

'The traveller's offer brought it to a head.'

They'd been through a lot in the last week. She should have taken a step back, evaluated whether they should even consider the traveller's offer. 'You know I can't choose between you and Bella.'

'Things change.'

'I haven't.'

He turned to face her. 'I understand Bella has to be the focus of your energy, your determination, your love. But when you shut me out, it eats away at me.'

'Now I realise I was doing that, I'll take care not to. Ever again.' She moved closer, hugging him. 'I promise.'

Would she be forced to choose between her daughter and this man she dearly loved? What if there was no world where she could have both?

CHAPTER 39

The next morning in the kitchen, Miss Harris had already made tea and was plonking cutlery onto the table as if it would fight back. 'Being detained by the police … I still can't believe it.'

'That was unfortunate,' said Freddy. 'I'm very thankful that Miss Lacey's ankle will heal, given time.' This was code for, 'Thank goodness my great aunt won't leave the house for a while.'

The maid raised an eyebrow. 'I took her account of the gunfight with a large pinch of salt.' She opened a window to let out the cooking smells. 'I've read about those gangs. The police won't take them on.'

'Miss Lacey has a wonderful imagination,' said Hugo.

'She does.' Miss Harris picked up her mistress' morning tea tray and left.

Sophie put a pan on the stove, her mind full of Hugo and Freddy. Her relationship with them hadn't settled, even after so long. She needed to prioritise them differently but equally. Make a conscious effort.

Charlotte was lapping up tea. Such a dear, undemanding

soul. Or did she only seem undemanding because mostly she couldn't talk?

Outside in the front garden, Mr Burgess was chatting with the gardener, their voices drifting in through the open window. 'Those spots on the lilies are nasty.'

'Looks worse than it is.' The gardener's London accent was broader than the butler's. 'If I prune out the infected stems, they'll be fine next year.'

Sophie cracked eggs into the pan, picturing the Manor gardens. Bella in the bower, surrounded by bushes and flowers in bloom. Sitting on the stone seat, swinging her legs, her blonde hair ruffled by a warm breeze—

'The eggs are done.' Hugo removed the pan from the stove. 'You're … distracted.'

'I was thinking about the gardens in Shorten.'

'They might be restored to their former glory by now,' said Freddy. When they'd left, with the gardeners diverted to fight the militia, weeds had conquered the flower beds.

'Gardening's therapeutic.' When Sophie had lived with her aunt, they'd kept a small herb garden. 'Predictable, changing with the seasons.'

Hugo plated up the eggs. 'Shame that doesn't apply to timelines.'

'Perhaps it does in a way,' said Freddy. 'Given how similar many parallel universes are, repetition must play a significant part in their creation.'

Sophie set Charlotte's plate of toast and eggs on the floor, her thoughts returning to the previous evening. 'Most of what the traveller chose to share was so vague as to be meaningless. What did he mean about protecting innocents? Are we innocents?'

'He recited it like a slogan,' said Hugo.

'Charlotte doesn't trust him,' added Sophie. Charlotte had

growled at the traveller, snorted and whined, her feelings crystal clear.

'I could go to Shorten by myself,' said Freddy.

Hugo's eyes registered his surprise.

'Would you?' blurted Sophie.

'In extremis. But if you both stayed and … failed, I'd never know, would I?'

Sophie helped herself to toast. Freddy would be safer in Shorten and could protect Bella, and splitting up was so unpredictable, it might get past Janus—

'Logic can't decide this,' said Hugo, watching Sophie.

The toast in her mouth turned dry. With an effort, Sophie swallowed it. The traveller's offer of safe passage bestowed the near certainty of reaching Bella. How could any parent refuse that? But it felt … wrong. She met Hugo's gaze.

This was no longer just about them, or even Bella. Janus had found a way to limit the summoning algorithm, and he was surely whittling away at the one that prevented him physically harming travellers. If he succeeded, how many would be tortured for his entertainment? Sophie's heart was heavy with dread yet that wouldn't, couldn't sway her. This universe, every universe, would be better with Janus gone, and they could end him. 'We hold our nerve, wait for the cylinder to be sold on from the pub.' She paused. 'We decline the offer of safe passage.'

That evening, they returned to Claridge's, met up with Tesla, and waited in the foyer. A woman in full mourning was sitting near the exit. Probably the lady who'd been in the dining room yesterday.

The traveller limped in, using a plain walking stick. 'Good

evening. Let's find a quiet spot.' He addressed Tesla. 'I don't wish to be rude, but could you excuse us for a few minutes?'

Tesla looked put out and strode off.

They chose seats at the far side of the foyer. Rather than sit on the floor, Charlotte stayed standing, eyeing the traveller.

'What you decide today is of the utmost importance.' The traveller's voice was low and urgent. 'Timelines are changing so quickly, they're fracturing. Universes that should take eons to collapse are folding in on themselves.'

Despite the summer temperature, Sophie went cold. His words reverberated, a melodramatic harbinger of doom. Entire universes folding in on themselves? Whatever that involved, it didn't sound good.

'How do you know?' said Freddy.

'Numerous reports from our people.'

'So, they survived,' said Hugo, 'managed to leave.'

'There are signs before the end,' said the traveller. 'As the damage progresses, different parts of the timeline connect and merge. A dinosaur appears in a city. A mountain village finds itself at the bottom of the Mariana Trench in the Pacific. One instant you're in a forest, the next you're on a mountain, and you're older or younger. There are infinite variations. A whole timeline can shift years backwards or forwards. Stabilise, then die.'

This was nonsense, right? A desperate push to frighten them into accepting his offer. Sophie played along. 'How does it end?'

'Once a timeline's changes accelerate to a certain point, it implodes, as happens with ancient stars.'

'How does that affect living things?' Hugo sounded as if he didn't want an answer.

'Time and space act as they do in a black hole. Matter is torn into its subatomic components.'

Sophie stared at her lap. Plausible sci-fi stuff but again, impossible to imagine — or verify.

'Janus' tampering is causing the fractures, and they're spreading out from imploding timelines. They all lead here, to you.'

Flattery? The traveller's final card? Unlike all other versions of them, in countless universes, they were special. Beyond unlikely.

They all stayed silent, eyes fixed on the traveller.

'If you summon him, he'll kill you before you draw breath.'

Fear clawed at Sophie. Whatever his agenda, instinct told her the traveller believed that.

'When you return to your home universe without the artefact, you'll pose no threat, and Janus should stop wreaking havoc.'

'*Should* stop,' said Freddy. 'So, there's no guarantee.'

'A high probability.'

'Define high,' said Freddy. 'Ninety per cent? Sixty?'

'I can't be more precise.' The traveller searched their faces, including Charlotte. 'Have you decided?'

Charlotte nodded, but it wasn't her regular, upbeat nod. More a grim gesture of defiance. Freddy's lips firmed into a brave line. Hugo's expression was bleak.

Sophie steeled herself. 'We decline your offer.'

Something showed on the traveller's face. Sadness? 'This moment was inevitable.'

'We make our own choices,' said Freddy, 'and meet the consequences on our own terms.'

'If only it were so,' said the traveller. 'This is a final warning.'

Sophie peered at him. 'For what?'

'We're decided,' said Freddy.

The traveller stood up and pulled something from his inside jacket pocket.

He's going to kill us. The words thundered in Sophie's mind. Before she could grab the pistol from her pocket, Charlotte sprang up and leaped on top of the traveller, grabbing his hand between her teeth. Charlotte could move almost supernaturally fast. Her companions jumped to their feet as the traveller fell to the ground, grappling with Charlotte.

Across the foyer, someone screamed.

The woman in full mourning sprinted over to the traveller. He was sitting up, trying to scramble backwards to escape Charlotte. The woman picked up a chair and slammed it onto the traveller's head with such force that the chair splintered. He buckled, blood pouring from his temple. The lady strolled away as if nothing had happened.

Charlotte moved off the traveller, holding a pen in her jaws, the grey nib pointing out of her blood-smeared teeth. No, not a pen. The weapon that had paralysed them in Rome, blinding them with light.

He'll recover. We should go. Charlotte's tone was unruffled in Sophie's mind. Charlotte dashed across the foyer, zooming past flabbergasted guests. Sophie followed her towards the exit with Hugo and Freddy. Around and behind them, hushed conversation grew louder, more hysterical. Sophie tried to block it out. Which was more shocking? A mad dog, or a lady in mourning assaulting a man with a chair? Was the woman a dog-lover? Someone with a grudge against the traveller? Or just unhinged? Whatever her motivation, Sophie was grateful.

Tesla waylaid them by the exit. 'What on earth happened?'

'He meant to murder us,' said Freddy.

As they left the hotel, Tesla stood in the doorway, watching them go.

Sophie shivered as she hurried down the road, though the air was balmy and the sky almost clear. But for Charlotte, she'd be dead. They'd all be dead.

Charlotte was trotting on the pavement with the heart-stopper in her impressive teeth, that were still stained red. Startled pedestrians stepped aside to let her pass.

'I should have followed the lady with the chair,' said Hugo. 'It can't be coincidence she was in the dining room when the traveller first turned up.'

'Not necessarily,' said Freddy. 'There must be other guests who were present on both occasions.'

They stopped to gather their wits on a street corner. Charlotte dropped the half-eaten heart-stopper into Sophie's palm. It was cracked and warm to the touch, like a dodgy electric plug. Sophie stashed it in her bag and stroked Charlotte. 'You were amazing.' They set off again.

'He'd really have killed us. In the middle of Claridge's. I can't take it in.' Hugo held onto his hat as he hurried along. 'All those people in the foyer would have witnessed it. He didn't care.'

'He'll have bailed,' said Sophie. 'Gone back to his ship.' The guy had sounded reasonable, but it had all been an act. 'He must have murdered Mrs Alveston.' The horrible scene in that hotel room resurfaced. 'When he couldn't find the cylinder, he gave her a heart attack.'

'How and why was the burglar involved?' said Freddy.

'The article in the paper mentioned he had a criminal record,' said Hugo. 'Perhaps the traveller hired him?'

Distracted, Sophie stumbled on a loose paving stone. 'In Rome, the traveller was unflappable. Here he was fidgety, stressed. Though that could have been his bad leg.'

'He was convinced the fissures in time and space lead to us,' said Hugo. 'Why would they?'

'We might be the versions most likely to succeed or...' Freddy tailed into silence.

'Or what?' said Hugo.

'This timeline is the next to collapse.'

Charlotte was trembling and Sophie patted her. 'We haven't seen dinosaurs plodding up the road. And Janus has been meddling with timelines since he became sentient, so he can enjoy his passengers' struggles.'

'That meddling is trivial compared to what he's doing now,' said Freddy.

They reached Park Street and Charlotte approached a patch of grass with a familiar determined gait. Sophie stopped walking and dug into her handbag for one of Charlotte's small plastic sacks.

'He may be losing patience, being less careful,' said Hugo. 'As with Richard the Third.'

Random. Sophie sorted the poo bag. 'Remind me.'

'In Shakespeare's play, Richard acts with caution to gradually secure power but there comes a tipping point when he just goes for it.'

Freddy scratched his stubble. 'If the time police's database has been compiled over millennia, that makes the traveller's uncertainty about Janus' meddling even more troubling.'

Sophie dropped the plastic bag in a litter bin. 'Why?'

'The timelines fracturing...' Freddy hesitated. 'It hasn't happened before.'

'Safe passage would be irrelevant if the Shorten universe fractured.' Hugo's tone was flat. 'And what about home?'

All matter torn into its subatomic components. The longing to hold her baby in her arms was so intense, Sophie felt faint. Please let the traveller be lying.

Freddy screwed up his eyes.

'Hopefully, it'll happen so fast, we'll be oblivious,' said Hugo.

Charlotte pawed at Sophie's bag and spluttered, maybe trying to talk. 'Do you think the heart-stopper's still working?' Sophie asked her. Charlotte gave an emphatic nod. 'If we drop it down a drain, contact with the water will ensure it won't harm anyone.'

'Or we should reverse-engineer it,' said Freddy. 'What an opportunity—'

'Not an opportunity,' said Sophie. 'It would explode in our faces.'

CHAPTER 40

The following morning on the terrace, Marion resumed her target practice. Dressed in a house-coat, she fired from the comfort of a bath chair. The birds in nearby trees squawked and scattered, the targets clinked, and the sun shone through the London mist, bathing the garden in gentle light.

Hugo peered out of the bedroom window. 'No sign of the end of the world, so why do I feel uneasy?'

'I feel the same,' said Sophie, 'as if the clock's ticking.'

Clink. Marion hit another target.

Sophie placed Charlotte's paperback on the page-turning machine and Charlotte lay on the floor to read. Charlotte had operated the device for so long that using it was part of her muscle memory. The soft click whenever she pressed the button for the next page was restful, a reassuring rhythm, but Charlotte couldn't settle, and she sat up.

'This is the traveller's mind games. His doom-laden predictions are playing like earworms in our heads.' Last night, the traveller's words had twisted Sophie's dream about

Bella, and Freddy's dead ancestors had paraded through the gardens.

'If the walking stick was going to get sold on, it would have happened by now.' Hugo turned away from the window. 'And your bracelet would have fired up.'

Sophie sat on the bed and fastened her boots. 'It's been barely a week. Maybe whoever has it, is holding out for a good price?'

Freddy did a token knock on the door that connected the two bedrooms. His fledgling beard looked okay now. He flopped down in the armchair.

Hugo sighed. 'We can't impose on Marion much longer. We need jobs and cheap digs.'

'There are vacancies for clerks in the paper,' said Freddy. 'I'll get started on query letters.'

Brought up with computers, Sophie's handwriting was terrible. 'Typewriters can't be that different from keyboards. I can do secretarial work.'

She shot Hugo a wicked glance. 'You'd be a fab butler.' She was only half joking.

Hugo rolled his eyes.

Charlotte pawed at the door, wanting breakfast, and they trooped downstairs in brooding silence. On the console table in the hall was a letter addressed to The Hardy Adventurers.

Hugo opened it. 'Tesla's leaving for Paris tomorrow. He wants to meet at six this evening for a farewell dinner, and suggests a new venue, Brown's. *A venue untainted by recent events.*'

'Wells is still out there,' said Sophie. 'We should play it safe and write back, politely declining.' The efficient postal system would ensure he'd receive their reply within hours.

Freddy set his mouth. 'Tesla might yet devise a plan to recover the cylinder.'

Tesla was exceptionally clever, but he'd failed to come up

with a single useful suggestion. Sophie looked to Hugo and Charlotte for support and found none. Right. She'd been outvoted.

They'd be meeting with Tesla.

~

Brown's foyer was more like a Victorian home than a hotel. Quirky, vivid cushions enlivened the sofas, and impressionist paintings lined the walls, dreamy in the muted sunlight that streamed through elegant Georgian windows. The dining room was smaller than the one in Claridge's or the Langham and had a more informal vibe, with plainer chairs.

It was early for dinner, and there were just two other guests. One was an Indian man in a turban and a formal suit with tails, and his companion was a monkey. The monkey was wearing a red, boxy hat with tassels that swayed as it munched olives with a haughty air. Evidently used to fine dining.

Sophie whispered to Charlotte, 'They won't allow you to sit on a chair.' Charlotte shrugged.

The only unusual thing about the man was his rings, the stones so large on his fingers, they didn't look real. Sophie tried not to stare. When Marion had claimed that a maharaja and his monkey were staying at Brown's, Sophie hadn't believed her.

Sophie chose a seat facing the exit, checking the pistol in her pocket. If Wells turned up, she'd be ready.

Five minutes later, Tesla came in. He ordered a bottle of red wine, a starter for himself, and everyone else opted for a main course. He clasped his hands together. 'So, what happened in Claridge's?'

Freddy summarised what the traveller had told them

about an impending apocalypse. 'We hope he was exaggerating.'

Tesla peered at Charlotte. 'To attack him, he must have frightened you.'

Charlotte adopted her innocent face.

Sophie explained about the heart-stopper. 'What did he do after we left?' she asked Tesla.

'He'd suffered an injury to his hand and there was a nasty cut to his brow, but he didn't stay for the nurse.'

Charlotte was keeping quiet, scrutinising Tesla.

'All dogs are interesting,' he said. 'You're … particularly interesting.'

Charlotte didn't react, not wanting Tesla to know how or why. He loved sharing his latest discoveries. Couldn't risk him sharing about her.

'She's very clever,' said Sophie. 'It's the poodle in her.'

Tesla nodded to a waiter to pour the wine.

'I'll stick to water.' Sophie needed her wits about her.

'What prompted your decision to leave London?' asked Freddy.

'Self-preservation, Mr Lacey. You've narrowly avoided being poisoned, been set upon by a criminal gang, and have fallen foul of the police. The cylinder is not worth losing my reputation, let alone my life. I have much to do.'

An unwelcome stab of recognition. Tesla's view of their situation was bang on.

'You haven't thought of a way that we could distract the McDonalds and retrieve the cylinder,' said Freddy. A glum statement not a question.

Tesla shook his head.

Their food arrived. Sophie transferred her steak pie onto a side plate and put it down for Charlotte, then tucked into peas and mash.

Tesla picked at his salad. 'I may travel in time in due course.' He sounded cautious yet matter of fact.

How humbling that they'd encouraged Nikola Tesla to visit the future, an experience which could inspire more inventions.

'If you say Janus' name near Marble Arch, his ship should appear,' said Hugo. 'We'd go with you, but our presence would prevent you calling it.'

Tesla set his plate aside. 'I'd rather travel from the United States.'

'The ship lands where a universe is thin or has a tear,' said Hugo, deploying his *Star Trek* level of knowledge.

'For some reason it favours huge arches,' said Sophie.

Tesla sipped his wine. 'A splendid classical arch is planned in Washington to commemorate the centennial of George Washington's inauguration. A good place to start.'

'Once you're in the ship, ask a mundane question,' said Hugo. 'If you receive a flat, logical answer, we've succeeded in ending Janus. If you get a hint of personality, he's in there, and you'd be wise to walk away.'

Hugo took his notebook and pencil from his pocket. 'Even if Janus is gone, you'll still need to be precise about your destination. This universe is a variant of universe 666.' He flicked to a page with the corner turned down. 'The designations are all incredibly long numbers. These are the last ten for this universe. If you repeat them, you'll return here.'

'Inauspicious.' Tesla looked at the string of numbers.

'How so?' said Freddy.

'Not divisible by three.' Tesla got to his feet.

'Don't you want to write it down?' said Sophie.

'I can remember it.' He gave them a respectful nod. 'I'll pay on the way out. Good luck.'

They all shook hands, and he left.

Freddy wiped his mouth with his napkin. 'A brilliant mind, but prone to superstition, giving groundless significance to a random number.'

Sophie touched her brooch, nestled beside the outline of Bella's rattle under her dress. Superstition could help morale. 'I'll pop to the loo before we go.'

A waiter directed her down a corridor, and she checked for Bad Wells. The traveller hadn't cared about attacking them in a swanky hotel. Likely Wells wouldn't either.

To her relief, the corridor was deserted and so were the loos. Returning to the dining room, Sophie's thoughts flitted to Tesla, then Freddy and Bella. Would she inherit her father's love of maths? Would she ever know him, or her mother? This terrible yearning would never fade. How long could they wait for the cylinder to be sold on? Months, years? When would they be forced to accept it was irretrievably lost, and leave 1889?

Take their chances in Juno?

CHAPTER 41

Sophie returned to Brown's dining room. She'd hardly sat down when Charlotte whimpered. Charlotte's attention was on a woman approaching their table. There was something familiar about her.

The woman's hair was dark, not blonde, and she wasn't wearing glasses... The waitress from the Langham! Today, she wore an elegant grey gown, styled for the evening, with a low neckline and puff sleeves. Her hair was up in a fashionable bun, though it wasn't neat, as if she'd dressed her hair without a maid. But those eyes...

Sophie's heart turned over. This had to be Wells. The same distinctive eyes as the male version. Cobalt blue.

Hugo and Freddy stood up fast, Freddy knocking over his wine glass.

Saw her in Claridge's. Purple dress. Waitress. Black clothes and veil. Charlotte's voice in Sophie's head was succinct and calm. Giving information, not a warning. Not yet. She was sitting on the floor, on edge, ready to pounce. *Same scent as other versions.* Charlotte's sense of smell, like regular dogs, was 100,000 times more sensitive than a human's. Sophie gripped the side of her chair. Charlotte had always known this woman was Wells, just hadn't been able to tell them.

Wells had been watching and plotting in plain sight. So, why did she attack the traveller? Help them?

'Do you mind if I join you?' Wells' manner was confident, polite.

Sophie's mouth was open. She shut it, slid her hand into her pocket and closed her fingers around the handle of the pistol, grasping the cold metal.

Wells smiled, an urbane twitch of her mouth that conveyed nothing.

Her silk drawstring bag was too small to hold a gun. Wells' skirt, on the other hand, with its layers of flounces, was fuller at the front, like Sophie's, and might have pockets.

'Are you armed?' asked Hugo, cutting through the veneer of gentility.

Wells sat down, the movement graceful and assured. 'Four against one, and you're wearing Guild armour. The odds are in your favour.'

Her response should have been reassuring, yet fear curdled in Sophie's stomach.

Freddy resumed his seat, his gaze still on Wells. 'Does the Guild make good quality armour?' Given the circumstances, Freddy's small talk was impressive.

Wells' jaw tightened. 'Please abandon this charade. You know what the Guild is.'

'We don't,' said Sophie.

'A friend gave us the vests.' Hugo reluctantly sat down. He appeared unruffled, but his eyes betrayed him. Fear edged with panic.

'I suppose the armour does resemble a vest,' mused Wells. 'Guild standard issue. I miss mine.'

Why was she talking to them? Sharing anything? Charlotte was eyeing Wells with the intense focus of a predator.

Except Wells was too wily to be prey. If this stayed polite, they might survive this, even learn something useful. Sophie briefly touched Charlotte's collar. One suspicious move, and Charlotte would pounce in an instant. Give her mistress time to use the pistol.

'Hannah Georgina Wells, I presume?' said Hugo.

Wells waved away a waiter. 'Henrietta Georgina. Hattie for short. We should keep things formal, don't you think?'

'May I present Mr and Mrs Harrington,' said Freddy, though Wells surely knew their names. 'Frederick Lacey.' In sticky situations, his default setting was civilised.

Yes, keep this polite but on point. Sophie looked their adversary in the eye. 'Does this Guild train assassins?'

'Among other things.'

'You're employed by the Guild?' said Hugo.

'Not anymore.'

'You fired at us at Marble Arch?' said Freddy.

A curt nod.

Sophie's mouth had dried. She took a sip of water, her gaze not leaving Wells. The traveller could have murdered Mrs Alveston, but so could Wells. 'Were you behind the murders in Claridge's?' Sophie asked.

'I'm afraid so.'

Sophie exhaled, trying to keep calm.

'And the burglar who died?' asked Freddy.

'An employee.'

'And you poisoned our tea,' said Hugo.

'How did you detect the poison?' Wells' tone suggested genuine curiosity.

Sophie sensed Charlotte stiffening, tensing up another notch. 'We have an interest in poisons, and a keen sense of smell.'

'Are you acquainted with the lady who wears a knuckle-duster?' said Freddy.

Wells blinked, puzzled. 'Oh, her rings?' She cleared her throat. 'I apologise for her assault.'

'She was with her friends in Harrods,' said Sophie. 'They're into expensive jewellery.'

'They don't pay for it.' Wells' answer was deadpan.

Surprising. Those wealthy women had been shoplifters?

'I'm assuming you hired the men to attack us outside the pub?' said Hugo.

Another curt nod. 'Your security bands track the artefact but are unreliable.' Wells sounded certain.

'How do you know about our ... security band?' Sophie was acutely aware of the bracelet concealed under her sleeve.

Wells' lips thinned. 'How else would you have traced the artefact to the Elephant and Castle and not found it?'

'By artefact, you mean the summoning cylinder?' Freddy wanted to be sure.

'I do.'

'Why did you help us in the Langham?' said Hugo. 'Hit the traveller with the chair?'

'I need more information about the artefact.'

'Is that why you're speaking with us?' said Sophie.

Wells fixed her with a cold stare. 'I recently discovered who I'm working for.'

'I don't understand,' said Hugo. 'You must have agreed to ... deal with us when you were in Janus' ship.'

'Janus instructed me through a third party.' Wells scanned their faces. 'We have a common enemy.'

'You believe he won't hold up his end of the bargain.' Freddy's voice was impressively even.

Wells laughed, an ugly, humourless sound. 'If I complete the contract, he'll ensure my silence by proxy. If I don't, my fate will be the same.' She sounded resigned. A prisoner on the way to the gallows.

'He'll send an assassin to kill an assassin,' said Hugo.

'Quite.'

'You know where the cylinder is in the pub?' asked Freddy.

'I do,' said Wells.

Sophie's stomach churned more. 'Janus must be aware you're with us.'

'This isn't on his itinerary, nor was the kerfuffle in the Langham.' Wells' eyes flicked to Charlotte. 'But for the need to disable the agent, I'd have spoken to you then.'

'He's an agent?' said Hugo. 'In what organisation?'

Wells hesitated. Had she slipped up? 'I'm sure you can guess.'

The answer fell into place. 'He works for the Guild,' said Sophie. 'The Guild polices timelines.'

'How can the artefact end Janus?' asked Wells.

This was why she was here. She'd overheard their conversation in the Langham dining room with the agent. *There is a remote possibility that you could end Janus, and that cannot happen.*

'Did I misunderstand?' said Wells. 'If the artefact can't end him, I'll destroy it.'

Sophie gasped. 'You mustn't.'

'I must,' said Wells, 'or it'll be used to summon him.'

'The artefact can end him,' said Freddy.

'How?' said Wells. 'It's not a weapon. The smiting myths are just that. Myths. Tales from the Roman festivals that grew with the telling. Theatrical smiting of Janus' enemies.'

Smiting? The show in Rome had involved thunder and lightning, a blazing tenement block in the sky, and a memorable non-sentient Janus. There'd been no smiting. 'We're not familiar with the smiting myths,' said Sophie.

Wells shot her a sceptical glance. 'His walking staff breathes fire or turns creatures into stone.'

The festival-Janus they'd seen had been a soldier with a

sword. Maybe in other years, he'd worn a cloak and carried his walking staff?

'That would have made for an impressive display,' said Hugo.

Wells shrugged. 'The notion that Janus sees all fates except his own is also invented, based on a lost play.'

Myths were sometimes based on fact. 'I hope that idea's true,' said Sophie.

'Hope gets people killed,' said Wells. 'Are you relying on a fable about the artefact? Is that why you think it can end him?'

She was fishing for info. 'We won't share details,' said Sophie.

'Then this is down to me,' said Wells. 'One good deed before death stops by.'

Before she could stop herself, Sophie blurted, *'Because I could not stop for Death, he kindly stopped for me.'* The poem had lodged itself in her brain long ago. She'd thought it buried and forgotten but Wells' words had brought it back.

Wells clasped her hands on her lap. 'Emily Dickinson. Ironic that all her work will be published posthumously.'

A shared appreciation of a poem was a flimsy foundation for trust, yet the alternative was Wells destroying the cylinder. Sophie glanced at Hugo, Freddy, and Charlotte. 'A bargain?'

They all nodded.

'If you share Janus' itinerary,' said Sophie, 'we'll explain about the cylinder.'

'Do you have it with you?' asked Hugo.

'I do.' Wells made no move to hand it over.

'You're working for him,' said Hugo. 'We can't trust a thing you say.'

'I enjoy a challenge, but I'm not deranged. If you've had

dealings with him, you surely understand. You have no connection to my club so we should adjourn there.'

'Confirm to us you're no longer doing Janus' bidding,' said Freddy. 'Show us his itinerary.'

'I will, at my club. I've already tarried too long. He can't suspect we're talking.'

'Have you ever failed to complete a job before?' asked Hugo.

'My first private client was a vampire and lost his head. His death ended the contract, so I was free to walk away.'

What? A bizarre joke?

'The Albemarle Club is just along the street. Do you wish to be announced with your actual names or your pseudonyms?'

Hugo had been right. Their assumed names hadn't fooled Wells.

Freddy looked at the tablecloth. 'Our actual names.'

Wells stood up. 'Ask for Mrs Neal. I'll wait for an hour.' She glided out of the dining room.

Sophie watched her go, relief warring with curiosity.

Charlotte's furry face was solemn, as puzzled as her mistress.

Freddy exhaled. 'Such distinctive eyes. The same as Nice Wells.'

'But everything else is rather different,' said Hugo. 'Sorry, poor gallows humour.' He tapped his fingers on the table. 'A professional assassin rather than a novelist. I wonder how that happened?' Now they were momentarily safe, he was going down rabbit holes.

'It doesn't matter,' said Sophie. 'She's lying about her club. In the 19th century, private clubs in London were men-only.'

'She's not,' said Hugo. 'Well, not about that. The Albemarle was the first to admit both men and women. Scandalous at the time. And in a few years, it'll bear witness to the scandal that dooms Oscar Wilde. His affair with the Marquess of Queensberry's son.'

'Hugo, focus,' said Sophie.

Charlotte stood up, ready for action, and Freddy got to his feet. 'We can't let her destroy the cylinder.'

'She'll die if Janus doesn't.' Sophie stood up too. 'That's a basis for trust.'

'I could go ahead with the gun,' suggested Freddy.

Sophie grimaced. 'No way.'

Hugo left his seat and rested his hands on the back of his chair. 'Two things tip the balance. Without seeing it, we can't confirm her club isn't on the itinerary. *If* it isn't, then it's a location Janus has overlooked.'

Sophie squinted at him. 'And the second thing?'

'The vampire.'

'Please explain.' The shock of Wells turning up had frozen Sophie's brain.

'Except for a mission where her client apparently died,' said Hugo, 'Wells has a perfect record of completing her deadly contracts.'

'She invented the vampire,' said Sophie.

Hugo shrugged. 'The point is, if she's never walked away from a contract before, this is a hundred per cent unpredictable.'

Freddy hesitated. 'It could still be a trick, though one I can't fathom.'

Sophie gave him the pistol. He had the best aim.

CHAPTER 42

*I*t was still light, and during the two-minute walk from Brown's, Wells didn't show.

The entrance to the Albemarle Club had a modest burgundy awning over the front door, a discreet plaque, and one uniformed doorman. Freddy returned the pistol to his pocket.

'We're guests of Mrs Neal.' Freddy's voice was tight with tension, but the doorman gave him a courteous nod and gestured them inside.

As they stepped into the marble foyer, Sophie missed the weight of the weapon in her skirt and reached for Hugo's hand. His palm was cool against her skin, and she drew strength from his touch. Charlotte was walking so close, her fur was brushing against Sophie's gown.

Wells stood up from a burgundy sofa. 'Come this way.'

An attendant took the men's hats to a cloakroom, and they warily followed Wells into a deserted lounge lined with bookcases. Wells gestured at burgundy leather chairs around a walnut coffee table. Charlotte sat on the floor near her mistress and wiggled her nose, intrigued by the faint scent of cigars.

A waiter hovered.

'Brandy,' said Wells.

Everyone else demurred. No way were they going to relax like old friends.

'The club struggles to recruit and keep members as the food is poor,' said Wells. 'It's comfortable enough.'

'How long have you been, um, in your line of work?' asked Sophie. Keep her talking, assess her.

'I served the Guild for five years.' Wells drank some brandy. 'I left eighteen months ago.'

'Tell us about the Guild,' said Hugo.

'More indiscretion won't change my fate,' she muttered, almost to herself. 'The Guild was founded centuries ago in Babylon to stop individuals changing timelines.'

'How many agents are there?' said Sophie.

'I'm not sure. A lot.'

Sophie changed tack. 'We appreciated you helping Charlotte grab the heart-stopper.'

'How do you know about heart-stoppers?'

'We've seen the device before.' Freddy's answer was skilfully vague.

'The latest design can sustain a fair amount of damage without breaking,' said Wells. 'It's fortunate it didn't kill your dog.'

Charlotte looked at her front paws and Sophie gulped. Was that heart-stopper more advanced than the one in Rome? They'd dropped it down a drain. 'It's vulnerable to water?'

'Full immersion for more than a few minutes still breaks them.'

'The agent was an odd sort,' said Freddy. 'Gave us a formal warning.'

'Verbal notice before using lethal force is mandatory. A stupid protocol. Gets agents killed.'

'Is that why you left?' asked Hugo.

Wells swirled the alcohol in her glass. 'Partly.'

They were getting answers but not all the truth. 'You don't enjoy the work?' said Sophie.

'Sometimes.' Wells drank her brandy with no effort to be ladylike, taking hearty sips.

'You're aware the agent offered us safe passage,' said Hugo. 'Would he have kept his word?'

'If that was the assignment.'

Sophie bit her lip. If they'd known for certain the offer had been genuine, refusing it would have been even harder.

'Presumably, there are docking facilities for agents' ships here,' said Freddy.

'There's a designated area.'

'Where?' Hugo moved forward in his seat.

Wells hesitated. 'Not far from Marble Arch.'

'We were taken by surprise when the agent tried to kill us,' said Sophie. 'We changed a previous timeline, but he and his partner saved me from drowning.'

Wells shrugged. 'You couldn't have been the assigned target.'

'They destroyed the cylinder there,' said Freddy.

'Another summoning artefact?'

'Thrown in the river Tiber.' The cylinder sinking below the surface replayed in Sophie's head. 'Then the agent used his heart-stopper to paralyse us, not kill us.'

Wells' eyes flicked to her. 'As you weren't the target, you'd have been treated as an innocent.'

'How do you define an innocent?' said Hugo.

'It's a Guild term for bystander.' The corners of Wells' lips lifted in a bitter smile. 'Agents protect innocents when they can. The Guild mantras never leave you.'

Sophie pictured the agent's face as he'd taken the heart-stopper from his pocket. 'I don't think he wanted to kill us here. Once we'd declined his offer, he thought he had to.'

'He claimed other versions of us had accepted,' said Freddy.

'Have you met your other versions?' Hugo asked Wells. 'It must feel strange.'

'It's fatal. A paradox that shouldn't exist.'

'Do you know why?' said Hugo.

He was going down another rabbit hole, but Wells wasn't fazed. 'It's linked to something called quantum entanglement. All versions of the same individual, despite being in different universes, are connected. If two are in the same universe, and physically too close, the one who doesn't belong loses cohesion and is winked out of existence.'

Freddy grimaced. 'What a horrible theory.'

'It's more than a theory,' said Wells. 'I called on the other version of me to retrieve the artefact. I waited some distance away until he left. I was still too close.' She finished her brandy. 'I narrowly avoided being snapped into oblivion.'

Charlotte lay down, had decided Wells didn't pose an immediate threat. Sophie, though, wasn't sure. Wells' eyes were hard and so was her mouth. Too small for her face.

'A different version of me paid the down payment for the contract in my home universe,' said Wells, 'though where they acquired so much money, I've no idea.'

'Your version here has made a fortune playing the stock market,' said Hugo.

'He has no plans to cross universes again,' said Freddy.

'Sensible man.'

'Janus sent versions of you to kill us in ancient Rome,' said Hugo.

'Do tell. Forgive me, professional curiosity.'

Freddy summarised, including the released snakes and

their traumatic escape in the bathhouse. 'Presumably, other versions succeed or use other methods.'

Wells sat back in her chair. 'Or are executed by the Empire.'

'Empire?' said Sophie. Had she misheard? The only empire that came to mind was from *Star Wars*.

'Unauthorised outsiders are presumed to be spies,' said Wells.

'How is this Empire connected to ancient Rome?' Hugo asked her.

'If you were trying to steal an historical artifact, you must have been in an imperial universe. They were made by the Empire, for the Empire. I can't believe you don't know that.'

'We call it by a different name,' said Hugo. 'The builders, because they built Janus' ship.'

'Is this Empire around now, I mean in the 19th century?' said Sophie.

'Very much so.'

More info might tip the balance against Janus. 'Does the Guild work for the Empire?' asked Sophie.

Wells raised an eyebrow, evidently finding the suggestion absurd. 'In ancient times, the Guild looted Empire ships and equipment on a grand scale but the Respect Treaty put an end to that. The Empire retains exclusive jurisdiction in their universes and timelines. They're off-limits to the Guild and vice versa.'

'Medieval Georgia,' said Hugo.

Sophie met his gaze. That's why the Guild hadn't interfered when she'd wiped out the army. That universe had been off-limits.

'The agents in Rome must have been on a covert assignment,' said Wells, anticipating Sophie's next question. 'Off the books.'

'So, the Guild doesn't abide by the treaty?' said Freddy.

'It treads a fine line. If the Empire had caught the agents, the Guild would have disowned them.' Wells' sharp eyes studied him. 'When Imperial equipment is found outside the Empire, the Guild's obliged to return it. If that's impractical, dangerous artefacts are stored and guarded.'

'Why not just destroy them?' said Hugo.

'That happens if they pose an unmanageable threat. Otherwise, they're kept for academic study or historical interest. If new equipment is discovered and is of value, the Guild unofficially acquires it. That protects the Guild and the treaty. The research department has an asset to reverse engineer, and the Guild can deny all knowledge of the job, the equipment, and the agent.' She regarded them with a slight frown. 'How did you get involved in this?'

Hugo gave her a wry glance. 'It's a long story—'

A man in a formal dinner suit strode towards them. 'Mrs Neal. A vision to delight the heart.'

Sophie gaped. Oscar Wilde. She'd studied his plays at school.

Wells jumped to her feet. 'I'll only be a moment.' She guided a bemused Wilde out of the lounge, her arm through his.

CHAPTER 43

It was growing dark, and the Albemarle Club staff were closing curtains and lighting gas lamps on the walls. Sophie glanced at the lounge doorway where Wilde had hurried out with Wells. 'Oscar Wilde and Wells … are together?' How bizarre was that?

'I thought Mr Wilde, um, batted for the other side,' said Freddy.

'In our universe, he was gay or bisexual.' Hugo drove his hand through his hair. 'He married, had children. Here, he could be straight.'

'Or their friendship's an elaborate deception,' said Freddy, 'to put us off our guard.'

'I don't think so,' said Sophie. 'When he rocked up, Wells looked … concerned.' Wells surely cared for him.

Hugo drummed his fingers on the arm of his chair. 'Whatever this version of Wilde is like, we should warn him.'

'Wells is a dangerous woman,' said Freddy.

'She is, but that's not what I mean,' said Hugo. 'If we tell him about his future disgrace, he might avoid it—'

'She's back,' said Sophie.

Wells strode towards them. No sign of Wilde. 'Apologies. Where were we?'

'Can we speak with Mr Wilde?' said Hugo. 'We have information that might help him in the future.'

'He knows about his downfall.' Wells sat in the same chair.

'How can he possibly know?' said Sophie.

'Because I've warned him.' Wells took an envelope from her evening bag.

'Where has he gone?' asked Freddy.

'Home. He can't be part of this.' Wells smoothed out a letter on the coffee table, two pages side by side.

Sophie's breathing sped up. Places, dates, and times in neat copperplate handwriting. Their names, and Tesla, and locations they'd visited. She scanned down the list. The Albemarle Club wasn't there.

Hugo pointed at the final entry. '*Sunday 14 July, 9am, Thornbridge House, and noon at Marble Arch.*' He swallowed. 'That's tomorrow.'

Freddy paled. 'My great aunt's house.'

'The Thornbridge entry is based on an incorrect assumption,' said Wells. 'That after so many failed attempts, I'd use the weapon of last resort.'

'The heart-stopper,' said Freddy.

'Heart-stoppers are standard issue. The weapon of last resort boils blood. Nothing protects against it. You can't select targets within a group. All in its line-of-sight dies. Kills in a vile way. Female agents carry it, but as the nickname suggests, it's only used in dire need.'

Sophie felt sick, reliving medieval Georgia and the dying army. The metallic smell of blood, the screams... 'It's not a weapon you can control, and it doesn't work in all universes.'

Wells rummaged in her bag and brought out a small jewellery case. She snapped open the lid. Inside was a shiny red ball, the size of an egg. 'This channels and controls the ability to boil blood in any universe.' She closed the box and returned it to her bag. 'Once set, it cannot be fought or avoided.'

Charlotte whined, low in her throat. In medieval Georgia, when a woman from the Empire had enhanced Charlotte's DNA, the procedure had bestowed an ancillary benefit: Charlotte's blood couldn't be boiled. Was that rare or commonplace? Sophie shifted in her seat. 'The Empire has a way of protecting blood from boiling.'

Wells' chin jerked up. 'How do you know that?'

Sophie wasn't going to broadcast Charlotte's private medical details. 'Rumours.'

A line appeared between Wells' delicate brows. 'Agents swear an oath not to reveal that sort of detail.'

'I'm guessing the Guild stole the procedure from the Empire.' Hugo tapped the Thornbridge entry with his finger. 'If Janus expects you to boil our blood, you've used the weapon before.'

Wells stiffened. 'In extremis.'

Freddy's eyebrows shot up. 'When did you decide…' he hesitated, '…not to use it on us?'

'I have a problem with killing children and animals.' She made it sound like a weakness.

Charlotte stared at her.

'Your dog…' said Wells. 'He or she is unusual.'

Charlotte gave an almost imperceptible shake of her head. Wells continued to subvert their expectations, but Charlotte didn't entirely trust her. 'She's female,' said Sophie. 'Highly trained.'

Wells didn't probe further. She gestured at the letter. 'Only the most basic information.'

Freddy rubbed his chin. 'Janus is altering countless universes, the changes triggered by your versions' choices and ours. Everything is constantly changing. The less he told you, the more likely some facts would remain correct.'

Wells' brow puckered. 'The timings are diverging at a rate I haven't seen before.'

'The agent claimed Janus' meddling is causing timelines to fracture much more quickly,' said Hugo.

Wells swallowed, taking that in. She'd been on the far side of the foyer in Claridge's, hadn't overheard their second conversation with the agent.

'Could that be true?' asked Sophie. Once their sworn enemy, Wells might now be a reliable fact-checker.

'All worlds end, but after an unimaginably long time. The Guild monitors corrupted universes, though just for academic interest. That must have changed.' Wells' voice was flat, certain.

The end of worlds… Bella's universe could fold in on itself. Sophie's heart ached, constricted by a growing dread.

'A glowing spider's web is an early signal that a corrupted timeline is failing,' said Wells. 'I saw it two days ago. Have you seen it?'

'No.' Hugo wiped a bead of perspiration from his forehead. 'Why a spider's web?'

'It only resembles one. It's a crack in the fabric of time and space.'

'You learned this from the Guild?' Freddy's face was ashen.

'I have only a basic aptitude for science.'

Wells was surely manipulating them, but Sophie couldn't help warming to her.

'Do individuals without the gene see this web?' asked Hugo.

'Most creatures can.' Wells chewed her lower lip. 'The

web heralds the death of a timeline far in the future, or it used to…'

'Janus is sending versions of you to who knows how many universes,' said Freddy. 'Could that have distorted space-time?'

'The number of individuals who cross universes is inconsequential given the scale of, well, everything. However, my activities and the actions of the other versions have been steered by Janus for his own ends, with his foreknowledge. That could mean the corruption is localised.'

Hugo exhaled. 'If it's localised, what are the consequences?'

'For you, and everyone in this timeline, immeasurably better.' Wells shot him a weary glance. 'Only I wink out of existence.'

'I don't believe it's localised to you or your other versions,' said Freddy. 'The agent said all the fissures lead here, to us.'

Wells gripped the arm of her chair. 'Are you sure that's what he said?'

Freddy nodded.

'Other versions of you are searching for the artefact,' said Wells. 'Why do the fissures lead here?'

'We don't know,' said Hugo.

Reassured by Wells' directness, Sophie voiced an audacious idea. 'If we share details about the cylinder, will you help us end Janus?'

'With pleasure.'

Sophie looked to the others. Freddy and Hugo nodded. So did Charlotte.

'The cylinder has a repair function,' said Sophie. 'It remotely resets the builders' — the Empire's — ships. Puts them back to factory settings.'

Wells frowned. 'So?'

'Used on Janus' ship,' said Hugo, 'Janus would also revert to his original settings.'

'He'd no longer be sentient,' said Freddy, keeping his tone clipped and business-like.

Sophie clenched her fists, thinking of Bella. 'Basically, it would kill him.'

Wells froze, then unexpectedly laughed. A genuine laugh, redolent with delight and surprise.

Freddy's lips flattened into a grim line. 'We summon him, then reset him.'

Wells stopped laughing. 'Summon him? You can't be serious? A sentient Janus would—'

'Be horrific,' said Hugo.

'He'd only be summoned for a moment, before we reset him,' said Sophie.

'A moment is all he needs.' Wells' expression was stony. 'I'm missing something. You seem like rational people.'

Were they? Or were they teetering on the edge of logic, falling towards an impossible goal?

'The instant you summon him, you're dead,' said Wells. 'What could possibly be worth that?'

Wells just needed to know the gist. 'Keep it general,' said Sophie to Freddy, wanting him to explain. She was emotionally drained, couldn't find the words.

When Freddy hesitated, Hugo summarised how Janus had cut them off from Bella. 'With Janus gone, we can travel to her safely, and anywhere else.'

Wells looked down, her reaction unclear.

Surprised? Sceptical? Likely both.

Wells slowly returned the itinerary to its envelope and folded it into her bag. 'I'll meet you earlier than the designated time at Marble Arch. At eleven.' She stood up. 'And I'll bring the artefact.'

Sophie blinked at her, astounded. When had Wells

decided to hand it over? Sophie got to her feet and extended her hand. Wells accepted the handshake and shook hands with Hugo and Freddy.

'Before we work together…' Wells turned to Sophie. 'I need something in return.'

Sophie stepped back, wary again. 'What?'

'Your body armour.'

CHAPTER 44

That night, Sophie dreamed about the cylinder. In the depths of a pine forest, it stood upright on a frozen lake. The ice sparkled, and the reset button fired a pulsing emerald light into a black sky. Bella was skating on the lake in lazy circles, the skirt of her coat rippling in an invisible wind. This was an older Bella, carving loops with her skates, as if tempting the ice to crack.

Sophie's first waking thought wasn't of Bella but of the day ahead. Awareness, dread, then resolve. This could be their last day — in any universe.

Wells had been adamant that summoning Janus, far from ending him, would end them. Why had she agreed to hand over the cylinder? Shaken hands on it?

As Sophie slipped out of bed, firing erupted from outside the bedroom window. Marion.

Charlotte instantly woke up and leaped to her feet, and Hugo groaned. 'That's a bad alarm clock.'

Sophie kissed him. 'I'll miss it, and Marion.' She picked up her brooch from Rome. *Four souls forever bound by love*, the stallholder had said. Would they also be together in death? She hugged Charlotte who nestled in closer.

Hugo sat up in bed and rubbed his eyes. 'Do you remember from Rome the buttons' functions?'

'The middle one in the row summons him. Viewed from the front, where the cover opens, the first button does the reset.'

He met her gaze. 'I didn't think we'd get this far.'

'Now it's happening, it feels inevitable.'

'What did you quote at me when we were first stuck in Shorten? *Nothing is inevitable until it happens.*'

'Some historian said it.' Tears threatened and Sophie swallowed them.

Freddy came in, fully dressed. 'I couldn't sleep, thinking about Bella and Clarissa and dying universes.'

'Janus' meddling is already beyond reckless,' said Hugo. 'What if today he goes all in?'

Freddy swallowed. 'I can't imagine that.'

'We can't control what he does,' said Sophie. 'Just what we do.'

The others didn't respond. They didn't believe they could control fate. Any more than she did.

After breakfast, Sophie packed the carpet bag, set it down in the hall and pinned on her hat.

'I so want Wells to bring the cylinder,' said Freddy, 'I've made myself believe she will.'

'For a price.' Sophie wasn't wearing her body armour. It was in the bag.

Freddy took his hat from the stand. 'How things change in 24 hours. I'll regret Wells' demise.'

'Not as much as ours.' Hugo put on his hat.

Hugo's dry wit would survive to the end. Sophie bent down and snuggled Charlotte again. 'You could stay here?' Charlotte's dismissive harrumph was so loud it echoed off the walls.

'I should keep the pistol,' said Freddy.

'Only the cylinder can kill Janus,' said Hugo.

Freddy squared his shoulders. 'If the worst happens, we have enough bullets to send us into oblivion.'

Sophie tensed. 'Don't think like that.'

Freddy gave her a determined stare.

The bracelet pinged and the dot was clear on Sophie's mental map. 'It's outside the Elephant and Castle.' Would Hattie deliver on her promise?

Marion and Miss Harris came out of the drawing room. Marion's rich green gown looked fabulous with her red hair. She leaned on the ebony cane and smiled.

How wonderful. She'd come out of mourning. As Sophie focused on Marion, the map shrank to the side of her vision and the disorientation lessened. Sophie sighed. It would have been easier if she'd discovered that trick earlier.

'Are you sure you won't take the gun bag?' asked Marion.

'If we fail,' said Freddy, 'no number of guns will help.'

'I so wish I could come with you,' said Marion. 'You mustn't trust this Wells person.' They'd told her what they'd arranged, and Marion had shared every detail with the servants. While Marion believed them, Miss Harris and Mr Burgess thought their 'interesting business' just a fanciful story to keep Marion amused.

Freddy kissed his great aunt on the brow.

'Before you go,' she said, 'I'm confused about something.'

Unsurprising. The turnaround with Wells had been a lot to process.

'Your daughter is lost, far away,' said Marion to Freddy,

'but the child's mother...' She gestured at Sophie. 'She's not married to you.'

'The situation is ... unconventional,' said Freddy. 'Um, I was previously married to Mrs Harrington.'

Marion appeared to accept this, though if 1889 was like Shorten, divorce was almost unheard of. Would she have been shocked by the truth? It still shocked Sophie, and she'd been there. That long ago night, believing they had hours to live, she and Freddy had seized the moment... She'd regretted it terribly afterwards — until Bella came along. She could never regret Bella.

'I shall pray for you,' said Marion.

'We appreciate that,' said Hugo.

Marion's prayers would probably fly into a void, but someone might hear. Sophie concentrated on the small map in her head, and it jumped to full size. 'The cylinder hasn't moved from outside the pub.'

The butler strode into the hall, his eyes on Marion's green dress. 'Your outings have improved Miss Lacey's mood.'

The maid gave Sophie a heartfelt smile.

Today, the smog was a faint grey cloud, obscuring roofs and the tops of trees. Above it, the sky was a sumptuous duck-egg blue. Which was lucky. Even a drop of drizzle would have done for the cylinder. The map in the corner of Sophie's mind vanished. 'Hopefully, Wells is on a bus or in a cab, heading this way.'

Sophie strode with Charlotte towards Hyde Park and Marble Arch, flanked by Hugo and Freddy, and her heart began to race. *All worlds end, but after an unimaginably long time. That must have changed.* What was happening in the

Shorten universe? At home? She was struggling to focus. Would Wells honour their agreement?

Charlotte was prowling, scanning the road, and Sophie's brain kept racing. *Janus' meddling is already beyond reckless. What if today he goes all in?* If Janus realised Wells was betraying him, would he send another assassin?

They reached Marble Arch. It was deserted, most people at church. The coal smell was stronger, the smog blurring tree blossom at the edge of the park. As they approached the fountain, something bright glittered. Fear hollowed out Sophie's stomach. On the basin was a beautiful, multi-coloured web. The park and the bird song receded, and her fear fell away, replaced by a blissful longing. She walked in a daze towards it.

But it vanished, and so did the longing, leaving a terrible emptiness. Sophie gazed around the park, hearing again the chatter of the birds. She'd forgotten where she was. 'No.'

'What?' asked Freddy.

'A glowing web.' Hugo was less than a pace from where it had been. So close to touching it…

Charlotte was further away. 'Did you see it?' Sophie asked her. Charlotte shook her head.

Sophie cautiously felt the basin. A real spider would have left traces of its silk. 'Just as Hattie described it.'

'Since when are we calling her Hattie?' said Hugo.

'Since now,' said Sophie, thinking of Marion, and Tesla, and everyone on the planet. 'We really are in this together.'

Hugo grimaced. 'Even if we succeed with Janus, we may be doomed anyway.'

Sophie chewed her lip. 'We might still have time.'

'If Miss Wells doesn't honour our agreement, we should return to Thornbridge,' said Freddy. 'Take everyone into Juno. Perhaps between universes we could be alright.'

Sophie didn't reply. A slow end in Juno would be worse.

CHAPTER 45

Half an hour after they arrived at Marble Arch, Sophie's bracelet chimed, and the map appeared. The cylinder was near the park. A moment later, Hattie marched towards them, her frilled purple skirt swaying with each step. In her arms was what could be the cylinder, wrapped in a tartan blanket. Sophie's heart swelled with hope.

'Apologies for the delay,' said Hattie. 'The cab didn't wait. I had to borrow one from the workshop.' She offered the bundle to Freddy, and he parted the blanket, peeked inside, and closed it. Then he cradled it like he'd once cradled Bella.

Sophie focused on Freddy and the map shrank. On impulse, she tapped the gemstone and the map vanished. Great. Only now had she figured it all out.

She took the body armour from her bag and handed it over. Hattie strode away, disappearing behind an oak tree, presumably to put it on. Freddy stood the cylinder on the grass where the ground was level and Sophie removed the blanket. Underneath the ball cover, the grey buttons were spaced in a triangle, not a line. Sophie gasped in dismay.

Freddy's mouth worked but no words came out. Charlotte gave a low whine, seemed to shrink.

Sophie put an unsteady hand to her brow. 'It's not the same cylinder.'

'It's the same walking stick,' said Hugo.

'The buttons are different.' Freddy described it, despair cracking his voice. 'We don't know which button does what.'

They should have anticipated this. They knew from Rome that cylinders were upgraded, changed.

Hattie was hurrying back. She registered their expressions and tensed.

'Even if we guess right with the summoning button,' said Sophie, 'we could hit the wrong one next and return him. I'd have to summon him again before resetting him.'

Hattie's face was pale under her purple hat. She gestured at the fountain. 'Destroy it.'

In response, Charlotte pointed to the edge of the park and made a 'let's go over there' gesture. Hattie did a double take.

'Out of range, we might puzzle this out without summoning him,' said Freddy.

'Do you know what the range is?' asked Hattie.

Sophie pictured the country lane in Shorten. 'If it's the same as calling the ship, about a hundred yards.'

Freddy picked up the cylinder and Sophie covered it with the blanket. They hurried across the grass and through the trees. Beyond the road, they turned right, and paused beside a four-storey building, the arch out of sight.

While Freddy kept the cylinder steady, Sophie opened the blanket, then the cover. 'Could the summoning button be at the top?' she said. 'More important than the others?'

'It's an equilateral triangle. There is no top.' Freddy hesitated. 'It's only the top as in "further away" when the cover opening lip is facing us.'

On the previous model, the buttons had flashed when they were pressed. Red for summoning, black to return him. In Sophie's dream, the reset button had been emerald. The festival firework letters in Rome had been green.

'Waiting for inspiration isn't going to help.' Hugo walked a few steps to monitor the arch.

Deep breath. Sophie touched the button at the top of the triangle and it pulsed orange. 'A new colour.' She swore under her breath.

Charlotte stood on her hind legs to see the buttons, resting her front paws on her mistress' arm. Like regular dogs, Charlotte distinguished between variations of yellow, so could see orange. Dogs saw black, white, grey, and blue, but not red or green.

'You weren't expecting orange?' Hattie was even paler.

'Any unchanged colours may lead us astray,' said Freddy. 'The functions could have been reallocated.'

Sophie struggled to keep calm. 'Is anything happening at the arch?' she called.

'No.' Hugo's voice was wobbly with relief.

Sophie touched the button on the bottom left. It pulsed blue, matching the intense summer-blue of the sky.

'Anything different?' yelled Freddy to Hugo.

'No.'

Sophie tapped the last button, and it flashed white. 'Now?'

Hugo strode back. 'No change.'

Freddy stared at the triangle. 'All new colours.'

'This is Russian roulette,' said Hugo.

Freddy squinted at him. 'A card game?'

Hugo shook his head. 'Not a game. There are six chambers in a gun barrel. Just one has a bullet. The bad guy spins the barrel, a chamber's selected, and the gun's pointed at a victim. When the trigger's pulled, if there's a bullet in the chamber, it fires.'

'I've never used a weapon that worked in that way,' said Hattie, presumably thinking of her futuristic pistol.

'If the chamber was empty and the bad person re-spins the barrel, the odds don't change,' said Freddy. 'But after we press the first button, our odds are better.'

Sophie grimaced. She was rubbish at maths and in times of high stress she had brain freeze.

'The odds change to one in two,' said Freddy. 'Fifty per cent.'

'Not helping,' said Sophie. 'It'll be a guess.'

'I've nothing left to lose.' Hattie's tone was measured and calm, her resignation — and resolve — impressive.

And in Sophie, shaky with fear, another emotion surfaced.

Envy.

CHAPTER 46

*B*ack in the park near the arch, the mist was fainter, the sun brighter, and Sophie shaded her eyes. Don't think about Bella. Keep in the moment.

Freddy set up the cylinder. Hattie stayed behind him, her attention on the arch, and Charlotte determinedly sniffed the ground beside Hugo. Right in front of them, a girl wearing a skimpy animal skin appeared from nowhere. She bared her teeth. Charlotte growled and Hugo staggered in shock. The girl vanished.

Different parts of the timeline were connecting, beginning to merge. How long before they were torn into atoms? Sophie flipped up the cover and her finger hovered over the top button. 'Orange might be connected with the arch flashing gold, the colour when he was summoned in Rome.'

Freddy hesitated. 'The white button could be neutral? Perhaps the reset button?'

'For me, white means purity and also death, like lilies at funerals,' said Sophie. 'That's a sort of reset—'

'The meaning that societies attach to colours varies hugely,' said Hugo. He addressed Hattie. 'Do you know the Empire's favourite colours? What those colours symbolise?'

'It probably doesn't help, but all their artefacts are grey.'

'Their research teams live in white buildings,' said Freddy. 'If they find white comforting, it wouldn't symbolise a ship not working properly.'

'I'm not sure,' said Sophie. The interior of the builders' headquarters in Georgia and Rome had suggested little interest in aesthetics, including colours.

'Hugo, look out!' yelled Freddy.

Hugo whirled around, too late to avoid a woman in a pink gown and powdered wig barging into him, her made-up face creased with alarm. The next instant, she disappeared.

A low, metallic hum cut through the air, and there was a buzzing sound. A swarm of bees? Sophie recoiled in shock. A soldier in camouflage fatigues was desperately scrambling, fleeing from an enormous insect. No, not an insect—

'It's a drone!' shouted Hugo. 'There's nowhere to hide. Move!'

But before Sophie could react, the soldier collided with her. As she fell, he stared, his jaw slack with surprise. Something violently shoved him on top of her, and he screamed. The scream snapped off. He and the drone were gone.

Sophie got to her feet. Her dress was wet, splattered with the soldier's blood. Nausea rose up and she swallowed hard. The timeline's splintering and merging was speeding up. She looked with increasing panic at the triangle. Orange button at the top. Bottom left, the blue button, white on the right…

Hit the button. Any button—

Clang. The arrival bell.

Sophie jumped, her finger an inch from the orange button. 'I didn't touch it!'

A green door filled the main arch. Just as Janus' ship had

camouflaged itself in the students' union, appearing as a lift, this door was huge and mock-gothic Victorian.

Rattling. The door swung open.

Hattie scanned the deserted park. 'Who summoned him?'

'No one,' Hugo gasped. 'He's got around the algorithm. Run!'

Freddy grabbed the cylinder and blanket and everyone sprinted.

Sophie was panting hard before she reached the edge of the park. Running in a corset wasn't getting any easier. Charlotte lay down and everyone else hid behind the nearest tree. It would make no difference. The master of time would know where they were.

Voices came from the arch and Sophie risked a peek past the trunk. Men in suits and bowler hats and women in bustle gowns were spilling out of the green door like a crowd from a stadium.

Hattie swayed on her feet. 'They're me! They're all me!' The men were the same height with identical faces. The women were shorter and had Hattie's face. Some carried umbrellas. All carried pistols. More and more of them jostled through the door, filling the park.

'Dear God,' said Freddy.

'How can they all be here?' said Hugo. 'Why aren't they winking out of existence?'

'I don't know.' Hattie leaned back against a tree trunk, her breathing shallow. 'I don't feel any pull towards them which is … impossible.'

Freddy gave Sophie the cylinder and blanket and cocked his pistol. Charlotte let rip a deep growl, preparing for attack, but Sophie was transfixed, unable to look away from the surreal scene. Some versions of Wells were shouting instructions, others were gesticulating, a few were screaming. And still more were striding out, elbowing into the crowd.

The arch glitched. Disappeared and reappeared.

'Janus must be delaying the timeline's collapse, sustaining the paradox.' Hattie extracted two pistols from her skirt pockets. The weapons were a conventional shape but entirely smooth with no visible trigger. 'He surely can't keep control for long.'

As if they'd heard her, the other versions of Wells went silent, and as one they turned towards the tree line. No leaves rustled and there was no birdsong. Fear soured Sophie's throat. She tightened her grip on the cylinder.

'There's too many,' said Hugo.

They sprinted down the street, trying to flag down a cab, but none stopped. Behind them, versions of Wells appeared by the trees. Hattie crossed the road, narrowly avoiding a speeding carriage, and her companions followed. When Freddy's hat tumbled off, he didn't pause.

They ran on. The first of the pursuing pack careered onto the road, stopping the traffic. Hattie took aim over her shoulder and fired.

'What are you doing?' said Sophie. 'They're you!'

'They're in hock to Janus,' said Hattie. 'They're not me.'

While Freddy took pot shots, Sophie clutched the cylinder to her chest. In the lead, Hattie veered right, cutting down a side street. Her ship wasn't far from Marble Arch. Could she escape in it? Could they? If they could leave the lynch mob and this universe, they'd still have the cylinder.

Hattie darted down another road, going north of the arch. Sophie kicked harder, though her lungs were bursting. Her heart pounded in her ears and a different pounding came from up ahead. The Guild agent was on horseback in his town suit, galloping towards them like a spectre through the mist. He shot at Hattie but protected by the body armour, she didn't falter. She returned fire.

The horse reared, throwing off the agent, who landed with a thump. He lay there, not moving. The horse neighed and trotted off.

'Is he dead?' yelled Sophie. She wasn't going to stop to check.

'He'll have been wearing armour,' Hattie shouted. 'Though the fall might have killed him.'

The pursuing crowd was baying and firing, and Sophie did a hasty check on Hugo, Freddy, and Charlotte. A miracle they hadn't been shot.

They'd circled the park and were now back on grass, the arch to the south. From the clear sky, thunder boomed, deafeningly loud, and the ground shook with a deep roar. Sophie stumbled, and the blanket fell off the cylinder. A putrid smell swamped her mouth and nostrils. Cloying and dense, it seeped through her clothes into her skin. Decay and death and despair. Daylight faded and screaming erupted from the mob. Something massive was blotting out the sun.

Janus was standing over the Marble Arch monument. Towering above the park and the surrounding roads and buildings, his ankles were higher than the arch. He'd planted his massive, sandalled feet on either side of the monument, crushing versions of Wells who'd recently emerged from the door. Other versions had plunged into twenty-foot-wide fissures snaking along the grass.

In one hand, Janus held a grey key. His other hand was on his staff. He slammed down the base of the staff, killing more versions of Wells. His grey cloak swirled, casting everything beneath it into darker shadow. His head was far higher up, but so large, his features were clear. An old face with a silver beard and flowing hair, yet his eyes were missing, just ragged black holes.

Anger tore into Sophie's brain, ancient and malevolent, deforming neurons, tearing the nerve cells inside out. Black was white. Facts were lies. Love was hate.

They were tiny compared to him. Pathetic. Pointless. Nothing mattered. Not them. Not Bella. No one.

'He's playing with our minds,' shouted Hattie. 'Shut him out and run!'

Sophie hadn't registered she'd stopped. Hugo was lying curled up, blocking his ears. She hauled him to his feet. 'Run!' she yelled. Freddy was already sprinting. So was Charlotte.

Hattie was nearing a dense group of trees. 'My ship's over there.' She reached the grove and was lost to sight.

Sophie's lungs were hurting so badly, she couldn't breathe, but she kept going. A hundred yards to the trees. Ninety—

Fire blasted from Janus' staff. The gloom around them sparked and lit up, an intense orange light that stung Sophie's eyes. Leaves on the trees up ahead calcified and the trunks became stone. The grass turned white. The grove was silent, dead.

No. Hattie was in there!

Her mind numb, Sophie skidded and changed direction, skirting the spectral trees. She took a frantic breath, and though it was futile, she ran faster. Behind her came the sound of cracking stone — branches breaking under their own fossilised weight.

Janus' giant key glowed.

'I AM THE END.'

His voice didn't just carry through the air. It drilled into bone. Vibrations shattered through Sophie's skull, jarring her teeth. Hugo grabbed her hand and Charlotte howled. The sound ripped into Sophie's heart.

The ground cracked and a chasm opened. Charlotte and Freddy were on the other side. There was no time to think, to assess the risk. Sophie and Hugo launched themselves across the gap. Their feet scraped at the far edge, struggling for purchase. They threw themselves forward. Sophie twisted to fall on her back, clasping the cylinder on her front, her heart thumping. The cylinder couldn't smash. Their last chance…

Stupid! Stress had shredded her brain. No risk of summoning him. He was here. She flicked up the transparent cover and hit the top orange button.

Nothing happened.

That must summon him. She pressed the white button on the right. Nothing. The returning button? Had he got around that—

Janus stamped his staff, and Sophie was engulfed in pain. Fire invaded her body, searing her bones and skin from the inside out. Her throat blistered, and she tasted heated blood as it poured from her mouth. Janus was burning her, burning everyone.

She fell to her knees, clutching the cylinder. Blood flowed from her nose, and she writhed, the cylinder rolling out of her arms as she vainly tried to protect herself with her hands. Hugo was sprawled, holding his head, blood coursing through his fingers. Freddy was next to him. Where was Charlotte? Sophie threw herself down between Hugo and Freddy. Being with them was important, but she couldn't remember why, thought dissolving as the pain and heat tore through her. A single image remained in her brain. The frozen lake and Bella skating…

The lake shattered, every shard of ice a stab of fire.

Four souls, forever bound by love. An unfamiliar voice cleaved through the agony, and a blur moved through the thick, red haze.

Falling, emptiness… The pain retreated, like a wave drawing back into the sea, and Sophie's terror faded too. Her lungs pulled in air that was soiled with filth and smoke, and she coughed and spluttered.

She managed to kneel and slowly, the crimson haze blurring her vision cleared. Charlotte was lying on her front beside the cylinder, one paw under the cover. *Blue button.*

Sophie tried to take it in. Had Charlotte pressed the last button? Had it worked? Had it reset Janus?

The sky was just as red, and the colossal Janus had a new, scarlet tinge. His massive head tilted — a flat disc, not a face.

Then he was gone.

The multitude in the park vanished. Wiped away in the blink of an eye.

Breathe. Sophie staggered to her feet. Everything hurt but that meant she was alive.

Hugo and Freddy were helping each other stand up. They were okay. They were okay.

The red sky was lighter, the sun shining.

Charlotte tapped the cylinder's lid, and it closed with a click. *Like my page-turning machine.*

Sophie's tongue hurt to talk, but she whispered, 'You saved us.'

He forgot about my protected blood.

Sophie hugged Charlotte with weak arms and trembled with relief and gratitude.

Charlotte's blood couldn't be boiled, even by a god.

CHAPTER 47

*P*olice officers ran down the road towards Marble Arch. Traffic was at a standstill, and they'd been forced to abandon their cabs.

In the park, birds who'd survived the onslaught were squawking, perched on calcified branches. The scarlet sky had faded to pink, and the grey smog was back, a welcome ragged band above the tree line. Within the central arch of the monument, the green door of Janus' ship was open, as if waiting for the many versions of Wells. But none were left and with so many unnatural paradoxes resolved, the life cycle of this timeline might be slowing, staving off the end. Nature on a grand scale restoring balance.

Charlotte and the upgraded cylinder had saved them. On the previous model, Charlotte would have seen the black button, not the red. And if the old reset button had been green or pink, invisible colours to her, she'd have had to remember it was the first button in the line when viewed from the front. That delay could have killed them. Sophie pulled her close.

We did it!

Speaking still hurt. Sophie croaked, 'Charlotte, you did it.' They high fived.

'Is Charlotte talking?' Hugo's blood-shot eyes shone with relief and joy.

Sophie nodded. 'Even though the danger's over.'

'It's over?' Hugo blinked, as if noticing her for the first time.

Freddy patted Charlotte. 'I hope talking's permanent.'

Sophie dearly hoped this was forever, changing … everything. She thought of Charlotte as her baby, yet whenever Charlotte spoke, she revealed more of her personality and her confidence. She was all grown up.

'Charlotte, can you read my thoughts?'

I don't need to. What you don't say, I can see on your face.

Sophie hugged her again. Hugo and Freddy joined in the hug and for a long silent moment they stood together, savouring the moment. They'd survived. And soon, they'd be united with Bella. Sophie hardly dared believe it. Then she caught sight of the spectral grove. 'We should pay our respects to Hattie.'

They trooped back to the trees, dreading what they'd find. Lying on the white earth around the grove were smashed stone birds, fallen from the sky. On stiff branches, bird statues silently faced the park, calcified with the trees. Inside the grove, scattered on ashy dust, were more pieces of birds.

Sophie scrunched up her eyes, thankful the gruesome graveyard didn't include Hattie.

'Perhaps her ship wasn't too near the trees,' said Freddy.

They hurried through the grove and peered out the other side. White soil gave way to scorched dirt, then to brown grass that just looked parched. No ship. And no building or object that could be part of its camouflage, like the rundown shed inside Juno's arch in Rome.

Charlotte snuffled at the ground, then sniffed the air. *No barrier.* She could smell the system that concealed the Empire's bases and if Hattie's ship was using a similar mechanism, Charlotte would know.

Freddy gestured at the open space. 'If her ship had turned to stone, the cloaking system would surely have failed.'

By the slimmest of margins, Hattie must have survived, escaping to another universe.

They retraced their steps. Sophie's brooch fell off and she picked it up. The fastening pin had broken. She trailed her forefinger along one of the gold lines stretching out from the centre. *Four souls, forever bound by love.* 'When Charlotte saved us, I swear I heard the stallholder who gave me this. Apparently, she was a seer.'

'I think seers were more than fortune tellers,' said Hugo. 'I can't remember what else they did.'

Sophie pocketed the brooch, keen to keep it safe. 'Could it have helped Charlotte press the button?'

Hugo raised his eyebrows.

'The mind can play tricks under stress,' said Freddy. 'My brain feels as if it's made of treacle.'

They reached the cylinder lying on its side, the grey casing flattening the grass, and Freddy retrieved it. Sophie found her faithful carpet bag, though not the blanket.

Charlotte snuffled at a tuft of grass. *Smells better.*

'No sign of the Guild agent,' said Hugo.

'Escaped in his ship like Hattie.' Sophie patted Charlotte. 'You couldn't have done this without her.'

Sophie paused, taking in the tranquil park. So much for the agent's apocalyptic ravings. 'Bella, here we come!'

Freddy coughed up flecks of blood. 'We should clean up first.'

Charlotte was her regular dapper self. Everyone else could have been extras in a horror film. They went to the fountain and rinsed their faces and hands. The water was pure and cold and energising. Sophie's dress was splattered red but washing their clothes would have to wait. She turned. Two police officers were walking towards them. Time to go.

They jogged to the arch. As they stepped through the door, Sophie held Hugo's hand and said his name. They were in the musty wine cellar Nice Wells had fallen into. Sophie put down her bag.

Charlotte sniffed. *We should ask to go to Shorten. If his voice hasn't changed, we should leave.*

Sophie gulped. 'Charlotte thinks Janus might still be here.' The prospect of safe passage to Bella was wonderful. Maybe too wonderful?

Freddy kept hold of the cylinder and eyed the exit. 'I don't want to say his name, though I suppose I have to. Janus, shut the door.'

'Door shutting.' The voice from the ship was crisply British and monotone.

Compliant, and not a hint of personality. Sophie exhaled. 'That was promising.'

The gothic door swung shut, making the same rattling noise as the lift doors. The sound effect was stuck on one setting.

'Could it be a trick?' said Freddy.

Sophie folded her arms. 'Janus, show us the real exit.'

'This is the real exit,' said the androgenous, expressionless voice. A rectangular metal panel appeared and slid open, heavy and functional like an aeroplane door. After a few seconds, it slid shut.

The voice had less modulation than bots at home. Too expressionless? A clever hoax? Sophie cast about for a test to prove Janus had truly gone. 'This ship is more advanced than Juno, even after the reset?'

Freddy nodded. 'Built after Juno.'

If the ship had no agenda, it should change its rules on request. 'Janus, answer Hugo Harrington as you would me,' said Sophie. 'Do this on every crossing.'

'Done.'

'Janus, please allow Hugo Harrington to summon you,' said Freddy, 'and let him see you when you land.'

'Unable to comply.'

'Explain why,' said Freddy.

'That security protocol cannot be overridden.'

'I can live with that.' Hugo grinned. 'The core security algorithms are still in place.'

Sophie welcomed an intense, heady relief. How had they managed it? How had they cheated fate?

'Janus, show the real ship,' said Hugo.

'This is the real ship.'

The cellar vanished, replaced by a bigger cargo bay than Juno's, the roof twice as high. Racks and boxes stretched into the distance.

Freddy laid the cylinder on the floor and took the destination note from his trouser pocket. 'Janus, take us to Universe 422, variant ending 2394488655667.'

'Preparing.'

'Janus, cancel the destination,' said Hugo.

'Done.'

'What are you doing?' asked Sophie. Had Hugo's promotion from pet status gone to his head?

'Juno randomly selected our Shorten destination for the other versions of you, Charlotte, and Freddy. The ones that didn't make it.' Hugo playfully jabbed Freddy in the chest. 'We should identify the precise universe where you were born.'

Freddy did a sceptical face. 'How can we do that?'

'Janus, do you have a record of our DNA?' said Hugo.

'No.'

The ship's record of their crossings had been wiped. Further confirmation Janus was dead. Not sentient in any universe. A new wave of relief. Whenever evil had been kept at bay at home, defeating the Nazis in World War Two, or free nations fighting off other tyrants at a terrible cost, those victories were only won in that universe. In others, a spectrum of outcomes still played out, in the past, the present and the future. Yet Janus was dead in all of them. Forever.

But Hugo was frowning. 'Earth to Hugo,' said Sophie.

He did a 'go with this' gesture. 'Janus, can you analyse our DNA?'

'Yes.'

'Analyse Freddy Lacey's DNA and match it with the universe where he was born.' Hugo crossed his fingers.

'Preparing … done.'

Hugo grinned again and took his notebook and pencil from his jacket pocket. 'Janus, confirm the core number of that universe and the variant's last designation numbers.'

'Universe 422, designation 9686778786812.'

Charlotte stared at Hugo. *I love you.*

'Janus, select that universe,' said Hugo.

Just seconds later, the heavy door slid open. Outside was the lane. Shorten.

'Janus,' said Hugo, 'how long—'

'Relax.' Sophie embraced him. 'We don't need to know.' However long the crossing had taken, her eyes and throat — her whole body — felt fine. The ship had healed her and kept the illusion of instant travel. 'Go with it.'

Beyond the exit was the thick trunk of the oak. Circling its base, half covered in snow, were rotting leaves, blown into a ring by the wind. Beyond the tree, under a pale cloudy sky, was the lane and the tall, bay hedge.

'No more adventures.' Sophie stepped out, her breath a ragged cloud drifting off to join the morning mist. Charlotte bounded forward and peed on the Janus stone. Yes, she'd changed, but she was still a dog.

They'd commissioned the stone to help accidental travellers. The arrow underneath Janus' symbol — two youthful faces — showed the way to the Manor. Beside the tip was a friendly face, like an emoji.

Hugo and Freddy drew deep breaths, relishing the fresh air, while Sophie shivered in her Victorian summer dress. She'd be even colder in her shorts and T-shirt. Her fingers tightened on the handle of the carpet bag. The hike to the Manor wouldn't be fun.

She turned back to the oak, checking for the oval opening near the base that resembled a fairy door. Despite believing it silly, she touched it for luck.

Stamping her feet, she strode towards the road, trying to warm up. Then stopped. The tarmac was sandy brown, not black. 'The tarmac's a different shade.'

'Be specific,' said Hugo. 'For me, it's all faded colours.' Without the gene, that's how he saw Shorten.

'It's definitely brown,' said Freddy.

Charlotte crept close to the road, her body low, alert to a potential threat. She extended a paw and touched the tarmac. *Not as dark*. To her, brown was muted black.

Carrying the cylinder under his arm, Freddy bent down to see better. 'Can it hurt us?' he asked Charlotte.

She shook her head.

'It needed resurfacing,' said Sophie. The lane had loads of potholes.

They set off along the road. As they rounded the bend, they came to a pothole. The lane hadn't been resurfaced. 'What's tarmac made from?' Sophie asked Hugo, confident he'd know.

'Sand and crushed rock, stuck together by crude oil. The

oil comes from heat and pressure acting on organic remains over millions of years.'

'So, tarmac's naturally black?' said Sophie.

'Until now,' said Hugo, 'in this universe.'

Freddy looked nervously up the lane. 'Many timelines must have sustained some sort of corruption.'

'I assumed it would directly affect humans,' said Hugo, 'but we've only existed for a fraction of the planet's history.'

Sophie's thoughts flitted to her parents. They didn't know about Bella. Convinced she wouldn't survive 1889, Sophie hadn't wanted to leave them with two loved ones to mourn.

Hugo bent and felt the tarmac. 'Same texture.' He straightened. 'Perhaps Shorten got off lightly.'

Please let Bella be okay. And please let home be the same. Sophie's parents … she couldn't live through losing them again—

'If even half of what the Guild agent told us was true,' said Hugo, 'it'll have its work cut out in a shedload of universes.'

A lurch of guilt. Sophie ignored it. They hadn't trashed time and space. Janus had.

Freddy bit his lip. 'The agent claimed corrupted timelines shift backwards or forwards. What year is this?'

'We set up the Janus stone recently,' said Hugo. 'If there's been a time shift, it'll be into the future.'

Sophie's stomach turned over. Bella could be grown up, elderly, or dead. No. Not after everything they'd been through.

Charlotte pawed the road. *Horse poo and petrol.*

Sophie told the others what Charlotte could smell. 'That's a 1920's combo.'

'This is a rural lane,' said Hugo. 'At home, people still ride horses for pleasure.'

'So, it could be the 1920s,' said Freddy, his face grim. 'Or a century later.'

CHAPTER 48

Shorten Manor's ironwork gates were open, and Sophie stared up the gravel drive at the house. Rebuilt.

'It looks the same as before the fire,' said Hugo.

Stone-framed mullioned windows, the crenellated roof, Elizabethan gables, and later extensions. Resplendent, like a defiant phoenix. Sophie flexed her feet, aching from the chilly trek up the lane. When had this house been finished? A few weeks back, or a hundred years ago?

'It's all right!' Freddy pointed at a fledgling Virginia Creeper at the bottom of a gable.

Recently planted, it would be years before the shrub covered the wall, resembling its predecessor. You could make buildings appear old, but you couldn't fake nature.

Sophie threw her arms around Hugo, and Freddy and Charlotte joined in the hug.

'Home.' Freddy's voice resonated, as warm as the hug.

Then he stepped away, his face sombre. 'Somewhere, there's a universe where my father isn't dead.' Richard Lacey had been shot on this drive by a militiaman. Freddy took a shuddering breath. 'If there is such a universe, what other things would be different?' Charlotte leaned against his legs.

'Finding the right universe could take the rest of your life,' said Hugo.

Sophie had loved Richard. She loved Freddy right now. 'Your father would want the best for you,' she said, 'Being happy with Bella and Clarissa.'

Freddy wiped his eyes.

Closer to the house, an unfamiliar gardener paused his weeding and stared at them. Charlotte in her dog coat, not to mention their blood-stained Victorian clothes, were a strange sight. A new bridge straddled the moat, leading to a smart front door, and beside the door was a drawbridge, currently unused. Handy if things went south again. The previously murky water in the moat was incredibly clear and clean, home to a family of ducks, while the gardens were tidy, waiting for spring.

Freddy rang the shiny bellpull, and Sophie caught her breath in a flurry of nerves. Would Bella even remember them?

Maud Watkins, Sophie's former lady's maid, opened the door. Her black dress was shorter, way above her ankles, and her hair was bobbed. Not so long ago, Maud had been scandalised by women cutting their hair. She gawped at them.

'What date is it?' Freddy asked in a rush.

Maud pulled herself together. '24th November, Sir.'

'What year?' said Freddy.

'1929.'

A wave of relief. Sophie hugged her. 'Good to see you.' When the housekeeper and butler had retired, Maud had been promoted.

'Come in. I'll fetch Lady Lacey.' Maud scurried off.

The house smelled of seasoned wood and paint. 'I've lost track of dates,' said Sophie. 'Has time shifted?'

Freddy closed the front door. 'We left Shorten on 5th February 1928. With Rome and then the 19th century, plus crossing times, we've been gone eleven months. It should be January 1929, not November.'

Okay, this was clear-cut. 'Eleven months away and Shorten's jumped forward nearly another year.' She dropped the carpet bag and sat in the hall armchair. It could have been so much worse. '24th November... Bella's birthday's in five days.' Sophie had stopped shivering but now she was trembling.

'She'll be nearly three. If she's forgotten us, we'll start again.' Freddy blinked hard. 'And it's not really her birthday here. Just the month and day when she was born in your London.'

'She's still little,' said Hugo. 'All is well.'

Sophie stood up. Breathe slower. 'Let's not mention the time-shift. It'll only freak everyone out.'

Anne hurried into the hall. Her cream silk dress was loose and straight, her skirt barely reaching her calves, and her salt and pepper hair was styled in a severe bob. Roaring 1920s fashion had finally reached Shorten.

Freddy strode over and embraced her. Though displays of emotion weren't the Shorten way, he was beyond caring.

Clarissa rushed in with Bella who was holding a battered teddy bear and running. When they'd left, she'd taken her first steps. She was wearing soft slippers that matched her green velvet dress, and a white pinafore. Her fair hair had darkened to the same sandy blonde as Freddy's, yet her blue eyes and the shape of her mouth were all Sophie.

Freddy knelt in front of his daughter, their eyes level. 'Hello.'

Bella's eyes widened, and she pointed at him and Sophie, then at Hugo and Charlotte. 'Mama.'

Sophie burst into tears. Bella did remember her! Sort of. Mama apparently encompassed them all.

'Hello, Henry.' Freddy shook the bear's hand. 'He was my bear.'

Bella nodded solemnly, reminding Sophie of Charlotte.

Sophie knelt too. Take this slowly. 'We've been gone a long time.'

'We talked about you every day,' said Clarissa, her attention on Freddy. Her cheekbones were more pronounced, and she had mauve shadows under her eyes. Caring for her fiancé's child, never knowing if she'd see Freddy again, must have been torture. But this was the start of a fresh chapter for her. Marrying Freddy and starting her own family. Clarissa wiped her eyes.

Bella sucked her thumb, thoughtful and curious.

Sophie couldn't hold back more tears and saw her through a smeary mist. 'Would you like a cuddle?'

Holding the bear, Bella stepped forward.

In the small drawing room, after Sophie and Hugo took it in turns to shake Henry the bear's hand, Freddy explained how they'd made crossing universes safe.

Anne winced. 'The chances of you surviving were … tiny.'

Hugo turned from staring into the fire. 'I'm trying not to think about it.' The fire had been lit in welcome and for solace, not for heat. The central heating worked fine.

'Could there be universes where your father's alive?' said Anne.

Freddy met her gaze. 'Finding one without unpleasant differences could take many decades.'

Clarissa froze. 'I'd accompany you?'

Freddy squeezed her hand. 'I'm not leaving you again.'

'Richard wouldn't want you to spend your life … searching,' said Anne. 'It's a comfort to know he's safe. Somewhere.'

'In other universes, what differences might there be?' Reassured, Clarissa was now curious.

'Major and obvious,' said Freddy, 'or subtle, with unforeseen consequences. You could be different. Bella might be too.'

Sophie opened her mouth, then closed it. They'd returned by accident to a universe where her parents hadn't died, and she hadn't noticed other differences. Must have been a fluke.

Bella babbled, Charlotte yawned, and the flames beyond the steel lattice fireguard gently danced.

'What colour is tarmac?' Hugo asked Anne.

Anne raised an eyebrow. 'Brown.'

'It varies, depending on the universe,' said Hugo.

Sophie shot him a warning glance. No point in worrying Anne. When this universe had been corrupted with a trivial change, humans hadn't noticed.

Maud came in, cradling a newborn.

Sophie jumped to her feet. 'What a beautiful baby! Yours?'

'Yes, Miss. She's a hardy one.'

'What's her name?' said Hugo.

Maud's cheeks turned faintly pink. 'Deborah Ellen.'

'I'm honoured.' Sophie's middle names.

'I want her to grow up respectable, with more than one name,' said Maud, giving Sophie a cheeky grin. 'But fearless.'

'Can I hold her?' said Freddy.

Maud hesitated. Okay, still unusual for men to cradle other people's babies.

'I've had plenty of practice,' Freddy assured her.

Maud handed him Deborah, and the child wriggled, sensing an unfamiliar smell and a new set of arms.

'How is Mr Watkins?' Hugo asked Maud. John Watkins was Maud's husband. Back in the day, he'd been Hugo's valet.

'He's well, Sir.' Maud's eyes gleamed with pride. 'He's the butler now.'

CHAPTER 49

Three days later and it was Bella's birthday. She'd been 13 months old when she'd arrived at the Manor. Eleven months on, and the same amount of time shifted forwards, it didn't matter this wasn't her 'real' third birthday. A Shorten birthday was still mighty fine, when Sophie had feared she'd never see her daughter again.

Bella had grown out of the key-rattle that had helped her mother brave so many calamities, but it remained on its chain around Sophie's neck, underneath a 1920s dress borrowed from Clarissa.

In the small drawing room, Bella tore the tissue wrapping paper off Clarissa's present. She held the doll at arm's length, studying it.

Made of rubber, the toy had brown bobbed hair, a linen bonnet and, like Bella, wore a pinafore over a dress.

Charlotte considered it. *A nice doll.*

The eyes looked more natural than Marion's dolls. Not as creepy.

'We must think of a name,' said Freddy.

'Dolly.' Bella put it next to Henry the bear and opened

Anne's present. Ever the rebel, Anne's gift was a tin train with, *Your son's dream toy* emblazoned on the box. Bella arranged the train around Dolly and picked up Henry.

'Are you ready for tomorrow?' Freddy asked Clarissa. 'No wedding jitters?'

'Not unless you're planning another silly trip down the lane.'

Freddy smiled. 'The vicar's moved the date back for the last time.'

~

The next day in Little Shorten, as bells rang out in a merry peel heralding Freddy and Clarissa's marriage service, Sophie and Hugo headed towards the side of the church. Everything here except tarmac was the same, but they wanted to check on Janus' symbol.

There it was. The same gargoyle over a stained-glass window that featured a horse and its rider. Though the horse was grey and generic, the rider was memorable, with his royal blue shirt and hose, buff sleeveless doublet, and brown, knee-high boots. A black, wide-brimmed hat obscured his brow, and his sandy hair tumbled over his shoulders.

Sophie stepped closer. The rider's smile was mischievous. 'He reminds me of Freddy.'

'Perhaps an ancestor. The window's the same.'

Sophie had previously hardly noticed it, more concerned with Janus' symbol, with its warning not to travel. Today, the gargoyle had snow on the two faces, flecks on the stone waves of their hair and in their ears.

Hugo turned away from it, fastening the top button of the coat he'd borrowed from Freddy. 'Ironically, after the demise of the master of time, I need time to adjust. I've got used to living with fear.'

'We've been living on adrenaline for years. It's not surprising we're disorientated.' Sophie was wearing one of Anne's coats and a cloche hat. Designed to hug the head, the hat didn't suit long, loose hair, so Sophie had plaited hers into a pigtail.

She took Hugo's arm and hurried into the church and towards the front row. The Manor servants and locals occupied the rest. Freddy stood up and waved at Hugo. His best man was cutting it fine.

The Reverend Alfred Wetherby smiled at them. His hair had turned white since they'd met at a long-ago cricket match. Though a kindly soul, he was old-school when it came to dogs and young children in church, so Bella, baby Deborah, and Charlotte were with a nanny.

Anne gestured for Sophie to sit beside her. Anne's make-up, finally socially acceptable, softened her features, and her blue coat flattered her eyes. Sophie was glad of her own borrowed coat. It would be many decades before the church installed heating.

The organ struck up Wagner's *Bridal Chorus* from *Lohengrin* and Clarissa walked down the aisle in a calf-length white dress and a short veil. She acknowledged the well-wishers, but she only had eyes for Freddy, who had a broad grin on his face.

In the Manor's large drawing room, at a table laid for the wedding breakfast, Sophie cuddled Bella on her lap. She could still hardly believe they were here, together, and couldn't resist squeezing her daughter every few minutes, checking she was real.

'Going home with you will be interesting,' said Anne, as if they'd be hopping on a plane. Decades ago, Anne had arrived in Shorten from the 1980s. Even if the timeline hadn't been trashed, the 21st century would be different from what she remembered. 'And we'll be back for Christmas.'

They planned to celebrate Christmas twice a year, in Shorten and at home.

'It'll be great seeing Marion again,' said Sophie. Freddy's great aunt was coming to the Manor for the holiday, but this would be a different Marion. One who hadn't nearly been poisoned, or arrested, or held her nerve in a gunfight.

CHAPTER 50

A week after Freddy tied the knot with Clarissa, three cars waited on the Manor drive. One was a sky-blue Rolls-Royce. The pretty colour softened the boxy shape, and the roof ensured that the chauffeur and passengers weren't exposed to wind and rain. The other cars were rickety ex-patrol vehicles, left over from the recent civil war when the Manor community had fought a militia.

The last car carried luggage, mostly Clarissa's. Alarmed by Freddy's talk that the timeline of modern London could have changed, she'd brought a heavy suitcase of clothes and toiletries. Sophie had exchanged the carpet bag for a kitbag that was just big enough to also hold Bella's stuff.

The weather was dry, but Freddy was taking no chances. He'd had a waterproof container made for the cylinder and was travelling with it in the Rolls.

'Anne, you go with Freddy and Clarissa,' said Sophie.

Anne hesitated.

'After so many years, time travel might be stressful,' added Sophie. 'It'll help to be driven down in comfort.' And they'd had bad luck in the lane before. Bella should go in the heavy

Rolls too. Sophie handed over her daughter, then climbed into the back of the next car with Charlotte. Hugo was sitting in the front passenger seat, the vests wrapped in tissue paper on his lap.

Sophie's vest, though, wasn't there. Right now, Hattie Wells was likely wearing it.

~

The cars stopped by the Janus stone, and they all got out. The verge was shiny with frost and their breath made rings in the air. Sophie held Bella's hand.

The chauffeurs turned the cars around. Reynolds, Seddon, and the other chauffeur left their cabs, staying close to the vehicles. Reynolds acknowledged Sophie and she gave him a respectful nod. He was keen to see a different ship.

'Juno, we wish to travel,' said Sophie.

'What's supposed to happen?' Clarissa peered at the verge.

'I told you,' said Freddy, 'it starts as a black shape.'

'Juno might know we only want to call her, not travel,' said Sophie, 'so might not appear.'

'We have gifts for other travellers.' Freddy recited Juno's many names in Latin.

Nothing happened.

'We should wait,' said Sophie. Juno took her time to appear.

Bella scrunched up her face. 'I'm hungry.'

Sophie dug into the kitbag and found an egg sandwich.

A loud clunk and the rectangular black void formed on the verge. Anne gasped and Bella screamed, dropping the sandwich.

'It's okay.' Sophie cuddled her daughter. 'It's saying hello.'

'Clarissa Lacey, Hugo Harrington,' said Freddy.

'Oh!' said Clarissa. She stepped back onto Hugo's toes. He steadied her.

'Reynolds, Seddon, Gove,' said Sophie. The chauffeurs gaped. Reynolds and Seddon had seen the fancy lift, but not Juno.

A humming noise, and the blackness faded, changing into rippling red bricks. The bricks separated to form the Roman arch, revealing the familiar courtyard inside.

'Pretty,' said Bella.

How fast children adapted. Initially terrifying, the ship was now just interesting. The arch and courtyard, Juno's default illusions, were as out of place in a sleepy country lane as Janus' lift with the crystal chandelier. Juno was smaller, not flush with the tall hedge, and Sophie walked around it with Bella. From the rear, the ship appeared to be a single room.

'Juno, may we return the items we borrowed?' said Freddy.

Click. 'Yes.' Juno's matronly British voice was clear and clipped.

'We'll stay here,' said Anne, taking Clarissa's arm.

Sophie guided Bella over to Anne. Juno had never taken off without instructions, but why take the risk? Bella was too young for accidental time travel.

Charlotte skipped inside and Sophie followed, holding Hugo's hand. 'Juno, answer Hugo Harrington as you would me.'

'Done.'

'Juno, show us the real ship,' said Hugo.

'Done.' The courtyard dissolved, replaced by the barrel-shaped cargo bay lined with racks and boxes.

'Our items are returned by Mr and Mrs Harrington and Mr Lacey,' said Freddy. 'Can you guide us to the original storage locations?'

Three lights came on down the ship and they marched towards the first. Freddy laid the handgun and the string bag of bullets on the rack.

Further down the bay, under the second light, Sophie lifted the lid on the bronze box, slipped the bracelet off, and placed it on the cushion. She put in a new note: *This bracelet has one working ruby, the oval-shape. That provides a mental map to the cylinder when the cylinder is outside. Focus intensely on a person to make the map smaller. Tap the stone when the map is on to switch it off.* She shut the lid.

At the next illuminated box, Hugo put in the vests and Freddy added his note. *Guild body armour. Works for all creatures.* Within the box, a bright green light drifted down the vests.

'Juno, the light cleans stuff?' asked Sophie.

'It does.'

Despite wearing them every day in 1889, they hadn't dared wash the vests, fearing that could damage whatever substance within the fabric repelled bullets. Going by the tear in the neck, another Sophie had worn the vest before… Sophie accepted what Einstein believed, that time wasn't linear, but understanding that was too hard, never mind applying it to multiple universes. 'I can't get my head around how the bracelet and vests can be found by us in the past, or other versions of us, before we've returned them.'

Charlotte leaned against Sophie's legs. *It is difficult.* The intricacies of time paradoxes and parallel universes were beyond even the cleverest labradoodle. *I hope my vest can help another Charlotte.*

Sophie resisted an illogical urge to grab back the vests. She chided herself. They didn't need them.

'Juno, designate the vests and bracelet as private,' said Hugo.

'Assign them to individuals with any of these names,' said

Sophie. 'Freddy Lacey, Frederick Lacey, Hugo Harrington, Sophie Arundel-Harrington, Sophie Harrington, Sophie Arundel, Sophie Lacey.' At least one version of her had married Freddy. 'And a canine, Charlotte.' That's what Juno called her. Charlotte's full name was registered at the vet at home. 'Charlotte Arundel.'

'Done,' said Juno.

Charlotte blinked. *I'm glad I have your old name.*

Sophie ruffled Charlotte's head. 'I'm glad too.'

They disembarked and moments later, Juno vanished.

'Janus.' Freddy had overcome his loathing of saying the name.

The golden lift appeared instantly. Used to a tardy Juno, Sophie was taken by surprise.

'A palace!' said Bella.

They'd wrestled with how much to tell her. If they shared that the lift was an illusion, she'd demand to see the real ship. Yes, Janus wasn't there, but the less time they spent awake in there the better.

'Reynolds, Seddon, and Gove,' said Freddy, to allow the chauffeurs to see the lift. 'Hugo Harrington, Clarissa Lacey.'

Anne walked across the verge and touched it. 'I never thought I'd be here again.'

Framing the doors was the familiar mural, with urns and stylised leaves, and at the top was the old-fashioned round dial, showing three floors. By the dial were the same prancing stags.

'I don't see any pictures on the doors,' said Sophie, 'or maths symbols.'

Charlotte nodded.

'Perhaps that function was a later upgrade?' said Hugo.

'It camouflages itself after a while,' said Reynolds to the other chauffeurs. 'Fits in with the colours of the countryside.'

'Why isn't it more in keeping with the lane?' said Clarissa, 'like a shepherd's hut?'

Freddy stepped nearer as the door clattered open and the arrival bell rang. 'For us, it's always been a lift. Perhaps even reset to factory settings, it gives return travellers the same illusion. To establish trust?'

'Nice Wells always saw a green door,' said Hugo. 'Familiarity is reassuring.'

Sophie shook her head. 'I think he still has nightmares.'

After the chauffeurs transferred their luggage inside, Anne cautiously stepped in with Hugo and Charlotte, gazing up at the chandelier. Clarissa scrutinised the chandelier too, holding tight to Freddy's arm.

Sophie hesitated on the threshold. Even with Janus gone, taking Bella inside was a leap of faith. She made herself go in, bringing her daughter with her.

The illusion of the elevator had expanded to accommodate them. It was now a foyer with occasional chairs.

The doors rattled shut and the fresh, cold of the lane was replaced by neutral, sterile air.

'Obey Hugo as you would me,' said Freddy.

Hugo read out the destination number.

CHAPTER 51

In Janus' ship, Anne sat down in the nearest armchair. 'I know you said this was safe—'

She was interrupted by the doors rattling open, and the arrival bell.

Beyond the threshold, students in jeans and hoodies walked past with earbuds in their ears. Others talked into their phones. No one showed any interest in them or the open lift.

Sophie breathed a sigh of relief. If this universe had been corrupted, it wasn't in a way that was big or obvious.

Freddy took Clarissa's arm and stepped out. Hugo followed with Charlotte and Anne, and Sophie came out last, holding Bella's hand.

'This isn't that different,' said Anne.

'Fashions must have changed since the 1980s,' said Sophie.

'When I left, the fashion was for big hair.' Anne's eyes softened, remembering. 'I had a wild spiral perm.'

Okay, that was hard to picture. Anne's 1920s bob was so smooth and elegant.

Anne's coat skirted her ankles and was loose and plain, like Sophie's and Clarissa's, and following Sophie's advice, the women hadn't brought their cloche hats. A few students stared at Charlotte who was effortlessly smart in her grey coat, but it was Hugo and Freddy who looked more out of place. Male students didn't generally wander around in expensive town coats.

'All of us squeezing into the flat might be too much,' said Freddy. When he'd first crossed universes to the students' union, Elliot and Lorna had allowed him to stay over. As a result, they knew about the time-travelling. 'I'll tell them about Janus, collect our wallets and phones.'

'Everyone has phones?' said Anne. 'That's different.'

As Freddy crossed the hall, the ship's doors closed. A few seconds later, the golden lift was gone, replaced by the modern grey one.

Clarissa's attention was on a girl in jeans and a T-shirt who had tattoos on both arms. 'What's the matter with her?' Clarissa whispered. She took a step back. 'Is it infectious?'

'They're just tattoos,' said Sophie.

Clarissa raised an eyebrow. 'That sailors have?'

'Um, yes,' said Sophie, though she wasn't sure.

While they waited for Freddy, Bella made to sit on the grimy floor. Sophie found a stacking chair and Bella settled on it, playing with Henry the bear. Five minutes later, when her father returned, she jumped to her feet.

Freddy handed out their wallets and phones. 'This universe has shifted forward ten months.'

'So, with Shorten going forward eleven months, we're now only...' Hugo paused. '92 years and 1 month ahead of Shorten.'

'Roughly,' said Freddy. 'It's 5th November.'

'We left for 1889 on 2nd November,' said Sophie. Their

month away had been swallowed up by the two universes shifting.

'Say this universe had gone backwards,' said Hugo, 'would we have met the same versions of us?'

Mind-boggling. Sophie tried and failed to imagine it. 'Presuming the laws of physics have stabilised after the Janus Wells-fest … if meeting another version of yourself gets you winked out of existence, I'm guessing meeting your actual self would too.'

'They should have degrees in this,' said Anne, with a straight face.

Charlotte glanced at her. *Is she joking?*

'I'm not sure,' whispered Sophie.

'Lorna insisted we keep the spare key to the flat,' said Freddy. 'They're sorry our adventures are over. Well, Elliot is.'

Elliot had wanted to time travel for a while. Sophie turned to Anne. 'Could they come to the Manor for Christmas?'

On the train to London, sitting beside Anne, Sophie plugged in her phone to charge. Opposite them, next to Hugo, Bella was occupied with a colouring book they'd bought at the station. Freddy and Clarissa were across the aisle, the cylinder in its box on their table. Too precious to store on a luggage rack.

Sophie found the website for Shorten Manor on her phone and showed it to Anne. As Sophie scrolled, Anne was silent, taking it in. The estate was open to the public, owned by the National Trust.

'We were right not to visit the Manor here,' said Freddy. 'It would have been odd, upsetting.'

Consigned to the aisle, Charlotte grunted her agreement.

'I love the suitcases with wheels,' said Clarissa. 'With no servants, what a godsend.' They'd transferred their things into modern suitcases in Derby station.

'The smoother shape of trains is impressive,' said Anne. 'What's happened to dining cars?'

'They got too expensive,' said Hugo.

Anne scrolled through apps on Sophie's phone.

'Can I have a phone that does this?' asked Anne.

'I shall make it so,' said Freddy, imitating a character from *Star Trek*.

'What is everyone doing on those telephones and machines?' whispered Clarissa. They were in the quiet carriage and other passengers were wedded to their tablets, laptops, and headphones.

'They're reading or playing games,' said Sophie, 'or working.'

'Working?' Clarissa sounded like a baffled actor in a period play.

'I didn't explain it very well,' said Freddy. 'Women and men of all classes work, and the machines are invisibly connected, so you can have face-to-face meetings and telephone conversations. You can write letters and post them through the air.'

A slight line appeared between Anne's eyebrows. 'Hugo, we mustn't impose on your family for too long.'

'My parents are fine about you staying,' said Hugo, 'and my mother will be ecstatic to see Bella.'

Hugo's mother had been upset when Bella had stayed far longer than expected with Freddy's 'traveller' family, off the grid. She had no idea how far off the grid, and Hugo couldn't enlighten her. Fiona Harrington would tell her politician husband who'd be duty-bound to inform the government, and the Guild agent's doom-laden warning, predicting catastrophically trashed timelines, would come true. The government would likely stop ordinary people travelling — including them — but scientists and soldiers would cross universes. The prospect of new technology, gaining the upper hand against unfriendly states, would be irresistible.

'Hugo's parents are used to unexpected visitors,' said Freddy. 'They kindly let me stay when Sophie gave birth to Bella.'

Hugo tapped his phone. 'Sending my mother our expected arrival time.'

Get Hugo to ask about Jack, said Charlotte. Sophie repeated the request.

'On it,' said Hugo.

'I'd forgotten Charlotte was sweet on the black retriever,' said Clarissa.

'Jack's fine,' said Hugo, reading the response.

In the train aisle, Charlotte moved closer to Sophie and rested her furry head on her mistress' lap. *I can't wait to see him again.*

CHAPTER 52

$\mathcal{A}$ week after their son returned with his wife and guests to the 21st century, Hugo's parents held an informal lunch party. The modern French windows in their kitchen made the most of the winter sunshine, but guests gravitated to the cosy Aga cooker and the appetisers on the generous rustic table. Jack and Charlotte were asleep in a secluded corner, soothed by evergreen hits unlikely to perturb any guest, including those born over a century ago.

Sophie handed out glasses of wine and sat on an upright chair opposite Freddy and Anne. Bella was on her father's lap, swinging around his old teddy bear.

'Your travels have changed you,' Anne said to Freddy.

'I'm still me.'

His mother sipped her wine. 'I know.'

Since Freddy had married, he'd become even more self-assured, and Sophie gave him a fond look, but his attention was on his mother. 'I see my childhood through different eyes now,' he said. 'You spoke about your life here. You didn't seem to miss it. Yet … you must have done.'

'Oh, I missed it.'

'I never realised,' said Freddy. 'As a result, I grew up happily anchored in my time and place.'

Anne smiled. 'If not going on about home helped in some way, I'm glad.' She stood up. 'I can't remember when I last tasted chilli con carne.' She joined Clarissa by the lunch table.

From across the room, came a small child's cry of outrage. Because of the time shift, Lucy's baby was over a year old.

Lucy took Janet off for a nappy change and Lucy's American partner, Tiana, went with her. Lucy had accidentally crossed to Shorten years ago, done well, risen to be head gardener. Tiana, a physics professor, had only recently found herself in Shorten. That's how they'd met. They'd managed to cross back, just before Janus got around the ship's algorithms.

As Lucy and Tiana left, Bella pointed towards the disgruntled child. 'I'm not a baby.'

Freddy made silly faces at her, making her giggle, and Sophie made silly faces too. Hugo sat beside them.

'Miss Hemmings is happy,' said Freddy. Lucy's pregnancy, arising from an unpleasant encounter with a militiaman, had been kept under wraps in Shorten, and Sophie had waited until Lucy's condition was obvious before confiding in Freddy. Sophie had also shared another important Lucy-fact — the true nature of her relationship with Tiana. Weathered by all his adventures, Freddy had been unfazed.

David Bowie's *Life on Mars?* started playing. 'We should have asked Hattie about Mars,' said Hugo.

Sophie shot him a quizzical glance. 'Why?'

'The Wells here must have got the idea for *War of the Worlds* from somewhere.'

'If Mars had advanced life, I'm sure we'd have heard.' Sophie had seen the movie, hoped it was fiction.

'There could be advanced life on the planet in other universes?' said Freddy.

'Tesla may have visited a universe with a different Mars,' said Hugo. 'In 1901, he claimed to have received radio signals from there. Many people believed him.'

Lucy approached, carrying Janet, and sat next to Hugo. Lucy's limp, the legacy of a militia ambush, had gone, thanks to Tiana's nagging. 'Why live with it,' she'd said, 'if you can get it fixed?'

Tiana put plates of chilli con carne on a side table and fetched Janet's car seat which doubled as a cot. Lucy settled Janet in it. The baby was asleep, her cheeks rosy from the warmth of the crowded room.

Clarissa came over with a tray. Freddy persuaded Bella to slip off his lap, and he accepted a laden plate.

Lucy sat back in her chair and smiled at Clarissa and Freddy. 'I'm so sorry we missed your wedding.'

Tiana grabbed Lucy's hand, her eyes shining. 'We're getting married in the New Year. Just the registry office and a meal at the pub. You're all invited. Obviously.'

'Congratulations!' said Sophie. 'We'll be there!'

'We're having a bigger wedding bash in our London next summer,' said Freddy. 'You're welcome to bring Janet.'

'We thought we'd wait a few years before crossing over to Shorten.' Lucy had wanted to return as soon as possible. Janet's arrival had evidently changed that.

Tiana gave her partner a broad grin. 'In the meantime, I'll teach Janet the science side of it, as much as I know.'

'More to the point,' said Lucy, 'she needs to understand not to blab.'

Janet kicked aside the light blanket covering her legs and Lucy tucked her up again.

Sophie kissed her own daughter on the brow. Janet and Bella would grow up sharing the coolest secret.

CHAPTER 53

*E*arly next morning, after his parents left on a business trip, Hugo flopped into a chair in the kitchen and sighed. 'I'll call work this week.' He'd been on sabbatical since before Rome.

Sophie was cooking breakfast. 'I'll start job-hunting.' That would be hard. What career could possibly match her skill set: time travel, helping to kill an evil god… She should modify the travel, swap medieval Georgia for modern Georgia, ancient Rome for the modern city, and with her unusual knowledge of history, she should apply to museums.

Freddy walked over to the French windows, and his daughter pressed Henry the bear's face up against the glass. He sipped tea, staring at the wintry garden. 'Surely work can wait a little longer?'

Charlotte nodded, and Jack copied her.

Yes, they needed downtime. Sophie set the table for Anne and Clarissa who weren't up yet and plated the first round of breakfast. 'I wish we knew why the fissures in time and space led to us.'

'We must have made one choice,' said Hugo, 'different to our other versions.'

Sophie gave sausages to the dogs. 'Which one?'

Freddy returned to the table. 'We'll never know.'

'Thanks to neuroimaging, we can watch how we make decisions,' said Hugo. 'Each choice happens before we're aware of it. Determined in advance.'

'Our brains, like everything, are part of the material universe. In every universe.' Freddy lowered Bella into the highchair.

Hugo looked up from his meal. 'So?'

'Take mountains and rivers. They exist in that form due to other physical elements that influenced their creation in the past. Our brains have also evolved over many thousands of years. Why would neural activity be exempt from the laws of physics any more than a mountain?' Freddy warmed to his argument. 'Take my decision to choose tea rather than coffee. My preference was the culmination of my previous choices, right back to when I was born.'

'About tea?' said Sophie.

Freddy didn't rise to her teasing. 'My birth was a result of my parents meeting, their births, and a thread of causation from the start of creation. Inevitable cause and effect.'

Inevitable. Sophie cut up Bella's toast. 'That's fine and dandy for us. Not for all the versions who died.'

Freddy watched his daughter messily eat scrambled eggs. 'Some versions accepted the agent's offer of safe passage, and survived.'

Hugo pushed food around his plate. 'Before he tried to kill us, the agent stated our decision was inevitable.'

'Maybe we were the last ones standing?' Sophie adjusted Bella's bib. 'The most stubborn?'

'The agent was going through the motions,' said Freddy. 'He expected our answer, based on our past actions. Consistent with the predictable, mechanical universe. And if we were fated to end Janus or not, we did what we had to do.'

Charlotte lay down. *I agree.*

'Atoms and electrons behave randomly at the quantum level. They're part of our universe.' Hugo drank his coffee. 'I'd like to think that makes free will more likely.'

'I've decided to believe in free will.' Sophie lifted Bella out of the highchair. 'Or what's the point of anything? Random acts of kindness? Striving to earn enough to eat? On a different scale, someone risking their life, and their family's lives, to inspire a country to fight an invading army. Without free will, nothing matters.' She cuddled Bella. 'I need free will to exist. To keep sane.'

Hugo laughed. 'A sane you is a force to be reckoned with. Unhinged … you'd be terrifying.'

Sophie bit her lip. Was he serious? She sat down and Bella climbed onto her lap, reaching for the repaired brooch pinned on Sophie's shirt. Collected from the local jewellers two days ago, the memento from Rome had withstood a lot but might not survive Bella's curiosity. Sophie eased away the small questing fingers and kissed her daughter's head, breathing in her sweet toddler scent.

'The brooch looked good on a Victorian outfit and looks just as good now,' said Hugo, maybe trying to soften his previous quip.

'It was wonderful talking with Tesla,' said Freddy.

'I love that he respected animals.' For Sophie, that was on a par with inventing incredible technology.

'When he was older, he doted on a pigeon,' said Hugo.

Charlotte blinked her approval. Though she'd stopped chasing them, she still found birds fascinating.

'I've been reading up about him.' Hugo tapped his phone. *'Owing a fortune to a hotel that Tesla lived in, he offered a black box as collateral. Tesla claimed it contained a weapon that could end all wars. He warned against opening it as it could explode. After his death in 1943, it was found to contain everyday scraps of metal.'*

Sophie didn't want to think of Tesla as old, let alone dead. He'd been so full of vigour and ambition. Time travel had been an incredible privilege but some of its legacy was a melancholy that might stay with her forever.

'A clever ruse to avoid creditors,' said Freddy.

'Perhaps,' said Hugo. 'But the FBI took the box, and everything from his home and labs. Apparently to Area 51.'

Freddy raised his eyebrows. 'Where the Americans are supposed to keep alien technology.'

'If the cylinder was in pieces inside the box,' said Sophie, 'the illusion of the walking stick wouldn't work.'

Their cylinder was intact, safe in the basement of this house. There was nowhere else to store it.

Hugo scrolled on his phone. 'The FBI has recently declassified a few documents about Tesla. The rest remains secret.'

'Are any of his inventions still in use?' asked Sophie. Tesla's genius deserved to be celebrated.

'His wireless technology is in this phone,' said Hugo. 'In radio-guidance systems, encryption, even drones. It's a long list.'

'In Shorten in the 1920s, people thought Tesla confused magic and science,' said Freddy. 'Arthur C. Clarke said magic's just science we don't understand.' There weren't many classic sci-fi novels Freddy hadn't read.

'If that's true, magic may be real.' Sophie kissed her daughter. 'How awesome is that?'

That evening, Hugo's drawing room fire cast a mellow light on Charlotte and Jack, dozing on a sofa, and on Bella cross-legged on the floor. Hugo was sitting on a different sofa and Sophie stood in front of the fireplace, rocking on her heels, and reading her phone.

'You haven't done that since school,' said Hugo.

'Done what?'

'Rocking on your heels when you're thinking.'

Sophie sat beside him. 'I've been researching those women who were shoplifting in Harrods. They were part of the most successful crime gang, ever.' She read aloud from her phone. '*Known as the Forty Elephants, the women stole from the wealthy during the 18th century and all the way through to the mid-20th. Their methods were so effective, most stores and house owners didn't realise they'd been robbed.*'

'Any photos of the woman with the deadly ring-punch?' said Hugo.

'I'm guessing she avoided being photographed, but she may have been Mary Carr, the gang leader.'

'I've investigated the British National Rifle Association,'

said Hugo. 'Queen Victoria opened their first competition on Wimbledon Common, ceremoniously firing a weapon. Competitors wore colourful invented uniforms and showed off their manly skills. Very popular with the female spectators.'

Sophie shook her head. The past really was a foreign country — in any universe.

'And I've researched Roman seers,' said Hugo.

Sophie touched her brooch, remembering the voice reaching through the pain inflicted by Janus. 'And?'

'Seers foretold the future, but they also interacted with the gods.'

Goosebumps rippled on Sophie's forearms. 'The stall-holder said the brooch was more powerful than any god.'

'It's fanciful, but perhaps she knew we could defeat Janus and her power through the brooch provided the vital nudge?'

'For me, it symbolises us, and Charlotte and Freddy. Precious for that alone.'

Bella pointed at Charlotte and Jack. 'Doggies.' Charlotte opened one eye and Bella jumped up. It was well beyond Bella's bedtime, but she was brimming with energy.

'I'm still pinching myself that we made it here,' said Sophie, relaxing into Hugo's embrace. 'If I'd ended up in Shorten without you, I'd have shrivelled up inside.'

Hugo stiffened. 'About that.'

Sophie squirmed around in his arms, sensing something serious.

'If I'd had to choose, I wouldn't have left you.'

'What?' He'd always been adamant he'd choose a regular modern life over her. 'This whole time you were *bluffing*?' The question came out angrier than she'd intended.

'I wasn't.' Hugo met her eyes. 'But once we ended Janus, and I didn't have to choose, I realised I'd been kidding myself.' He kissed her. 'You're part of me. Taking my own path, I'd have lived half a life.'

Sophie struggled to take that in. His certainty that he couldn't stay in Shorten had tipped the balance, reinforced her resolve to reject safe passage and try to end Janus. 'If I'd known, Janus wouldn't be dead.'

'I didn't know myself until he was gone,' said Hugo. 'What I thought I *should* want, wasn't what I wanted.' He shot her his killer half-smile.

But Sophie was too shocked to flirt. They were only here because Hugo had told himself a lie — over months, ever since Shorten in the civil war. 'If we'd followed the Guild agent to his ship, would you have realised before we got in?'

'I hope I would, but I honestly don't know.'

No more secrets. That's what they'd promised each other after their wedding. But you couldn't share a secret you didn't realise you were keeping.

'I guess what I ultimately wanted could be down to being in love,' said Hugo. 'Or perhaps it's the soulmate thing?'

'Whether versions of me chose safe passage depended on the corresponding versions of you. What choices they made.' Sophie squeezed his hand. 'We're tangled together.'

'All of us are.'

The dogs had woken up and were sitting on either side of Bella. Solemn furry sentinels. Bella had altered her mother's soulmate bond with Hugo, inserting a maternal seam down the centre. That seam could so easily have weakened the bond, or torn it apart—

A clink of glasses. Freddy and Clarissa came in with a bottle of prosecco, four glasses and a bowl.

'I thought you were in bed,' said Hugo.

'Not yet,' said Freddy, winking at Clarissa, who blushed. He poured the prosecco into the glasses and into the bowl for Charlotte. In Shorten, they'd caught Charlotte necking wine with no ill effects. A cool side-effect of DNA enhancement. She'd developed a taste for expensive champagne but stoically put up with prosecco and knew to only drink it with close friends.

Freddy raised his glass. 'To the versions of us who didn't make it.'

The others raised their glasses. Charlotte stood to attention, and Jack and Bella copied her.

'We'll always remember you,' said Hugo.

Charlotte slurped her wine and as Sophie sipped hers, she pictured their versions, similar but different. Countless souls in a distorted fairground mirror.

'I guess we'll never pin down how we cheated fate,' said Hugo, 'got past Janus.'

'Maybe Hattie's myth from the lost play was true,' said Sophie. 'He could see all fates except his own.'

Accident.

'Accident?' repeated Sophie. 'Charlotte, what do you mean?'

You dropped the cylinder. Cover was knocked open. I touched the button.

'Countless versions of me must have dropped it,' said Sophie, 'and countless versions of you must have tried but not reached the button.'

I don't know about the other versions.

'After you pressed it, you said Janus forgot your protected blood,' Sophie said to Charlotte.

A solemn nod.

'Also, unlikely.' Freddy sat on the floor beside Charlotte. 'Countless versions of you must have acquired that protection.'

It's frustrating, not knowing how I did it.

'Tapping the button would have required little or no

conscious reasoning,' said Sophie. 'Thanks to the book machine, you could do that in your sleep.'

'It could have been down to Charlotte's thoughts as she hit the button,' said Hugo.

'Were you thinking about your book machine?' asked Sophie.

When I read, I don't think about the machine. I think about the story. Charlotte's voice in Sophie's mind was soft and measured. *When I touched the cylinder button, my head was full of our story.*

'Our story,' said Bella.

Sophie gasped. 'Bella's repeating Charlotte's telepathic words!'

'Clever doggie.' For Bella, Charlotte talking was normal, must have been happening since their return home.

'Amazing,' said Freddy.

'What does Charlotte mean by our story?' Hugo asked Sophie.

'When Charlotte hit the button, she was thinking about us. Our lives, bound up together.'

'But other versions surely had the same thoughts?' said Freddy.

'Our Charlotte's thoughts were evidently a tiny bit different,' said Hugo. 'I guess it'll always be a canine mystery.'

That's okay. Charlotte stretched.

'I'm going to order a personalised T-shirt,' said Hugo. 'Never underestimate a labradoodle.'

'Order two. No five,' said Sophie, eyeing Clarissa and Bella. 'We should get ones for Jack and Charlotte too.'

Bella whirled on the spot, fell over with a thump, but instantly leaped up. Jack wagged his tail.

'She's so determined,' said Hugo. 'I wonder where she gets that from?'

'Obviously from me,' said Freddy, shooting a playful

glance at Sophie. He turned towards the mantlepiece. 'I should complete our vow.'

On the shelf was a frieze, their tourist souvenir from Rome. Two young faces looking in opposite directions and underneath, a square of wax. Freddy took the Janus frieze, laid it flat on the coffee table, and Hugo handed him a biro.

Pressing hard with the pen, Freddy wrote, *Quest complete.*

'What happened to writing it in Latin?' said Hugo.

'We're home and safe.' Freddy straightened. 'English is good enough.'

Sophie picked up the frieze. The room shimmered and Sophie tightened her hold on it. When her younger self had come across Janus' gargoyle on the church, the whole building had shimmered. There'd been no trees or flowers nearby, but she'd breathed in pollen, carried on a sweet, rain-drenched breeze, blown through a doorway from another universe.

Back then, she'd dismissed such things as flights of fancy. Now she knew that sometimes logic — or even sanity — wasn't enough. To know what was real, you had to open your heart to any possibility. She scanned the room and everyone in it. All was well. Something had passed by, but it was gone.

Her younger self hadn't known she needed to get away, to travel. Neither had the younger Charlotte. That was why she'd called the lift in the first place.

Charlotte looked up. *I didn't mean to start our quest, but I meant to finish it.*

Sophie gave a low whistle. 'Okay, Charlotte's reading my mind.'

Bella leaned into Charlotte and did a happy sigh.

'Unsettling,' said Freddy.

'Incredible,' said Hugo.

'Exciting.' Sophie grinned.

Charlotte tilted her head. *Wonderful.*

I hope you enjoyed *Endgame*.

If you did, let people know.

Reviews are the most effective way of building awareness of a book you've enjoyed.

While I love telling people about the *Shorten Chronicles,* honest reviews bring the books to the attention of other readers.

If you didn't buy *Endgame* direct from my Fantasy Bookshop, I'd really appreciate it if you'd leave a review (short as you like) where you bought it.

Thank you!

Historical Note

Endgame is speculative fiction, but some of this novel was inspired by fact:

- H. G. Wells (the author, not the assassin) wrote original and compelling science fiction, which continues to inspire authors and movie makers in the 21st century;
- In the 18th and 19th centuries and well into the 20th, the female crime gang, the Forty Elephants, made a fortune shoplifting in London;
- Many of Nikola Tesla's inventions (inspired by time travel or not) underpin our current technology.

Stay in the Shorten Universe

Endgame is the last main book in this series, but Sophie's adventures aren't over…

Murder at Shorten Manor, a standalone novella, is a cosy mystery that will keep you guessing until the last page.

It's Christmas 1929 at Shorten Manor, and Sophie and the gang are looking forward to some quiet family time. But when a servant is found dead and the police can't reach the Manor through the snow, it's down to them to find the murderer — before they strike again.

Even if that means less eggnog and a lot less Christmas cake…

Point your phone camera at the QR code and go straight to my Fantasy Bookshop. Click on 'Exclusive to this Bookshop,' then tap the down arrow to choose your preferred format.

Or search for Rosalind Tate on you browser.

Happy reading!

About the Author

Rosalind Tate lives in Gloucestershire, England, and holidays on the Cornish coast. She served in the British military, then worked as a journalist and a lawyer.

Rosalind's enjoys authors' and readers' conferences, talking about publishing and encouraging new authors. When she's not behind her computer, you can find Rosalind reading her favourite books, walking her dogs, swimming, or watching sci-fi and fantasy shows.

Rosalind has three grown up children, a tolerant husband, and two utterly gorgeous dogs.

Contact: rosalind@rosalindtate.com

rosalindtate.com

Acknowledgments

My late mother showed me how to be a writer, and infinite thanks go to my husband, Ian. Thank you for your patience, support, and sharp, proofreading eyes.

Huge thanks as well to my editor, Debi Alper, and my fabulous readers in *Team Charlotte* who ensure my stories are as perfect as they can be. In particular, I'd like to thank Colleen Curran Price, who realised that after Freddy's own time travelling adventures, he would forge a closer bond with his mother, with a new insight into how her life had been — taken from the 1980s to live in Shorten.

Thank you to our labradoodle, the wonderful Bella. You inspired the *Shorten Chronicles* after all. And thanks also to Bella's goldendoodle kid sister, for her author guarding skills. She's called … Sophie. *What?* Okay, when we adopted her, I was obsessed with Sophie Arundel, and our energetic puppy has some things in common with her literary human counterpart. She's sassy, runs fast, and is far too impulsive.

Finally, Toby deserves a mention. He was our first labradoodle and is no longer with us.

Well, in this world.

Rosalind Tate
Gloucestershire 2025

ENDGAME
BOOK SIX OF THE SHORTEN CHRONICLES

First published in Great Britain in 2025
by TOB Publishing

Copyright © Rosalind Tate 2025
® The Shorten Chronicles is a registered trademark

The moral right of Rosalind Tate to be identified as the author of this work has been asserted by her in accordance with the Copyright, Designs and Patents Act 1988. All characters in this book are fictitious and any resemblance to persons living or dead is purely coincidental.

All rights reserved. No part of this publication may be reproduced, uploaded, distributed or transmitted in any form or means, including scanning, photocopying, recording or other electronic or mechanical means, or stored in a database or retrieval system, without the prior permission in writing of the publisher, nor is it to be otherwise circulated in any form of binding or cover other than that in which it is published without a similar condition, including this condition, being imposed on the subsequent purchaser.

A catalogue hardback record for this book is available from the British Library:
ISBN: 978-1-0687976-8-2

Cover Design by 187 Designz
Website by sprkdesign

TOB Publishing

www.ingramcontent.com/pod-product-compliance
Lightning Source LLC
Chambersburg PA
CBHW020645120726
47906CB00001B/130